Prey to the Butterfly

Prey to the Butterfly

Thomas E. Coughlin

Fitzgerald & LaChapelle Publishing, LLC

Written and produced in the United States of America

Cover Photography: Elaine M. Coughlin, Chester, NH and
Richard Henderson, Nashua, NH

Cover Design: Lisa Atkins, Pelham, NH

This book is a work of fiction. Names, characters and incidents are
products of the author's imagination or are used fictitiously. The names
of actual places were used largely with permission or as a point of
historical reference. Any resemblance to actual events, locales or
persons, living or dead, is entirely coincidental.

FIRST EDITION

Fitzgerald & LaChapelle Publishing, LLC
814 Elm Street, Suite 401
Manchester, NH   03101
Phone: (603) 669-6112   Fax: (603) 625-1450

Dedication

For Elaine, Sean, Dawn and Monica Coughlin... family

Acknowledgements

The ownership at the Cliff House and Union Bluff Hotel, the Maine Diner, Rita Douglas, Kimberley M. Vaillancourt, Sonny and Sandra Diprizio, James and Shirley Eaton.

Introduction

I distinctly remember the moment of conception for the story I am about to relate. It was late February of 2007 and I was working in my office. It was the heart of tax season and my nerves were frazzled. My office phone rang and seconds later a soft-spoken, male voice asked to speak to Thomas Coughlin. I identified myself and impatiently waited on the purpose of the call. Immediately, the caller went into an explanation of why he needed to reach me. He had only just begun to explain the purpose behind the phone call when I halted him in mid sentence and informed him of my work situation: I was a certified public accountant in the depths of tax season and my time was not my own. It seemed the man had a story he wanted to share with me. He asked if I was the author who wrote under the name of Thomas E. Coughlin. I explained that I was both the author and the CPA and that there was no way I could clear any time for him until mid-April. Ronald Dingman politely accepted my excuse and promised to contact me in a month and a half. Hanging up the telephone that evening, I was convinced I would not hear from the man again. I was wrong.

Two days before the end of tax season Mr. Dingman telephoned my office. He reminded me of our short-lived conversation a month and a half earlier and asked if we could arrange a time and place to meet. Begrudgingly, I honored his persistence and agreed. He suggested that we rendezvous in the pub at the Union Bluff Hotel in York Beach. The reader should understand that I held out little hope of an interesting encounter with the man, let alone the inspiration for a future book. I agreed to sit down with Dingman solely out of a sense of obligation. It was late in the afternoon on a Thursday when I entered the pub at the Union Bluff and searched the faces in the crowd of customers. Within seconds a man seated at a small table against the wall gestured to me and I joined him. Ronny Dingman appeared to be in his early to mid-fifties. He had recognized me by way of a biographical photograph at the back of one of my books. Dingman had a serious face, seemingly not one prone to laughter. His hair was still nearly jet black and rested atop facial features dominated by a ruddy complexion. I remember thinking how little his soft-spoken voice suited his appearance.

Following a few minutes of meaningless banter, during which I learned he worked at the Cliff House Resort as head groundskeeper and had for nearly twenty years, he moved the conversation to more serious matters. He wanted to share a very personal story with me, a true story about two individuals he came to know through his employment at the Cliff House. He explained, with great earnestness, how he needed to make others privy to what he knew. It was his desire to let others in on the specifics of two lives that had played out before him some twelve years earlier. At some point I reminded him of the fact that I was, and always had been, a fiction writer and, therefore, the credibility of any account I provided would be tainted. This seemed to be of no concern to him. He merely thought the story should be told. Very early in the meeting, Mr. Dingman spelled out how he expected nothing in return from me in the way of compensation, aside from a free copy of anything I should publish. His only goal in this undertaking was the contentment coming from the knowledge that the story of Walter Plews and Felecia Moretti would not be lost to everyone who came after them. I sat with Ronald Dingman for something in the neighborhood of four hours that afternoon and into the evening, sitting in the same pub where twelve years earlier no small part of this drama had played out. By the time we parted that evening I already felt the excitement and anticipation of putting on paper the extraordinary events that unfolded here along the coast of Maine a dozen years earlier.

Over the next year I met with Ronny Dingman a half dozen more times, eliciting more details on individuals and occurrences and, yes, attempting to find any inconsistencies in his account of the events that supposedly took place in 1995. In the end I was never able to find an illogical breakdown in the continuity or detail of his account. For purposes of this novel, each of the individual's names have been fictionalized with the exception of Ronny's. There was little in the way of detail that was not provided by Ronald Dingman. This is how it was told to me.

1

His pickup truck groaned to a halt by the side of the driveway as the man arrived at the complex's tennis court. Exiting the cabin of the Chevy, Ronny Dingman was greeted with a rush of cold, Maine air. It was early spring on the southern coast of Maine, but spring in name only. Two hundred yards east of him the temperature of the Atlantic Ocean hovered around forty degrees and today's breezes were skimming right over the surface of the water. Ronny was foreman of the grounds crew that looked over this valuable piece of real estate that sat majestically on and about Bald Head, a formidable rock formation that gazed out over the blue Atlantic in York, Maine. He was employed by the Cliff House for over eight years, the last five functioning in a supervisory role. In these early weeks of spring it was time to make an assessment of any damage done to the property over the harsh winter of 1995. This review included stairs and walkways, the outside of the main and auxiliary buildings, and the various recreational facilities scattered over the grounds. Hence, his short trip down the driveway to the tennis courts.

The forty year old pulled down his Patriots cap, trapping most of his black hair beneath it and keeping it from flying into his eyes. After letting out an audible shiver he reached back into the pickup and grabbed a clipboard. A moment before his walk to the courts his attention was captured by movement from up the driveway. Squinting through the cold air, he focused on the image of a solitary figure moving up the road in his direction. Owing to the optical illusion created by the undulating surface of the private road, this lone female appeared to almost rise out of the ground, her lower body gradually coming into sight as she moved over the upgrade in the road. Dingman froze in his tracks, somewhat bewildered by the woman's appearance. It was unusual to see anyone arrive at the resort on foot, particularly at this time of year. The village was a good three miles away. The woman—she was young, perhaps in her mid to late twenties— seemed underdressed for the time and place. She was wearing a flimsy, cotton jacket over a summer tee shirt and denim jeans. No doubt, she was here to apply for a job. He had heard the Cliff House had placed an ad in the local paper a few days earlier to fill positions of non-returning employees from the prior year.

Pretending to rummage for an additional tool from the cargo area of his truck, he lingered beside the road, hoping to catch a closer glimpse of the woman. Seconds later she came abreast of the vehicle and he was able to view her in more detail. He theorized she was a pretty woman although he was not able to confirm this, thanks to the frenzied way her brown hair blew about her face. During the split second when her face did pop into view from behind her wind-tossed hair, he saw that her complexion was red from the effects of the cold, Maine air. Additionally, he determined she was quite fit, her jeans outlining the flattering contour of her lower body. The woman moved past Dingman without so much as a sideways glance, her eyes trained on the main building a hundred yards in front of her. Outwardly, she was oblivious to his attention.

Thirty minutes after his arrival at the tennis courts, Ronny Dingman sat with his back to a birch tree and out of the wind, reviewing his notes. Beside certain items scratched out on his yellow pad he had a notation to himself, a reminder to check the maintenance room for any supplies from the prior year before purchasing new inventory. A satisfied smile broke across his face when he remembered that this was his night out with the guys. It was Wednesday and that meant his bi-weekly meeting at the pub of the Union Bluff Hotel. Reaching into his back pocket, he produced his wallet and counted out the cash. He had forty-four dollars, more than enough for a few beers and a sandwich. He thought a night with the guys might be just what he needed to lift his sprits.

When Ronny cleared the front door of the pub he was happy to see Dave seated at their regular table by the window. It was their long-standing table of choice, affording them a partial view of the crashing surf on Short Sands. Dave Durette was a man of forty-six years and an accountant by trade. Balding, somewhat reserved, he was the elder of the group.

"When am I going to learn that when you guys say five-thirty it means six?" asked the man in his usual abrupt, gruff manner.

"We never claimed to be anything but lying jerkoffs. How long is it going to take before you finally catch on?" responded Dingman.

"Damn it. I've been sitting here like some pathetic loser for twenty minutes," cried out Durette. "Will Walter be joining us tonight?"

"Yeah. I confirmed that a couple of hours ago. But you know Plews... always last to arrive. Besides, I don't want him here too early. I want a chance to hear what Jacobs has to say about that blind date he set him up with. I didn't want to say anything to Walter about it until Chrissy boy had given us the straight dope." Ronny Dingman and Walter Plews both worked at the Cliff House. Walter was office manager at the hotel and had been for over ten years.

"Hey, that's right. That was this past week. Was that a pure set-up or did they double?"

"They doubled, so Chris will have every ugly detail for us." A barmaid arrived at the table at that moment and was asked to fetch Ronny a Budweiser.

"I can't believe you two actually got him to go for it. I mean, what has it been, ten years or something?" asked the accountant.

"Yeah, something like that. Hell, think of it. Reagan was in office the last time our Walter might have gotten lucky." The two men shook their heads and Durette reached for his glass of beer.

Dingman's glass of suds had just arrived at the table when Chris Jacobs made his entrance into the pub and scrambled across the room.

"Order me the usual while I go to the men's room and comb my hair," he commanded, placing a hand on each man's shoulder. The brisk, April wind had disheveled the thirty-seven-year-old bachelor's perfectly groomed locks and maintenance was in order. Jacobs sold medical supplies to hospitals and clinics in the region and, by all appearances, made a good living at it. He was handsome, trim, and always the best dressed man at this or most any other table he graced with his company. Ronny and Dave filled in the period of his absence with some sports talk. Jacobs returned to the table within a couple of minutes and grabbed the chair affording him the best view of the room, his antenna always up in search of any attractive females within hailing distance.

"So, how are things in the boring world of the married?" Jacobs asked as he settled into his chair.

"Same ole, same ole," announced Ronny.

"Ditto, ditto," added Dave.

"Sorry to hear that gentlemen, but on the positive side, being married means you always have a date," needled Jacobs.

"Never mind busting our chops here, jerkoff. We've been waiting on a full report on our man Walter's dream date," demanded Dave.

"Ah, the date. You had to ask me about the date," answered Chris, an uncharacteristic tone of sympathy in his voice.

"Bad?" asked Ronny.

"If only I could say it was only bad. Guys, it was brutal. It was like watching a defenseless animal being tortured."

"How do you mean?"

"Well, first of all, I had never met this Deidre broad before. Courtney, my date, provided her, and I just assumed she'd be okay. Life lesson number one: Never assume anything. I mean… it was ugly from the first hello until the last verbal volley from that bitch's mouth. This classless, little whore just never let up, making derogatory comments about Walt not just behind his back but right to his friggin' face. I had warned Courtney that he wasn't the best looking guy on the block but I guess she never passed it on to Deidre the bitch."

"I think we've all had dates like that at one time or another. You know, when you know in the first ten seconds that you haven't passed muster. You can only pray that the gal will be merciful and spare some small part of your ego," piped in Ronny.

"Yeah, I can relate," added Dave, no doubt recounting a personal experience from his own bachelor days.

"Sorry guys, but in the interest of total honesty I have to say that I haven't had the pleasure," announced Chris.

"Cut the crap, Jacobs. Are you trying to tell us that you've never been rejected by a female?" questioned Ronny.

"Never, not in the true sense of rejection. I've been turned down by a few married women, but only because of the fear of being caught by their husbands. However, I've never come away thinking that any girl or woman didn't want to be intimate with me," confessed the handsome salesman.

"Jacobs, you're so full of shit it's coming out your ears," growled Dave prior to swallowing the last vestiges of his beer.

Outside, the setting sun was casting long shadows from the Union Bluff out over the foaming Atlantic Ocean. The three friends ordered a second round of drinks but passed on the dinner menus, deciding to wait on the fourth member of their party, Walter Plews.

"I'll probably hate myself for asking but can you give us an example of how bad this gal was to our man last night?" asked Ronny. "Exactly how bad is bad?" Chris rolled his eyes and lowered his voice, leaning forward over the table, allowing him to communicate in a whisper.

"We were out for a little dining and dancing, nice place, so-so food. Walt had asked Deidre if she wanted to dance no less than three times and she had refused. She had been making eyes at this guy across the room for a while. I noticed it so I'm sure Walter noticed it. The guy wasn't about to approach the table given that Walt's got six inches and a hundred pounds on him. Then, all of a sudden, she gets up and walks over to this guy and asks him to dance. He accepts. They exchanged numbers, no doubt."

"God, what a bitch," snarled Dave.

"Okay, I get the picture. *No mas, no mas,*" added Ronny.

"Guys, the closest thing I can come up with to describe this goddamn nightmare is when you're watching the nature channel on television and they show a snake slowly swallowing its victim alive. The look in the prey's eyes... that look of absolute hopelessness, is the same look that was on our buddy's face by the end of the night. It was goddamn brutal!"

"Where do you find them, Jacobs? Where do you dredge up these bottom-feeding broads?" Dave asked, visibly upset from his friend's report. A brief lull in the conversation descended on the table as the friends digested Chris's account of the double date. It was the handsome salesman who broke the silence.

"You know, guys, I'm the new kid on the block. I think I'm missing a piece of the puzzle that is Walter Plews. What is his story when it comes to women? Has he never had a real relationship with a female?" Ronny and Dave made momentary eye contact before Dingman spoke up.

"Walter's been carrying this thing for a girl called Melinda Klaus for like eight or ten years. He just can't seem to get over her. I think part of it is because he keeps so much bottled up inside him. I mean, how long does it take to get over a broken heart? Six months, maybe a year? Walt's been brooding over this woman for as long as I've worked with him at the Cliff House? I mean, Jesus, move on for God's sake!"

"So he really loved this broad," said Chris.

"I'm thinking it even goes a little beyond love. It's almost unnatural," added Ronny.

"I take it she's married somewhere with six kids or something?"

"If only. No, Melinda Klaus is buried somewhere up around Portland. What happened was they were going out together for about a year and, I think, planning to get married. Then, out of nowhere, she breaks it off and stops seeing him cold turkey... no calls, no nothing. Meanwhile, she's doing all these good works by visiting hospices and working with the dying... people like herself. She does so much good that the Catholic Church actually looks into whether she might be a saint or something. I guess she did some pretty remarkable things with these sick people... borderline miracles. She didn't seem to mind treating our buddy like some expendable piece of crap though. Eventually the church dropped the saint thing. Walter went into a total funk about this time and a year later he gets word she's died. He never gets to see her or talk to her. At her request there's even a closed casket at the wake. Eventually he learns that she had contracted melanoma and couldn't bear having him see her waste away like that. It left him all screwed up in the head, still loving her and at the same time not forgiving her for cutting him out of her life like that."

"Damn! You know, jerkoffs, it might of been nice telling me all this shit before I agreed to double with the guy," added Chris before lifting his glass of beer.

"Jacobs, we're not here to make your life any easier," muttered Dave.

"Screwing with your head is the only pleasure we have left in life. Remember, we're married," needled Ronny.

Twenty minutes after the arrival of Chris Jacobs, the imposing figure of Walter Plews filled the doorway. The soft spoken hulk of a man stood six-feet, six-inches while his weight fluctuated between two hundred and eighty-five and three hundred pounds. Fifty pounds overweight, he had a round face made to appear even more oval by the short, brush haircut he sported. Walter's eyes connected with Ronny's and he ambled over to the table.

"Sorry, guys, running late again," he uttered apologetically while pulling out his chair. "Have you ordered anything to eat yet?"

"Hey, it's Wednesday night and on Wednesday nights we're a band of brothers. We don't do anything until the quartet is here," explained Ronny.

"I noticed you all ordered drinks," pointed out Walter.

"Brothers, but not friggin' monks," snarled Dave before saluting his friend with the gesture of his glass.

The table was more subdued than usual on this night, each man careful not to lead the conversation anywhere close to the topic of blind dates or unfeeling women. When the group grew uncomfortably quiet Chris provided his friends with an update on the politics back at his corporate office. Before long Jacobs had the men roaring with laughter as he recounted a joke played on one of the office's yes men. The prank involved a freestanding pair of women's legs broken off of a mannequin and a life-sized toy sheep strategically left in plain sight inside the fellow's office. It seems the individual in question was out of town for three days at a seminar only to return to find his office and lifestyle the object of amusement among his peers and, unfortunately, upper management.

"You know, guys, I thought of all of you today when I was outside freezing my ass off," injected Ronny during a lull in the conversation. "Suddenly being a bean counter or some butt kissing sales toady like Jacobs didn't seem so bad after all. Not with that breeze blowing in off of the ocean."

"Stop your goddamn whining, Dingman. At lunchtime I had to hoof it out to the car and get my lunch. Not exactly a pleasant thirty seconds," scoffed Dave sarcastically.

"Yeah, Dingman, can it. If we want any more shit from you we'll squeeze your head," answered Jacobs.

"Oh, and speaking of outside in the cold, and this only applies to Walter, by any chance did you catch sight of a certain female applying for a job today? This morning this gal came walking in by me from the road. The poor little shit was underdressed like she couldn't afford a winter jacket or something. She had a hell of a figure and may not have been too bad to look at from the neck up either. It was hard to tell with the wind blowing her hair all around her face." A look of acknowledgment registered immediately on Walter's face.

"I think I know who you're talking about. She starts next week in house-keeping. She dropped off her employment application forms at the office today and I caught a glimpse of her."

"What was your take on her, Walt?"

"Pretty girl… real, pretty girl. Her face was sort of red though, like she had a sunburn or something."

"It was like that when I saw her outside. I think it was windburn. Hell, I'm not sure she didn't walk all the way out to the hotel, and from God knows where," added Ronny.

"Talk about a sideways glance into a sad, pathetic life. Dingman, it sounds like the highlight of your day was catching sight of a pedestrian walking up the driveway," cracked Chris behind his engaging, wry smile.

"I never claimed to be a rock star… or even, dare I say, a medical supplies salesman," answered Ronny in a deadpan fashion. The table broke out in a spontaneous roar of laughter, the good-natured ribbing only unifying the brotherhood among the four men. Uncharacteristically, it was Walter's voice that chimed in after the uproar subsided.

"Then again, that girl's one hell of a pedestrian."

The better part of the next two hours was spent on nostalgia. An abridged discussion of actresses from the thirties and forties led each man to share with the table which of the screen stars they would pair themselves up with should time travel become a reality in the next twenty-four hours. Without hesitation Dave confessed that Barbara Stanwyck was his choice. In true Dave Durette fashion, he provided no explanation. For Chris, it was Vivian Leigh. He tied his fantasy in with the scene from *Gone With The Wind* where Clark Gable defiantly carried the beautiful actress up the stairs to the bedroom. Ronny surprised the table with his choice of Bette Davis, quickly explaining that he wanted the young Ms. Davis from her role as the sassy waitress in *Of Human Bondage* and not the frightening creature from *What Ever Happened To Baby Jane?* Lastly, Walter made his selection: Veronica Lake. He underscored his decision by pointing out her incredible beauty. Adding to that, he explained she stood under five feet in height. The soft-spoken hulk went on to say that he liked the idea of possessing the nearest thing to a 'living doll' imaginable.

2

The four friends exchanged good-byes in the doorway of the Union Bluff Hotel while, under a blanket of darkness, the sea roared not more than a hundred yards away. It was after nine o'clock. Walter walked the short distance down the road to his car in a parking space sandwiched between the movie theater and bowling alley, both now slumbering in dead silence until the eventual return of the swarms of tourists nearly two months away. He fumbled with the key to open the car door, his hands chilled by a constant stream of frigid air. Home was just under a half hour drive away on Wells Beach. Walter was the fortunate recipient of free lodging, thanks to the generosity of Delores Plews. His spinster great-aunt owned a sprawling oceanfront home in Wells. The house, nicknamed 'The Sand Castle,' was one of a dwindling number of turn-of-the-century ocean residences still standing along this expanse of exposed shoreline. Walter was the lone occupant of this massive, one-hundred-year-old house, save for the two weeks Aunt Delores came to visit every summer. In return, Delores Plews saved on most all custodial expenses and had the added satisfaction of knowing a blood relative stood watch for her over this considerably valuable asset.

Walter chose Route 1 for his drive home and avoided the winding shore road. He sped northward in a state of mild distraction, his thoughts careening between the conversation around the table minutes earlier with his friends and some of the loathsome details of his recent date with the woman named Deidre. So occupied with these thoughts was the man that it came as somewhat of a shock when he eyed his approach to Mile Road and the final leg of his journey. The last mile of his ride directed him due east past Billy's Chowder House and ultimately to the edge of the Atlantic Ocean. In less than two minutes he was maneuvering the car into the yard behind the house. He was home. 'The Sand Castle' sat before him in nineteen rooms of total darkness. On the far side of the structure thundered and advanced the Atlantic Ocean, there at Walter's doorstep and beyond, three thousand miles to the next continent. The house rested magnificently like an emerald jewel on the lip of the open ocean, a symbol of another time and generations gone, witness to two world wars and the jazz age. With its age came architectural nobility not present in the newer structures that likewise lined the sandy oceanfront, distinct, visual evidence that stateliness was beyond the purchasing power of the dollar.

Walter turned the key and pushed in the wooden door at the bottom-rear of the building, the movement breaking the dark silence and sending a familiar echo throughout the spacious rooms of the cavernous residence. He flicked on the light in the combination living room and kitchen and squinted as his pupils attempted to adjust. There was little he would need to do before retiring for the evening. His bedroom was close by on the backside of the building, away from the crashing surf, sandy beach, and bright rays of sunlight at dawn. He heated water for tea while tidying up the kitchen and popped a capsule in his mouth for a hereditary heart condition. Again, his thoughts returned to his date a few days earlier and the image of that Deidre woman. He wasn't sure if he had ever been told her last name. Following a few moments of discomfort, he replaced her image with that of Melinda's. He would be retiring early on this evening and decided to entertain himself with thoughts of Melinda Klaus. It was a familiar exercise for the man, losing himself in a memory from a distant time and place. On this evening he decided not to simply allow random images or memories of this special woman to monopolize his thoughts but, instead, to concentrate his reflections on a specific event. The truth was that the most romantic episode in the life of Walter Plews was also the most adventurous, partly because he was not one to search out challenging experiences. However, he learned some ten years earlier that fate would sometimes dictate the course of one's life and the extent to which one might venture outside of one's own comfort zone.

Walter was already attired in his sleeping garments when he made certain all perimeter doors of the house were secured. Sliding his body between the cold sheets, he shivered and prepared for another indiscernible night of sleep. Flicking off the table lamp, he closed his eyes and pushed his consciousness back to a time ten years earlier. It was 1985 and he had just entered into his first, real relationship with a woman. Melinda Klaus was a reasonably pretty girl, light-skinned, with a generous amount of reddish, brown hair. Her body-type was sometimes described as coming from peasant stock. Some characterized her as big-boned. Other, less sensitive people, simply labeled her as overweight. Walter and Melinda had only been out on two dates when she asked him to accompany her to Canada to attend the wake and funeral of a relative. She had been asked to represent her wing of the family and be present for the services of an uncle. She had found the prospect of traveling alone to New Brunswick completely intimidating and appealed to Walter.

The funeral service had taken place in the late morning of a weekday. It was followed by a catered reception that the two were pressured into attending. This caused their return trip home to be delayed until well after two o'clock. By the time their vehicle reached the border crossing point at Calais there remained less than an hour of sunlight on this early December day. Their re-entry into the country was a simple affair, their only declaration being their return home with one and a half homemade blueberry pies. Their arrival on home soil was also hailed by the swift onslaught of an ice storm, the kind particularly dreaded in this region of northeastern Maine. Within thirty minutes of their journey southward along sparsely populated Route 1, they were robbed of the information contained on roadway signs as the icy granules clung to the surface of all signage, rendering them unreadable.

Inside the cabin of Melinda's compact car, Walter had taken over behind the wheel. With his bulk spilling over the contoured driver's seat he carefully maneuvered the vehicle along the ribbon of ice that was Route 1 on this day. They were progressing at less than thirty-five miles per hour, one cog in a caravan of vehicles proceeding southward into the teeth of the storm.

"I have a feeling this ice has been falling for more than an hour or two around here," observed Walter while not removing his eyes from the road in front of him.

"I am so, so sorry for having gotten you into this mess, Walter. I really am," confessed the woman. She glanced over at the man and saw his eyes widen in response to a change in circumstances on the road ahead. Melinda glanced out the windshield and viewed a sea of brake lights illuminating a tree-covered landscape draped in dusk. "What's happening up there?" she asked.

"I don't know but I don't like the look of it." He eased his foot down on the brake pedal, sending the car into a controlled skid. They both breathed a sigh of relief as the Japanese import came to a stop. "Well, all we can do is sit here and wait until we start to move again," the man announced. He reached across the cabin and gave the woman's hand an affectionate squeeze.

A half hour after coming to a complete stop they remained frozen in place. Behind them a long line of headlights was now visible, extending in a line up an adjacent hill and beyond, out of sight. Immediately in front of their position sat a pickup truck, the small light inside the large vehicle shining through a sheet of ice clinging to the back window. Suddenly, out of the darkness emerged the outline of a male figure, moving through the car's headlights and up to the driver's side of the vehicle. Walter rolled down the window.

"The word from the front of the line is that a couple of trees are down across the road up ahead. They're estimating that Route 1's going to be closed three to four hours before everything's going to be back to normal. I'm going to go around. There's another way to get south and make it down to Ellsworth but I'll need you folks to roll your car back a foot or so to let me get out of line," stated a burly stranger from behind a bushy beard.

"How long will this other route take you?" quizzed Walter.

"Maybe a little over an hour to reach Machias and then, in this shit, at least another hour and a half to get to Ellsworth." Walter glanced over to Melinda and made a questioning gesture.

"It sounds better than sitting here for another three to four hours," she reasoned. Walter turned back to the man.

"Mind if we follow you?" he asked.

"Be my guest," answered the man before turning from the car and trudging back to his truck.

A minute later the two vehicles had reversed direction and Walter was following the pickup truck through the dark, Maine night. For the next half hour Walter guided the compact car through the tracts of the stranger's pickup. Visibility on either side of the vehicle extended only a few feet beyond the beams provided by the car's headlights. Instinctively, he kept his eyes trained on the two orbs of light that were the pickup truck's tail lights, seventy-five feet in front of him.

"Boy, I wish he'd slow down just a little," he confided to the young woman, seemingly finding it more and more difficult to keep up with the larger vehicle.

"The tires are all-weather but I put them on over a year ago," she confessed. A second later both felt the back end of the car skid out from behind them as they descended a modest decline in the icy road. Walter reacted immediately, pulling back his foot from the gas pedal and turning in the direction of the swerving vehicle. His tactic kept the car under a measure of control, limiting the skidding and allowing him to bring the compact to a complete stop thirty yards down the road. The two travelers let out with a spontaneous sigh of relief. Any feelings of contentedness were short lived as the two orbs of light that were their beacon disappeared into the cold, icy air up the road in front of them.

"Oh shit," Walter exclaimed, his eyes looking out into the dark, hostile night.

"We'll just take it real easy and stay on this road. It probably isn't too much further back onto Route 1," reasoned Melinda.

"God, I hope not," added the visibly shaken man. "I've pretty much kept my eyes glued on the road since we left Route 1. Have we passed any houses with lights on in the last half hour or so?"

"It's really hard to pick up on anything out here. You'd think they'd have some street lights out here in the hinterlands. But, to answer your question, I thought I saw a couple of houses with their lights on a few miles back…but they've been few and far between." The man looked across the front seat at the woman and then down at the gas gauge.

"Between a quarter and a half a tank. Things could be worse. Anyway, on the bright side, think how much better we will get to know each other after this nightmare is over," he muttered through a thoughtful smile.

"Thank you, Walt."

"Thank you for what?"

"Thank you for not getting all pissed off and taking it out on me. I know a lot of guys who would." He reached across the cabin of the car and affectionately pulled loose strands of hair back from her face, tucking them behind her ear.

"Perhaps I should get us moving… in case we're cradling a set of railroad tracks," he joked. He jerked the transmission back into first gear, finessed the vehicle back to the proper side of the road, and continued their journey.

The next forty-five minutes proved slow going with Walter desperately trying to avoid a repetition of the skidding incident. Hoping to happen upon something that resembled a town, they passed only two vehicles in that entire time. The few road signs they came in contact with were iced over and unreadable, similar to the conditions they had seen back on Route 1. By now they theorized that they had somehow passed south of Machias, a conclusion based on the passage of time, and merely needed to happen upon Route 1. It was at about this time when the car began a long, moderate descent, the road seeming to grow progressively narrower. This downward grade continued for a few minutes before the headlights picked up something on the road less than one hundred feet in front of them.

"*Walter!*" cried out the woman, grabbing his arm and ripping at the fabric. Instinctively, he pushed down forcibly on the brake, sending the vehicle into an extreme skid. Following a three hundred and sixty degree spinout the car came to rest laterally to the object blocking the roadway. A log lying parallel to the road told them that they had reached the bottom of a dead end street. Walter let out with a loud sigh and exited the car to survey their predicament. Within moments of his feet touching the ground he was aware of the bits of sleet slicing through the air, the granules of falling ice pinching at his face. Circling the vehicle, he was relieved when he saw no evidence of physical damage. However, he was concerned to observe that the accumulation of ice in this area was no less than four inches. Over his shoulder and about fifty yards away sat a large building, blanketed in darkness and barely visible through the icy precipitation. He paced away from the compact car, retracing the track left in the ice by the vehicle's tires. The trip up the road and out of this hollow would not be easy, he thought. Returning to the warmth of the front seat, Walter explained their predicament to Melinda and spelled out a strategy.

Melinda pressed down cautiously on the accelerator while Walter stood behind the car and pushed. It took only seconds to conclude that their number one strategy was doomed to failure. Walter was not able to obtain any traction under foot, providing little in the way of forward momentum for the vehicle. Following a full two minutes of the sound of the car's engine racing wildly he waived off Melinda and collapsed back into the passenger seat.

"I'm going to walk just a little way up the road and see if there's any sign of anyone being around," he announced.

"I'll come with you," she answered.

"No, Melinda, it's really bad out there." On close inspection she could see the reddened effect of the ice pellets on his face.

"Just don't go too far. Please, Walter."

"No, I promise. I'll go a hundred yards, max. There's a couple of houses just a little way up the road. I just want to see if there's any sign of life... like a car or a light on inside. The house behind us here is definitely unoccupied."

Following less than five minutes spent away from the car and out of sight of his female friend, Walter reappeared in the lights of the vehicle, his steps short and guarded to avoid falling onto the cold, icy roadway. She swung open the car door and he fell back onto the front seat.

"First, walking is treacherous. Second, the few houses on this road appear to belong to summer people, and third... it ain't summer," he reported bluntly. "Melinda, we appear to be screwed." The woman closed her eyes and took a deep breath.

"I tried putting on the radio while you were out on your walk. First, we're still getting a friggin' lot of Canadian stations... mostly in French. Absolutely no help. I did pick up a station that might have been Bangor. They talked about the ice storm. By the way, it's worse here near the coast... I assume we're near the coast but we really can't be sure, can we? Anyway, before the station faded away into the night under more of those French-Canadian stations, I think I heard them say that this icy junk is going to continue through tomorrow night." Walter stared across at her, a *deliberative expression written on his face. He shot a glance at the fuel gauge.*

"The gas is down to a quarter of a tank. We can't risk running it down too much more," he said.

"It's our only source of heat right now."

"Do you have a flashlight in the car?" he asked.

"Yes. Why? What are you thinking?" He looked back in the direction of the house beyond the obstruction.

"We'll gain access to the house… doing the least damage possible."

"Do you mean break in?" she questioned in astonishment.

"I'm afraid it's our only option. Melinda, this is getting serious. We could freeze to death out here."

Behind the single, focused beam of their flashlight the two travelers approached the sprawling house. Dressed in darkness, it appeared to be something from a bygone generation. They approached the building tentatively while the frigid wind whipped beads of ice against their faces and caused the nearby trees to whistle in acknowledgement of the ungodly weather. The front door and main entrance was wooden, the top half consisting of a series of small, rectangular panes of glass.

"I should be able to just break one of those small panes and turn the handle of the door," said Walter, as if asking his partner for permission.

"Be careful," she instructed while shielding her body behind his. Using the butt of the hardened rubber flashlight, he shattered the window on the third attempt, reached inside the opening, and unlocked the door. Stepping inside the building they were granted immediate relief from the cold, howling wind but were met with a room temperature not unlike the one outside in the elements.

When the beam from Melinda's flashlight fell upon a light switch, Walter quickly tested it. To their disappointment, nothing happened.

"The fuse box must be turned off. If I can find it we should, at least, be able to get some light in here," he declared. Next, they moved deliberately into the living area. By all appearances they were in the dining room. It was clear the house was tastefully furnished and tidy. A moment later Walter let the beam of light linger on the stone face of a fireplace. He glanced down at his companion and smiled. Stepping forward toward the far side of the room they noticed that much of the far wall consisted of glass. There was no visibility thanks to the layer of ice adhering to the outside surface.

"A sliding patio door," he said. They moved in unison into the next room, a living room. It, too, had a fireplace. The two circled the ground floor of the house and came upon an open kitchen. Walking over to a row of cupboards that lined an interior wall, Melinda swung the first open and signaled to Walter to provide illumination. Even in its darkened state it was evident that it was a working kitchen, not ultra modern or high tech.

"Looking for anything in particular?" he asked of her.

"Matches, candles, you get the picture?" she responded.

"I'm almost positive I saw a set of candles in the last room on the table." They retraced their steps and found a pair of tall, slender candles adorning the dining room table. Following the briefest of celebrations the two lost travelers returned to the kitchen.

"There has to be wooden matches somewhere in this kitchen or at least in the house," declared Melinda, her eyes starting to adjust to the darkness. Methodically, they moved the concentrated illumination from the flashlight along the walls until it finally fell upon an antique, metal match holder affixed to the molding of the pantry door. Melinda scurried across the kitchen floor in the next instant and examined the container for contents.

"Walter, we're in luck," she exclaimed, enthusiastically raising her voice.

Within minutes the two friends sat side-by-side on the living room couch, the single flame from a candle providing the only drab light in the room. The illumination from the flickering flame gave evidence of another of their problems, the temperature, as each breath fogged in the air before them. Following an audible shiver from Melinda, Walter sprang to his feet.

"We've got multiple fireplaces here, so maybe there's firewood somewhere close by," exclaimed the man. "I'll go outside and poke around. Maybe you can explore a little more and see if you can spot a fuse box." Melinda leaned over and kissed him on the cheek.

"Don't you go and abandon me now," she jested, following the innocent peck with a meaningful hug.

After a momentary examination of the missing pane of glass in the door, Walter stepped out into the relentless storm of ice. Instantly, he was struck by the wind chill effect on his face and ears. He set out to walk the perimeter of the building. Above the resonance of wind and hail he thought he picked up on the sound of waves crashing onto shoreline, suggesting the house was situated somewhere along Maine's extensive coast. Beneath his feet the accumulation of icy particles made a crunching sound still quite audible above the whistling tone of the wind. Reaching the back of the house he observed a massive deck. It was void of any furnishings. However, the beam from the flashlight appeared to pick up on an elevated mound at the far end of the expansive, wooden platform. He plodded ahead across the backyard for a closer look. Finally, hoisting himself up onto the deck, he pushed aside an inch of ice and saw the surface of a plastic, blue tarp. His heart pumped with anticipation while he peeled back the corner of the plastic covering. Under it, protected from the elements, was a generous quantity of split and dry firewood.

Melinda greeted Walter at the front door. He carried logs under both arms.

"All we have to do is find some paper or kindling wood and we're in business," he proclaimed, proudly carrying the wood inside and placing it down by the fireplace.

"Consider it done," she answered, presenting him with a small stack of papers. "They were here for Thanksgiving," she observed.

"And how do you know that?"

"By the dates on the papers, Sherlock." He glanced down to see a series of newspapers dated during the later half of November of 1985.

"My little Perry Mason," he sighed, planting a kiss on the crown of her head.

After a period of frustration with their inability to get the logs to ignite, the couple was successful. With both warmth and additional light now available they were able to relax and settle into this foreign environment. By now the couch had been pulled closer to the fireplace and both sat comfortably on it, their bodies snuggled together, their arms entwining one another.

"Tomorrow when it's light I'm going to carve out a wooden slat to replace the pane of glass I broke," said Walter.

"You know, Walt, this is going to sound crazy but I feel really close to the people who own this house."

"That doesn't sound crazy at all. I mean, we're here in their home… the home that could have saved our lives." With that said, he abruptly jumped to his feet. "Don't go anywhere on me. Don't move a muscle." The large man scurried from the room and returned seconds later with an empty pan from the kitchen. Then, without explanation, he exited through the front door and returned a few seconds later. Rejoining Melinda a few feet from the darting flames of the fireplace, he placed down the pan. It was filled with a quantity of ice.

"Fresh water in a matter of minutes," he announced.

"I swear you're like Michael Landon on Little House on the Prairie." He smiled back at her.

"Not as good looking as him though." She reached over and pulled his head to hers, pressing her lips to his and lightly probing the inside of his mouth. He returned her gesture, drawing in a deep breath as if trying to freeze the moment. Seconds later they were gazing deep into each other's eyes while, outside, an extended gust of wind caused the eves of the building to whistle.

The two stranded travelers were cradled together on the couch when Walter broke a long period of silence.

"I don't suppose you saw anything in the kitchen that might even be remotely edible, did you? I mean, they were here as recently as Thanksgiving."

"No, nothing at all. Trust me, I looked." They let out a unified sigh and slumped back into an embrace.

"The pies!" cried out Melinda, jumping to her feet. "We have those blueberry pies out in the car. They're probably frozen by now but it won't take long to thaw them out."

It was eleven o'clock and the stranded couple began preparations for sleep. They had devoured most of one pie and stored what remained in the kitchen, that being an unheated section of the house. Outside, the wind seemed somewhat subdued but the ice continued to fall and cling to everything exposed to the elements. Walter had laid out two blankets on the floor in front of the fire. They were salvaged from a trip upstairs to the bedrooms.

"Walter, dear, could I impose on you for one more thing," asked the girl in as seductive a voice as she could muster under the circumstances.

"You know you can."

"It just dawned on me that I still have my sleeping bag in the trunk of the car… from when the girls and I went climbing in October. Would you be an absolute sweetheart and bring it in for me?"

"Go outside… again?" She leaned into him, returning her lips to his. She followed the kiss up with a tweak to his ear, a gesture she had used on him since their

first date. He shrugged his shoulders and let out an exaggerated sigh.

"You women have way too much power. You really do." With that said, he climbed to his feet, slipped on his coat, and trudged the forty yards out to the vehicle. He returned to find the woman huddled under the two blankets, the better part of her clothing lying on the floor at the far side of the fireplace.

"Your sleeping bag is ice cold. It'll take a few minutes to get it warm enough to crawl into." She smiled up at him but withheld comment. "You know, Melinda, I was hoping that you might let me use at least one of the blankets tonight, given that you have the insulated sleeping bag now." He fell back on the couch and removed his overcoat.

"You needn't worry about the blankets, Walter." She lifted her body from under the blankets, divulging the fact that only a pair of pale blue panties remained on her torso. Walter felt his head grow light at the sight of the woman's milky white body. Encircling his neck with her long arms, Melinda pulled him downward to the floor. The fire crackled just feet away. It sent out ever-changing streams of light. The light danced over her nearly naked body, raising the seductive power of this gift from her Creator. He was caught in the crossfire of what he saw as a role reversal, a female acting as the sexual aggressor. However, his feelings on the appropriateness of the circumstances were of no relevance. At this moment in time he was powerless to resist, deny, or in any way avoid her wishes. His body and bloodstream invaded by the seductive influence of Melinda Klaus, Walter Plews was powerless to do anything but comply with her wishes.

"Walter, put a couple of fresh logs on the fire and then join me on the floor," she instructed. He complied, almost hypnotically, with her request.

Joining Melinda on the floor of the living room, he was immediately enveloped by her in the sleeping bag. It formed a sort of cocoon for the two. With the blankets acting as a buffer between their bodies and the cold floor, she drew him closer to her. Like a wild vine growing through and around a vertical object her limbs enfolded him. Enshrouded in this fabric cocoon and under the absolute spell of this member of the opposite sex, Walter complied with the wishes of this splendid, sexual creature, rendered helpless by her touch and magnificent, primal scent and taste.

Walter, breathing heavily and now sexually depleted by his own efforts, opened his eyes to the darkness of his quiet room. His spirits crashed as he rejoined the here and now, a present void of Melinda Klaus and everything she brought to his existence. Again, as he had done so many times before, he relived the events that followed. It was on a Thursday morning, thirty-six hours after being stranded, that a plow made its way down the road and freed the two lovers. The temperature had risen dramatically that morning, causing a thick fog to envelop the region. Days later Melinda made mention of seeing a cemetery up by the top of the road as they drove away but, owing largely to the fog, seeing little else. For his part, Walter had left the house in the best condition possible. The broken window was shored up by a wooden slat that would keep the elements and critters out until the spring and the owner's return. In addition, Walter and Melinda had pooled their expendable cash and left one hundred and eighty nine dollars to cover the cost of the window repair and the use of blankets, firewood and candles. Along with the money they left an apologetic note, attempting to explain the circumstances and the necessity of the break-in. Incredibly, owing to the density of the fog on that day and their reluctance to linger in the area of their illegal entry, they were not able to learn of its exact location. Their anxiety to leave the region quickly and avoid questioning over the break-in resulted in a shortage of details of the route out. They did not stop that day to refuel the car until reaching Ellsworth. The following spring they returned to Maine's Washington County in search of the house. Recreating the adventure in their heads, they scoured the areas around Machiasport, Roque Bluffs and Jonesport in the hope of finding the splendid house at the end of the long, descending road. They were never successful. Later that year, Melinda ended the relationship.

Walter lay in the darkness, alone in his corner of the imposing house. Less than one hundred feet away the Atlantic Ocean continued to surge and recede over the smooth surface of the sand. It was not even eleven o'clock when he nodded off to sleep.

3

*W*alter pushed his chair back from the desk and raised his arms over his head, stretching out the kinks. He had just completed a non-stop, three-hour sitting at the computer, entering data and adjusting financial information for upper management. Glancing down at his watch, he decided to take a break away from his desk. Outside the confines of his office the weather was unseasonably mild. After replenishing his cup of coffee, he made for the door and proceeded in the direction of the long set of stairs to the back of the building. There he would descend from the heights of the complex to the jagged, rocky floor of Bald Head. It was April, mid-week, and only a handful of rooms at the Cliff House were occupied. What better place to take a meditative break from his office work than on the open rocks, less than a stone's throw away from the foaming surf, he thought. Reaching the lined, jagged floor of stone, he made his way toward a familiar spot within the two acres of tidal cove, craggy divides, and weather-smoothed shelves. His meditative station of choice was at the foot of a protracted, ten-foot-high ledge. There, Mother Nature had carved out a natural bench where he could deposit himself and admire the breakers as they slammed endlessly against this ridge of solid rock. The big man collapsed onto the stony chair and drew in a sip of coffee. He remembered it was his night to meet the guys down at the Union Bluff Hotel, and the prospect of this brought a smile to his face.

A few minutes into his afternoon break, a seagull sailed by his head and winged its way in the direction of the main building. His eyes instinctively followed its line of flight. It was this that led him to pick up on the solitary figure standing on the patch of manicured lawn between the hotel building and the downward spill of rocks to the sea. Upon closer scrutiny, he saw that the person in question was the mysterious pedestrian reported on by Ronny a fortnight earlier. By now Walter knew her name, thanks to the payroll checks processed through his office. Her name was Felicia Moretti and she lived on Freeman Street in York.

Walter allowed his eyes to stray in her direction over the next few minutes. She was tall, thin, and stood motionless on the elevated strip of grassy terrain. Again, just as it had in Ronny's account of her arrival at the Cliff House, her brown hair blew wildly about her face. Initially, she appeared to be looking out to sea. However, on closer scrutiny, this enigmatic female's eyes seemed, at least for the moment, to be focused on him. The woman's attention sent a charge of nervous energy through his stomach. Turning away from her position above him, he reached for his coffee and swallowed a mouthful. Walter glanced at his watch and learned he had been away from his desk for nearly fifteen minutes. Then, in a casual manner, he glanced back in the direction of the woman. Her stare appeared to remain riveted on him. Prompted, no doubt, by a buildup of social anxiety, he timidly lifted a hand and offered an uncertain wave. The Moretti woman stood frozen for an uncomfortable moment before returning the gesture in the form of a whimsical flutter of her own fingers from a raised hand. A moment later she turned from Walter Plews and the open ocean and disappeared behind the building.

Ronny checked his watch as the pickup rattled its way along the shore road toward the village. It was just after four o'clock, giving him adequate time to run multiple errands in town and meet the boys at five-thirty. He had reached the first of multiple stretches in the road where the paved surface allowed for a view of the ocean. Suddenly, the solitary figure of the mysterious woman came into sight. Hugging the ocean side of the road, she walked facing the oncoming traffic, sending out an unambiguous signal that she was not soliciting assistance in her journey home. Dingman made an instantaneous decision to offer her a ride. The woman's head turned as the vehicle slid off into the shoulder and the pickup groaned to a halt.

"I can take you into the village if that's where you're headed," he called out through the truck window.

"Thanks for the offer, but I'm okay," she answered pleasantly.

"I work at the Cliff House, too... and I've seen you there."

"No, it's okay. It's a nice day and I've got plenty of sunlight left." He shrugged his shoulders and threw the vehicle back into first gear. She lifted one hand to shield her eyes. "It's nothing personal. Maybe keep me in mind when the weather's not so nice and I'm caught in a downpour," she added. The young woman followed her words with a genuine smile, a gesture clearly intended to spare the man's feelings.

Ronny arrived at the Union Bluff ten minutes early and laid claim to a table visible from the doorway. He opened a newspaper and waited on his friends. He almost expected an extended waiting period based on recent history so the entrance into the room of both Dave and Chris came as a pleasant surprise. The two men had met up on the street outside.

"Nice table, Dingman," sniped Jacobs while settling into his chair.

"Our usual was occupied."

"It's nice to not be the friggin' first one here for once... and sitting there like a penny waiting for change," piped in Dave. The three men ordered drinks and began sharing stories from the workplace. Chris reported that a salesperson had been added to the outside sales staff.

"I passed her a couple of times in the hallway in the past couple of weeks, probably when she was in interviewing. I thought she was hot. They lured her away from one of our competitors. Now I'm getting this real bad feeling that the powers-that-be may see her as a replacement... for me. Funny, after this revelation, she's not looking so hot anymore."

"Cheer up, buddy. Maybe after she's put the shiv in your back and taken your office, she'll let you hang around and be her toady. You know, like a living, breathing, office trophy," wisecracked Dave.

"She's got to be ten years younger than me if she's a day. Man, maybe, just maybe, I could answer to a woman if she was older than me, but never, ever, to a younger one. I mean, this little bitch can't be more than twenty-six," exclaimed Chris.

"Youth must be served," chimed in Ronny.

"Hey, guys, thanks for all the support." An instant later the table was in shadow and the trio looked up to see Walter standing over them.

"I actually thought I'd beat at least one of you here tonight," he declared before pulling up a chair. On the arrival of the last member of the group a waitress came by and left off menus.

The mood turned less serious as the foursome put in their food orders and sipped on their cold glasses of beer. On this evening the conversation darted from the Red Sox to the latest *Seinfeld* and on to the hottest woman on television.

"It's nice to see that those goddamn Republicans are actually doing something down there in Washington. This week they're working on increasing exports. Unfortunately for us poor bastards at this table, they're working on exporting every one of our jobs," voiced Chris, a vocal liberal on all things political.

"Hey, Jacobs, are you through spending your Clinton tax cut... you know, the one he promised before the election?" asked Dave, a staunch conservative.

"That was mostly the retirees who took it up the ass, and I don't see any senior citizens sitting at this table," came back Chris.

"Clinton's on board with the Republicans on the whole NAFTA garbage. Wave good-bye to your jobs gentlemen," added Dave as he raised his glass in mock salute.

"I think there's going to be a special place in the bowels of hell for the whole lot of them," uttered Walter in an especially sincere tone.

"Any chance of me changing the topic from politics to women?" injected Ronny. His suggestion drew a unanimously favorable response. "Guess who I finally had a chance to talk to this afternoon?" The men all shook their heads, unable to proffer a guess. "That woman I told you about two weeks ago... that walked up from town to apply for a job."

"And?" questioned Chris.

"This afternoon I was coming into town a little early to pick up a few things for work. I saw her on the road... walking home. I stopped and offered her a ride, and managed to get a real good look at her. She's a knockout."

"Did she take you up on your offer?" asked Dave.

"No. She said she didn't mind the walk in the good weather."

"She sounds a little uppity, particularly for a chambermaid. That is what she is, right? A chambermaid." asked Chris.

"No, she was nice about it. She didn't bust my balls and get all offended or anything. She said not to hesitate to ask again in bad weather." Jacobs suddenly found his friend's account comical and burst into laughter.

"Jesus, Dingman, you're like a prostitute who can't even give it away," he blurted out. "She opted to walk ten miles instead of share the cabin of a truck with you."

"It's not ten miles, smart ass," snapped back Ronny.

"Her name is Felicia," injected Walter sheepishly.

"You've spoken to her, too?" asked Dave.

"Not spoken, but she waved down at me when I was outside on break today."

"She waved at you, Walter?" quizzed Jacobs.

"Well, waved back. I noticed her staring down at me down on the rocks. I go there sometimes to take a break," he explained.

"Well, unfortunately, it sounds like you two losers are going to have to go on worshipping her from afar. Christ, you'd think she was a runway model the way you go on about her."

"Yeah, Chris, what are they thinking. Women like this chambermaid aren't worth making a fuss over… only girls like that Deidre bitch you hooked Walter up with a couple of weeks ago," spit out Dave. A hush fell over the table as the men simultaneously realized the secret was out. Walter fiddled uncomfortably in his chair.

"I figured Chris told you guys about my date," muttered Walter. "Chris, it's okay. Hell, we've probably all been down that road at some time in our lives."

"All but one of us," muttered Dave before draining down the remaining beer in his glass and gazing around the pub for the waitress.

The evening of talk and camaraderie was winding down when Chris laid claim to a lull in the conversation.

"I wonder if I could bring up something a little more of the serious nature? And, without question, I'd like to think it wouldn't go anywhere beyond this table." His tone was uncharacteristically serious.

"Oh, Christ, here it comes. Jacobs is finally coming out of the closet," needled Ronny, sending a wink across the table to Walter.

"You don't have to say a word, Jacobs. We've all suspected this from day one," added Dave. Chris answered with an exaggerated sigh.

"You know, suddenly, it's all beginning to make sense. A few months back when I grilled you on those yellow socks you wear every once in a while," injected Walter. "I can't help but remember how you got all huffy and insisted they were harvest gold and not yellow. How could I have been so blind and not picked up on that?"

"It's okay, sweetie. You can confide in us," teased Dave.

"Jerkoffs! I'm serious. I'd like a little feedback here. A couple of nights ago I called my sister down in Massachusetts just to make sure everything is okay. Early on I can tell that something is bothering her but I figure it's just something with her piece of shit boyfriend. Then, after a few minutes she tells me that she has to share something with me, but she doesn't want me to think she's gone completely insane. That's when she says that she thinks there's a ghost in the house. She and her boyfriend bought this Victorian house in Lowell about six months ago and they have come to the conclusion it's haunted." Gazing around the table he saw that his three friends were taking his words seriously. "My fear is that Janice is completely losing her marbles. Ghosts! I mean, what do I say to her? She's my little sister. Should I suggest she see a psychiatrist?"

"Chris, you know me. I may be an accountant but my heart is in science. I'm not some flake who'll believe any horseshit that comes down the pike," answered Dave thoughtfully. "This doesn't necessarily mean your sister's going off the deep end." The middle-aged man checked his watch. "I don't have time tonight to get into this, not with the ball and chain waiting at home. But, next time, guys, remind me to tell you about this part-time job I took about fifteen years ago."

"You ran into something like this?" quizzed Chris.

"Damn right I did. So I suggest you cut your sister some slack and give her the benefit of the doubt for the time being. There's so much crap out there that we just don't understand... and just because the scientific community frowns upon this notion doesn't mean it's not true. Hell, it's been less than thirty years since they finally conceded that a pitcher's curve ball actually curves!"

"The Bible's full of stories about ghosts," added Walter, calmly.

The four men stood on the sidewalk in front of the Union Bluff Hotel. The night was clear and calm, the Milky Way shining directly overhead. Walter made a point of patting both Dave and Chris on the back, a sign of the brotherly affection he carried for both men. Both returned the gesture.

"And you... you, I'll see at work tomorrow," Plews said to Ronny. The friends began to disburse in the direction of their respective vehicles when Walter suddenly turned back to his cohorts. "I can't tell you guys how much these Wednesdays mean to me," he called out over the sound of the crashing surf.

"Don't get all sentimental on us now, Plews. How many beers did our little Walter have tonight?" questioned Jacobs.

"It's okay, Walter, we all feel that way," reassured Ronny from across the street. Within sixty seconds all four men had scattered back in the direction of their individual lives, or the facsimiles thereof.

4

*W*alter let out with a satisfied sigh and leaned back into his chair. It was probably too early in the year to draw any concrete conclusions but he liked what he saw. Cash flow showed a marked improvement over the past two years and reservations were up considerably as the region and economy continued on its recovery from the recession of the early nineties. He had been lost in financial data for the better part of the afternoon. Glancing down at his watch he did a double take. It was a few minutes beyond three-thirty. Instantly, he knew he was in dire need of some fresh air. Outside the office window, the sun had started its descent behind the nearby line of trees and toward the western horizon. The big man crossed the office and drained the coffee pot of its contents, the last remnants of a late morning, ten cup filling. Circling the building, he made his way down the cement stairway, across the natural stone terrace, and down below to his rocky chair. Sixty feet away the sea crashed incessantly against the craggy face of coastline. The active sea was at odds with the warm, calm air. Walter sat still for the few minutes, content to breath in the moistened, fresh air and watch the Atlantic mount its timeless attack against this land mass. Finally, he drew in a mouthful of coffee. It's strength brought a grimace to his face. For some unexplainable reason, it was times like these that brought notions of Melinda to mind. Yes, he felt a definite closeness to her when isolated in nature. Looking over his shoulder and back toward the stairway he convinced himself he was alone.

"I was thinking about our time in northern Maine the other night… thinking long and hard, Melinda," he said softly. "That experience, those four days away with you were the best, most exciting, of my entire life. You do know that, right?" Walter eased the back of his head against the flat wall of the ledge and closed his eyes. The sun felt warm against his face. "I actually tried dating again, as you probably know. Talk about a disaster, right from the get go." The big man exhaled, an attempt to shake off the lingering sadness he felt descending over him. At that moment he felt a light object graze by his hand. He opened his eyes and observed a single, yellow flower on the ground by his foot. Reaching down, he plucked it from the slab of rock. There was no vegetation within a hundred yards of this spot, let alone flowers. Walter craned his neck in an attempt to assure himself he was alone. He appeared to be. "If I were a superstitious man I'd think that you were sending me a sign," he murmured. Seconds later a white flower drifted downward and came to rest in his lap. Springing to his feet, he gazed up at the outcropping of rock ten feet above and caught sight of Felicia Moretti perched above him, her legs crossed in Indian fashion.

"How did you get up there without me seeing you?" he asked in astonishment.

"My daddy used to say that people who talk to themselves all have money," she called down lightheartedly.

"Well, maybe I'm the exception to the rule. Man, you'd make a great sniper." She answered with a playful giggle and rose to her feet.

"Sniper, huh. Where could I go to school for that?" The tall, trim woman gazed down on him, the height accentuating the perfect lines of her body. Walter found himself frozen below, unable to come up with a suitable reply. She gestured to him to wait a moment and began making her way down from atop the ledge.

With his six-foot, six-inch frame shaking with nervous energy, Walter waited as the young woman climbed down to his position. Ten seconds passed before she approached him, her right hand extended in friendship and left hand holding a quantity of flowers.

"Hi, I'm Felicia. I work here at the Cliff House, too. I've been working here about three weeks." Walter was tempted to blurt out that he was already privy to that information and that she was the subject of his and his friends gossiping on more than one occasion, but managed to catch himself.

"I'm Walter… and you're the girl who walks back and forth to work from town."

"That's right, three and nine-tenths miles, one way, every day. That makes nearly eight miles a day. It's how I keep my girlish figure and, well, on top of that, I'm too poor to own a car." Again, Walter searched for a clever response but came up empty. Ultimately, he shrugged his shoulders and settled back onto his rocky chair. The angular brunette followed suit, settling in immediately beside him on the flatbed rock.

"I've been in York for almost a month and I've yet to make an acquaintance, let alone a friend," she confided.

"I find it very hard to believe that a pretty girl like you has any problem meeting people."

"If by people you mean men then, of course, that's true. However, I'm sort of a strange duck. I'm into making friends with a guy and then not acting on anything that might develop romantically from there. Most guys hear that and decide to move on. Then, there's making friends with other women. I've always had a problem in that area."

"That's probably because you're so attractive and a lot of women don't want to be around other women who are substantially more attractive than them," he explained.

"What a nice thing to say," gushed Felicia, leaning in his direction and placing her head against his shoulder. Walter felt his body further tighten from anxiety. Meanwhile, the young woman in his company seemed totally relaxed. Bringing the bouquet of flowers up to her face, she inhaled and extended them in his direction. He responded by sniffing politely. "By the way, am I keeping you from your work?" she asked.

"No, it's okay. I've got all my important work done for the day. That's why I came down here for the fresh air."

"The fresh air... and to talk to yourself," she countered.

"Yeah, sort of talk to myself."

"There's nothing wrong with that. I do it all the time." She spoke with her shoulder resting against him. A second later the girl abruptly pulled herself back. "I'm not getting you in any kind of trouble, am I? Maybe I shouldn't be acting so familiar out here in the open with you being an executive, suit and tie sort of a guy, and here's me just working in housekeeping."

"No, it's okay. I'm hardly a big, executive type. I've got a good job and I'm quite satisfied with my salary, but that's it."

Disregarding his explanation, Felicia jumped to her feet and brushed the loose dirt and particles of stone from the seat of her jeans.

"Walter, it has been a pleasure meeting and speaking to you but I can't put off the task at hand any longer. As much as I dread the prospect of it, I have to be hitting the road and starting the long, painful walk home."

"Painful? Why painful?"

"Stupid me. I turned an ankle walking to work this morning. It's nothing too bad but I have a strong feeling it'll be hurting like the devil by the time I get home tonight," she confessed. Remembering Ronny Dingman's experience with her, he half hesitated in his response.

"If you're comfortable with it, I could give you a ride," he offered.

"No, I can't be hanging around for too long. I need to attend to some things back at the house this afternoon."

"No, I could give you a ride right now."

"And you wouldn't get in trouble?" she questioned.

"My boss is always telling me I'm putting in too many hours. Hell, it's been three years since I've taken a whole week off." The pretty, young woman stepped forward and gave the man a kind-hearted hug.

"Maybe my luck is changing and I'm finally making a friend," she declared, her voice expressing no small measure of gratitude.

Walter banked a left turn at the bottom of the Cliff House driveway and drove south toward the village at Short Sands. As unlikely as this would have seemed only hours before, Felicia Moretti sat across from him in his passenger seat, still clutching her bouquet of flowers.

"I never asked you how you managed to come up with those fresh flowers. They're kind of out of season."

"They're called cosmos. You don't think I stole them from work, do you?"

"No, of course not. That never even entered into my head. It just struck me as unusual." When the cabin of the vehicle suddenly grew quiet, he glanced over at the woman. Felicia had lifted the grouping of flowers up to her face.

"You never told me your last name," she quipped from behind the blossoms.

"Plews. My name is Walter Plews." The attractive brunette giggled.

"Walter, that is a terrible, terrible last name," she commented playfully.

"My first name is no bed of roses, or cosmos, either." She laughed again.

"But the name, Walter, we can work with. When we're good friends I'll be calling you Walt, and there's nothing wrong with Walt as a name."

"You see us becoming good friends?" he asked.

"Of course, don't you?"

"I would have no reservations about making friends with you, Felicia. I mean no reservations." She reached across the car and tweaked at his ear.

The vehicle had just made its way onto Route 1A when Felicia advised the man that they would be taking a left hand turn down the road.

"I live on Freeman Street. It comes just before we reach the village where that saltwater taffy candy store and the movie theater are," she instructed. He did not dare tell her that he already knew her home address, thanks to her employment records, and only needed directions to actually find the street. Within seconds the car was coasting down the road with the village clearly in sight.

"Right up here on the left," she directed. He proceeded up the narrow side street for a couple hundred yards before being told to stop. "This is it," she then announced. They were parked in front of a well-maintained multi-family house. Another uncomfortable lull in the conversation was in progress when Felicia intervened.

"If you're not in too much of a rush, I could make you some tea or maybe some cocoa. We'll have the house to ourselves for a while. Gary won't be home until at least six." Walter's mouth dropped open in bewilderment.

"Gary! Who's Gary?"

"Gary's my roommate."

"You have a male roommate?"

"That's right… and he works until six. It's a really nice apartment. I never could have afforded a place like this by myself," she explained. Walter was unable to disguise his disappointment. "It's not what it sounds like. Gary's my gay roommate… my very, very gay roommate." He fidgeted in his seat. "Gary's the roommate who wears more makeup than me and flagrantly sticks out his pinky finger when he holds a cup. Walter, Gary is quite gay. Now relax. Anyway, do you plan on snubbing me or are you going to accept my invitation for a cup of tea?"

"I would love to join you for tea," he responded sheepishly.

Walter sat alone in the living room while his new acquaintance prepared their beverages in the kitchen and out of sight. The apartment was impeccably furnished and immaculately clean with the rug still showing signs of a recent vacuuming.

"I hope you don't mind milk and sugar with your tea. We don't have any lemons in the house," she called out from the next room.

"Milk and sugar will be fine. That's how I ordinarily have it," he answered. He took a moment to contemplate his circumstances. He was sitting in the living room of Felicia Moretti, the woman of mystery whose arrival Ronny Dingman had announced over drinks a few weeks earlier. This was the same woman who seemed such a perplexing mystery only twenty-four hours ago. Now, he sat in her warm living room, this integral place in her private life, waiting for tea. He lifted his eyes from the floor as she entered the room, tray in hand. Placing the tray down on the table before him, she prepared both beverages and handed one to him. She then surprised him by seating herself on the couch to his immediate left and not in one of two cushioned chairs nearby.

"If I may be so bold to ask, who was it you were talking to this afternoon down along the ledge?" Felicia asked. Walter was immediately taken aback, not just by the directness of the question but also by the intensity of the eye contact from the woman.

"So you actually heard what I was saying back there."

"I'm not hard of hearing." He sat perfectly still for a moment, as if considering whether to answer the question or just get up and leave.

"She was someone I knew a long time ago."

"And did she leave you?"

"In every sense of the word."

"What does that mean?"

"That means that first she dumped me, then she went and died on me a year later. From everything I was able to piece together she broke it off to spare me the pain and suffering of watching her go… along with keeping some of her own ego intact. She had melanoma."

"That's skin cancer, right?"

"Right." She nodded her head understandingly. "You know, I can't believe I'm sharing all of this with you. I barely know you," declared Walter.

"Sometimes we can meet someone and we know immediately that we can trust them. Then there are others we can know for years and never feel inclined to share anything with them," reflected the woman. "Now me, I don't speak much of myself or where I came from. I keep my past to myself."

"So you just sat there and let me spill my guts knowing you wouldn't share anything about yourself with me?" Felicia shrugged her shoulders and flashed him a coy smile.

His visit to the home of Felicia Moretti had run on for nearly a half hour and, instinctively, he felt the need to extricate himself from her company. Beyond this woman's physical beauty there was a seductive charm about her that sent a wave of cautionary fear through him. Walter's own sense of emotional self-preservation guided him to take leave of this place. His cup of tea empty, the heavy set man rose to his feet and politely made his way towards the door. Felicia moved gracefully over the carpeted floor behind him, her bare feet like cat's paws on the rug. He bid her a good afternoon and started down the stairs to the first floor. Reaching the second step in his descent, he felt her hand come down on his shoulder and summon him to stop. He turned to face her. Standing above him on the landing, he had to glance up slightly to meet her eyes.

"Now, Walter, I don't want you to put more significance on this than there really is," she cautioned. She pressed her lips to his. With the back of his head cradled in her hand, he submitted to her advance. The kiss lasted the briefest of seconds but still left the flavor of her mouth on his lips. She pulled back and surveyed his condition. Lightheaded, disoriented, brain-muddled, Walter took in the image of this seductive female and fought off the temptation to literally surrender every fragment of his self-respect and prostrate himself before her.

"Good night, Felicia," he managed to blurt out before turning and descending the stairway.

"You'll soon learn I have a flair for the dramatic," she sang out before breaking into a flurry of seductive laughter.

Walter let out a deep breath while surveying the surface of his desk. Strewn with an assorted number of correspondences, reports and tax forms, it was a blunt reminder of his lack of productivity since returning from the Moretti woman's apartment. His feelings at the moment were mixed. On one hand there was this exhilarating, sexual intoxification pumping through him, the residue of his brief interaction with this almost perfect stranger. Then, on the other hand, there was a sense of danger associated with Felicia Moretti. Instinctively, he knew to what extent this magnificent creature could bring on heartbreak and misery. What was it that Gibran had warned us about? That which gives us the greatest pleasure can also discharge the greatest pain. He glanced through his office window in the direction of the nearby line of trees. In doing so his eye was caught by movement in the upper corner of the glass. A small, black and brown spider had begun to weave the outer perimeter of her web. For the next few seconds he watched as the tiny insect systematically began the construction of this weapon of entrapment. After thirty seconds in a trancelike state, he pulled his attention away from the spider's activity outside the window and focused his attention back on the work spread before him on the desk.

5

The hands on the prominent, black clock on the far wall of the office read three o'clock. Walter lifted himself from his comfortable office chair and made his way to the coffee machine in the next room, debating with himself on whether to take his afternoon break on the ledge at the edge of the ocean. Two days had passed since he spoke with Felicia Moretti. Twenty-four hours earlier he had returned to his meditation spot in hopes of speaking again to the attractive woman. To his disappointment, she had not appeared the prior day and he was left sitting alone with his thoughts. He found himself losing an internal debate with himself on the wisdom of making his way down the long procession of stairs to the edge of the sea. In less than two months the rocky playground in the shadow of Bald Head Cliff would be peppered with tourists at this time of the day and his tranquil refuge would be lost. Finally, after a moment of hesitation, he exited the office and made his way around the building to the stairs.

Walter glanced around the jagged ground before depositing himself on his customary rocky bench. He was alone by the sea for the moment except for a solitary camera buff one hundred yards away beneath the cliff. He pulled out a paperback from the rear pocket of his trousers, turning the book open to the page of his bookmark. He began perusing the page in an attempt to pull the storyline and what had already played out from memory. Unconsciously, his eyes scanned up to the grassy strip of land above him, the spot where he had first spied Felicia Moretti. Each time, however, his pupils returned to the pages of his novel empty-handed. He was about to close the book when a single, white cosmo floated down from above, coming to rest in the inverted spine of the book. He spun himself to his feet and glanced up at the Moretti woman. She stood elevated ten feet above him, a gentle breeze blowing her brown hair back from her face. She wore a fragile smile while holding tightly onto a group of mixed flowers.

"How do you manage to keep sneaking up on me?" Walter asked in good humor.

"I guess I'm light on my feet. Then again, maybe the sound of the ocean provides more than just a little cover for me."

"I was just about to go back to the office," he acknowledged.

"Oh, I get it, Mr. Hard-to-get." Her words caused him to laugh.

"I've been sitting down here waiting for you..." He caught himself in mid sentence and dropped his eyes to the ground. He was blurting out a little too much information, he thought to himself.

"Waiting on little ole me? Why Rhett Butler, you handsome rogue," Felicia sang out in her best Scarlett O'Hara impersonation. He chuckled.

"Do you need a ride?" The brunette shook her head no.

"I love your coffee cup," she announced, pointing down at his right hand. "It looks like a diner cup. I love diners. Well, I should say I love diner food. What about you, Walter? Do you like diner food?"

"Who doesn't?" he answered. "My doctor doesn't like the fact that I like diner food."

"Unfortunately for me, I can't afford to be going out to eat every day, not with my sky high rent and expensive taste in clothes," she declared, gesturing down to her faded sweatshirt and well-worn denim jeans.

"Is someone else giving you a ride?" he asked guardedly, following up on her rejection of a ride ten seconds earlier.

"Someone else giving a ride to little ole me?" She answered, again with the southern drawl.

"Yeah, I was just curious."

"No, Walter Plews, you are my official driver. Now Walter, I'll repeat what I said a few seconds ago. I really, really like diner food."

"I could take you out to a diner if you wanted to go. It'd be my pleasure."

"I swear, Mr. Plews, how did you ever figure out I wanted little ole you to ask me out?"

"Just a wild hunch, that's all." He watched as Felicia scampered down from the layer of rock above. She was at his side a few seconds later.

"These are for you," she proclaimed, extending a handful of flowers.

"Thank you, Felicia." She reached up, tweaked at his ear and paused the briefest of moments for his reaction. He stood muted until she let out with a burst of laughter and scrambled over the rocks toward the cement stairway. "How soon would you like to go to that diner? Any night but Wednesday is good for me," he called out to her.

"How about this weekend?" Felicia called back.

"That works for me."

"Pick me up, five-thirty at my place on Saturday," she announced before disappearing up the flight of stairs.

Walter lugged his body up the extended series of cement steps and returned to his office. His thoughts were awash with Felicia. He thought about his next night with the guys and reporting on his budding relationship with the attractive Miss Moretti. He stared down at the analysis work he was doing on occupancy rates and immediately shuffled it aside. His concentration level was flat-lining. It was better to work on something repetitious and brainless like data entry while the image of Felicia Moretti was taking possession of his process of thought. Through his office window he could see the glinting light from the descending sun through the line of pine trees. A speck of movement caught in his peripheral vision drew his attention. He focused his eyes on the brown and black spider that had taken up residence outside his window. She had completed her web, a beautiful, intricately engineered snare. Now she rested almost completely out of sight on the edge of the sill. She was biding her time, waiting, patiently waiting.

6

*W*alter turned his Corvette onto Freeman Street and glanced down at the digital clock embedded in the dashboard. He was three minutes early for his date. The vehicle rolled deliberately up the narrow roadway, the engine barely audible. Within seconds he caught sight of Felicia standing in front of her building. He had anticipated having to call on her at the front door. His eyes widened at the sight of Felicia Moretti outfitted in a form-fitting dress and heels. Until this moment, Walter had only seen her in jeans and sneakers. She spotted the car and moved to the edge of the sidewalk. He brought the vehicle to a stop in the middle of the road and the sharply dressed brunette made her way toward the passenger side of the car. Walter bolted from behind the steering wheel and scurried to the far side of the vehicle. His date waited appreciatively while Walter fumbled with the passenger door, eventually swinging it open and ushering her in. He froze in place momentarily while she gracefully folded her legs over the passenger seat, his eyes riveted on her knees and perfectly cut calf muscles. Finally, he closed the car door behind her and hurried back to behind the wheel.

"You look beautiful, Felicia," he muttered.

"Thank you, Walter. I thought you deserved having your companion for the evening dressed in something other than jeans."

"I fully expected to have to pick you up at the front door. Imagine my surprise to see you waiting on me by the curb."

"Gary's home… and he can be a bit of an asshole. I thought I'd spare you that," she explained behind a warm smile.

"I hope you have an appetite," he called out while the car slowly accelerated.

"Any chance I could put in a special request?" Felicia asked.

"Sure, go ahead."

"Any chance you could take me down to Wells Beach before dinner and show me the Sand Castle?"

"Of course, if that's what you'd like. Hell, I don't remember even telling you about the Sand Castle." He shot a glance across the front seat of the car and eyed her smiling back at him. "I can't even keep track of what I have and haven't told you."

"That's going to make lying to me very problematic," she muttered half under her breath.

"Yeah, for sure," he answered. "Not that I plan on lying to you anyway."

Walter and Felicia were blessed with a beautiful, spring evening as they motored north on Route 1 through Ogunquit. The sidewalks were already dotted with tourists on this last Saturday in April. Reaching Wells, they turned eastward onto Eldridge Road and drove in a straight line until a cement wall blocked their advance. They had reached the Atlantic Ocean. Walter swung a left turn and the two proceeded alongside the foaming seawater until Plews pulled the vehicle onto a modest side street and brought the car to rest behind a sprawling, mint green, oceanfront home.

"Miss Moretti, I give you the Sand Castle," he announced, introducing the formidable structure as if it were a member of the family. The tall woman stepped out of the car, her eyes trained on the three and a half story building. Within seconds Walter was standing next to her, ushering her toward the partially hidden stairwell at the rear of the building. She walked beside him in silence while her eyes took in the architectural details of the edifice.

"When was it built?" she asked.

"Early in the twentieth century. We've never been able to nail down the exact year."

"I love it. I absolutely love it," she admitted in a voice brimming with sincerity. Directing her up the flight of stairs at the back of the house, he guided her around the main floor on a porch that harkened visitors back to another age and time.

"My great-aunt, she actually owns the house, my great-aunt still refers to it as the piazza," Walter said through a chuckle. "She's from another world. She's incredible... still sharp as a tack. You ask her and she can give you insight into Calvin Coolidge, Babe Ruth, Rudolph Valentino, F. Scott and Zelda, you name it. As a young woman she actually met Calvin Coolidge! I find that absolutely unbelievable," he declared.

"I'd love to meet her," Felicia said in a reverently low voice.

"She'll be here for a couple of weeks in July. If we're still seeing each other then I'm sure I could arrange it." The brunette glanced back at Walter.

"We're seeing each other?" she inquired accusingly. He grew flustered.

"No... I didn't mean anything by that... like we were actually seeing each other..." She brought her fingers up to his lips.

"Don't let me do that to you," she responded. "Don't let me get you all flustered. Of course we're seeing each other. It's the weekend and we're together... here... at your house." He let out with a sigh and took a deep breath. Felicia flashed him a beguiling smile and brought her body in contact with his. They were standing at the front of the house. Between the sweeping, arched openings in the porch's woodwork their eyes took in the expanse of sandy beach and tranquil ocean. Walter pulled a set of keys from his pocket and unlocked the main entrance. She preceded Walter into the house, her eyes scanning from room to room. The entranceway led directly onto a flight of stairs leading up to the second floor. Felicia paused thoughtfully inside the doorway, then turned right into the living room. Behind a picture window offering a one-hundred-and-eighty-degree view of the open ocean was a generous-sized room furnished large-ly in wicker. The woman moved through the living space in silence, proceeding into the adjoining dining room. There she stopped and examined the handsome, mahogany furniture dominating the middle of the room. Finally, she spoke.

"You have to be the neatest, most orderly man in the world."

"I barely ever use these rooms. I do all of my living one floor below," he explained. She lifted her glance to him and moved on. They walked together into the kitchen. Her eyes perused the room while a smile spread across her pretty features. Two steps inside the room she stopped in place, staring down at the surface of a black sink.

"Is this made of what I think it's made of?"

"If you're thinking slate, then yes," answered the man. Her eyes ran back and forth over the object. Above the body of the basin it read: *Monson Maine, Boston, Mass.* Transfixed for an extended time by this highly unusual kitchen fixture, she was finally able to tear her eyes away and continued her tour of the house.

"It reminds me of my grandmother's house," she declared. Her comment was, no doubt, in reference to the style of cabinetry and the age of the major appliances. With the lone exception of a microwave oven, the kitchen could have been frozen in time from the 1960's. The abbreviated tour of the house's main floor concluded in a sunroom. It appeared the room had been carved and enclosed from the original wraparound porch. "This is absolutely magnificent," exclaimed Felicia as she walked toward a wall of glass that effectively framed the foaming surf of the Atlantic Ocean. "How can you not use these rooms?" she asked in disbelief.

"It doesn't mean anything if you don't have someone to share it with," answered Walter. She directed her brown eyes to his but withheld a response, perhaps viewing him as too easy a target. It is said that the intuitive powers of women are far more developed than those of men. If that is the case then certainly an argument could be made that the fairer gender's ability to detect vulnerability in the opposite sex is more cultivated than its counterpart.

Felicia, seated on a wooden bench outside the Maine Diner, fidgeted beneath Walter who stood over her. Always the gentleman, he had surrendered his seat to an elderly couple who, like them, waited to be called inside to a table.

"Popular place," she uttered, commenting on the delay in being seated.

"Well, little miss fussy, you're the one who wanted diner food. It could be worse. We could be here in July with a million tourists," answered Walter.

"Would you prefer it if I demanded gourmet food at some overpriced greasy spoon? I hear there's some places not too far from here that'll have you running to the bank and taking out a second mortgage."

"Yeah, maybe I should be counting my blessings," he admitted in a whisper.

Their time spent waiting out an open table did not extend beyond five minutes. Soon they were escorted to a booth just inside the door and handed menus. Felicia placed hers face down within seconds and delivered a polite kick to her escort's shin.

"No dilly-dallying, Mr. Plews. When the waitress arrives back here I want you fully decided on your meal and ready to order," she insisted.

"You do realize that I'll have a nice black and blue mark tomorrow from that kick to the shin you gave me."

"God, you must bruise like a peach." He smiled across the table and squeezed her hand.

"Don't worry, you're worth it," he acknowledged.

"So now that we have a second, tell me a little about this girl you talk to when you're alone down by the ocean." His date had wasted little time directing the conversation to a subject personal in nature.

"Like what?"

"You could start with her name."

"Melinda. Melinda Klaus."

"Ahh... a *fraulein*. And you say this girl left you... and then she died. When you spoke about her back at the house I thought I detected a little bitterness. But, here you are... years later, still taking time to speak to her in private... and during your afternoon break mind you."

"I loved her deeply," confessed Walter. His words prompted his date to visibly pause and reflect on his sentiment. The momentary lull in conversation was interrupted by their waitress's arrival.

"Have you folks decided?" asked the middle-aged woman.

"A cheeseburger with ketchup, lettuce and tomato. Fries with a dish of brown gravy on the side, plus an orange soda," barked out Felicia in a spirited manner. The waitress scribbled down the order and turned her attention to Walter.

"I see you have meat loaf on the menu," he drawled.

"That happens sometimes. We don't wash off the menus until later in the evening," jested the woman, her eyes darting to Felicia then back to the man. Her literal interpretation brought forth an eruption of laughter from both Walter and his date.

"I'll have the meat loaf plate and a cup of coffee... regular." The waitress scooped up the menus and hastily made her way toward the kitchen. Felicia's eyes followed the woman across the room before returning to the man seated directly in front of her.

"So tell me more about this Melinda Klaus," demanded Felicia in the next breath, her voice both seductive and insistent. She watched as a painful expression took hold of Walter's face.

"I sort of told you everything there is to know about her that time I visited your apartment. I loved her. She dropped me. She died about a year after we split up. Presumably, she dropped me to spare me some of the anguish of having to watch her waste away. All I know is I've never connected with another human being the way I did with her." Walter paused and drew in an extended breath. For a moment he considered sharing his story of the ice storm with Felicia but instantly decided against it. He had never shared an account of those incredible two and a half days with anyone and was somewhat surprised with himself that he would even contemplate doing it with a woman he barely knew.

"So how about you, Felicia Moretti? What's your story?" The brunette's face turned serious as she peered across the table at him.

"I'm a proverbial rolling stone. I don't tend to spend a heck of a lot of time in one place before I get restless and move on. I also tend to grow somewhat bad-tempered when anyone tries to pry into my life. So Walter, forewarned is fair warned. I think my life and philosophy can be summed up in that old Gale Garnett song, *We'll Sing in the Sunshine.*"

"How do you mean?"

"I mean, the way I live my life is in the lyrics: We'll sing in the sunshine, we'll laugh every day, we'll sing in the sunshine, then I'll be on my way."

It was a short time after the Moretti woman's flippant explanation of her personal philosophy when the meal arrived at the table. Felicia greeted her plate with the gleeful exuberance of a five-year-old let loose in a candy shop. Walter, conversely, appeared to withdraw into a placid, meditative state, barely adding anything to the mealtime conversation. Following a period of largely one-sided discussion, Felicia engaged the waitress in light banter for the couple's remaining time in the diner. By the time the two strolled across the parking lot to the man's car, Felicia had had enough of the silent treatment.

"Okay, out with it. What's with you and this sudden clamming up all of a sudden? Did I say something to tick you off?" The man shook his head in the negative and adopted a vacant, facial expression. "Plews, either tell me what's rattling around in that thick skull of yours or I make a scene right here in the parking lot," she threatened. "Trust me, Walter, I'm shameless and I have a strong suspicion you're easily embarrassed." The blank expression on Walter's face quickly mutated into one of absolute concern.

"I told you, it's nothing," he insisted with a degree of irritation in his tone. Seconds later the slender brunette fell to her knees and clutched the man's hand.

"Oh please, Walter, please don't say it's over," she cried out in anguish. "I'll do whatever you ask of me. I can't live without you. You must know that. What will it take from me? You have my mind and body. Is it my soul that you want?"

"All right, I'll tell you what's bothering me, but get up," he pleaded half under his breath. "She's just fooling around," he called out to a party of elderly patrons making their way toward the entrance of the restaurant. Felicia continued on a few seconds more, kissing his hand feverishly.

"For God's sake, cut it out," he begged, the first hint of a smile finally showing on his face. "She's quite the little comedian," he called out again, hoping to reassure the senior citizens that they were not bearing witness to a complete, psychological meltdown. Felicia methodically lifted herself to her feet, burying her face into the middle of his chest and squelching laughter. He ushered his date into the car, letting out an audible sigh of relief when the doors closed beside them.

"Okay, Plews, out with it," the woman insisted before he could even insert the key into the ignition. He looked straight ahead through the windshield, avoiding eye contact with his companion.

"It bothered me when you started talking about pulling up stakes and moving. I like things constant in my life. I've just met you and I'm already developing a fondness for you, and here you are already talking about taking off. It just depressed me, that's all," he confessed.

"Walter, I love my apartment down in the village, in spite of my idiot room-mate. I really like my job. That probably sounds stupid to you, me being a chambermaid and all, but I do. I love living on the coast of Maine. So you see, I'm pretty happy right now."

From the parking lot of the Maine Diner, Walter turned the vehicle south, heading down Route 1. To her relief, Felicia quickly realized she would not have to provide the brunt of the conversation within the car. It was Walter who initi-ated a discussion regarding various matters at work. Once every topic of mutual interest at the Cliff House had been exhausted, he introduced the content of the latest discussions with his three friends at the Union Bluff Hotel in its place. Whether sincere or feigned, the Moretti woman displayed a genuine interest in the subject matter bantered around by these reasonably typical males.

"So, you complete idiots actually discuss which old movie actresses you would like to go to bed with? Aren't any of the guys married?"

"Yeah, two of them are… but so what. It's not like Bette Davis or Veronica Lake is going to step down from the silver screen and slip into one of their bed-rooms. It's just innocent guy talk," he pointed out, defending his pub brothers.

"I guess," she relented, reaching across the front seat and tugging on his ear.

An uncomfortable silence descended on the cabin of the vehicle as the car turned onto Freeman Street and cruised toward Felicia's house. The hour was still unthinkably early for bringing a social evening to a close and they both knew it. Walter's Corvette slowed to a crawl then stopped across the street from the house.

"You're invited upstairs for tea and maybe some of those fancy, English cookies. Let me repeat that. You're invited up for tea and cookies, not a friendly game of strip poker, or a hot and heavy make out session, and certainly not an evening of unbridled sex," explained Felicia. He laughed aloud.

"What about Gary?"

"By now Gary is up in Ogunquit up to God knows what! I may not even see him again until Sunday night." The gentle hulk of a man stared across the front seat, exhaled a deep sigh, and turned off the engine.

Felecia turned the key and pushed in the front door. The interior of the apart-ment was pitch black and it was a few seconds before her fingers finally made contact with the switch and a wall light illuminated.

"Oh, there's something I really want to show you, Walter. Why don't you make yourself comfy in that chair in the corner and I'll put on some tea," she suggested, pointing him toward a well-cushioned, velvet chair at the far side of the room. He lumbered across the living room, as directed, and eased himself down. Glancing around, he was taken with how meticulously clean and void of any clutter the room was. From the kitchen came the familiar sound of water being prepared for hot beverages. The pretty brunette's face peeked from behind the kitchen door.

"I'm not terribly comfortable in a skirt and nylons. Mind if I change into something a bit less confining?"

"No, go ahead," he responded from behind an orchestrated smile.

A full ten minutes had passed before Felicia re-entered the living room with a tray covered with cups, saucers and a plate of cookies. Walter lifted his eyes from an issue of the *Smithsonian,* observing that his hostess was now dressed in nothing more than a satin robe, her hair quite damp as if she had just emerged from a hot shower.

"If you'll slide that table over closer to the chair, I'll serve the tea," she said, gesturing toward a coffee table a few feet away. He rose from the chair and slid the table directly in front of her. The smell of faintly perfumed soap filled Walter's nostrils as Felicia placed down the tray and eased her guest back into the velvet, upholstered chair. "Now if you'll pour your own tea, I'll go to my bedroom and get what I wanted to show you." The man watched as Felicia left the room, her damp hair streaming over the neck of her robe and down her back. She returned in thirty seconds, a stack of cards in one hand. "I found these in an antiques shop a few days ago. Take a look," she insisted. She handed him a quantity of postcards before seating herself on the floor beneath him. Taking hold of the dated postcards, he deliberately reviewed one after another, careful to examine both sides of the faded cardboard. All the while, the woman simultaneously prepared her beverage and scanned his face for a reaction.

"Wow, this is an amazing collection of cards. Some of these I've never seen before."

"There's one that really blew me away," she exclaimed, rising to her feet. "Let me shed a little more light on the subject," she added. Leaning over Walter, she stretched upward and flicked on the brass floor lamp positioned behind the chair. Then, in one continuous motion, she deposited herself atop the man, curling her legs halfway beneath her torso. "There's a card with a 1914 postmark in here," she exclaimed, taking the cards and riffing through the stack. "There's a bunch of people that look like they're on a picnic and Bald Head Cliff is in the background." She proceeded to cull through the deck of cards, the weight of her body in full contact with Walter's sensitive pubic region.

"Yes, I remember that one," he acknowledged.

"Here it is," she stated eagerly, pulling the card from the stack. "It's dated July 19th, 1914. It was sent to Mrs. Effie Burgess, Dracut, Massachusetts. There's not even a street address! *We're getting some relief from the heat here. Will drop by next week. George.* Poor Effie is back in Dracut, no doubt roasting her backside off and here's George here, sprinkling salt on the wounds. What an inconsiderate jerk," snapped the woman. Her reaction to the card brought a round of laughter from Walter. "Now look at the other side of the card," she ordered. The man complied. "I'll bet half the people in this picture are dead by now. They look so happy in the picture and now half of them are dead."

"Half? You think only half are dead?"

"Maybe even more than half," she countered, revising her estimate.

"Try all of them! Sweet Jesus, the card is over eighty years old and nobody in the picture looks a day under fifty!" roared Walter. "They'd have to be over one hundred and thirty years old to still be alive!"

"Are you sure?" Felicia asked in a little girl's voice.

"Do the math," he answered through rolling laughter.

"I saw this old guy walking along Long Sands last week. He could've been over a hundred and thirty," she insisted, bringing her face in close proximity to his. He breathed in the fragrance from her skin, all the while conscious of the subtle movement of her body atop his own.

"He probably wasn't even one hundred, let alone one hundred and thirty," he responded, his voice tailing off. "Come on Felicia, no one lives to be one hundred and thirty." She relaxed her body, letting its full weight rest upon his. Walter's thoughts were now overrun with Felicia Moretti. He knew that beneath the satin robe wrapped around her body was nothing but her perfect flesh. She edged her body slightly higher onto his, her breath warming the man's neck.

"When we left the restaurant and you brought me directly home, I was struck with this fear that you wanted our relationship to end," she whispered to him while encircling his massive shoulders with one arm. "Walter, we won't let that happen to us, will we?" The woman waited on a response. She felt his upper body go limp while the sexual energy she conjured up caused his body beneath her to harden. Unable to verbalize a reply to her question, he drew in a deep breath, hoping to somehow decrease the heating of his blood. Walter quickly realized the exercise was futile. This female, still a stranger, was intoxicating him with her behavior, intoxicating him with her cunning, deliberate form of sexuality. "I want and need you in my life," she added. Unable to muster any sort of resistance to her erotic offensive, he followed a series of deep breaths with a response.

"I have to admit that...after dinner I was considering everything you had said and what it might feel like down the road...losing you and losing touch with you. I was thinking it might be easier just taking my lumps now before I'm totally gone."

"You have to trust me, Walt."

"It's not even a matter of trust at this point. Felicia. I don't have the strength or the inclination to walk away from you. If there's a price for growing close to you, then I'll pay it...no matter what." She answered his admission with a passionate kiss on the lips, her tongue reaching inside his mouth. The battle between their two wills was over, the outcome never in doubt.

7

It was a late afternoon borrowed from paradise in the village of York when Ronny Dingman motored his pickup up the roadway to the Union Bluff Hotel. The nearby shoreline at Short Sands was dotted with groups of teenagers meandering by the edge of the lethargic breakers. Locals knew there would be three days of rain later in the month due in payment for this splendid May afternoon and accepted it. The road was lined with more vehicles than usual in the off-season, sending Dingman in search of parking at the rear of the hotel. He emerged from the back of the building, only to pause and gaze out over the glistening ocean before him with the backdrop of a hillside clustered in well-kept beach houses on the quiet end of the Nubble. The rugged Mainer made his way into the hotel lobby then banked a hard right on into the pub. Inside, Dave Durette and Chris Jacobs had already laid claim to their table of choice. Durette mimicked checking his watch before waving his friend over.

"And where's our gentle giant?" called out Chris.

"He'll be along. You know Walter, always fussing over this or that report." Dingman called over to the nearest waitress and ordered a glass of his usual sent to the table.

"I hope you guys appreciate having me here tonight. If I were sane I'd be up in Portland in one of their singles bars. I mean… with this weather the skirts and shorts are out in force. The long, bleak winter is behind us. The girls are out strutting their stuff," reported Jacobs enthusiastically.

"Trust us, we're honored," croaked Durette through a mouth half filled with brew.

"And how's Walter? I'm assuming he's fully recovered from that whole Deidre experience last month?" Chris posed the question to Ronny.

"Our boy is quite the happy camper these days. My guess is that your friend Deidre is a long-forgotten memory by now."

"That takes a weight of my shoulders. That whole stinking nightmare of a blind date I set up for him was still bothering me. He's a buddy and a good guy and it really bothered me that I put that whole fiasco together."

"Put your mind at ease. These days Walter has nothing female on his mind but a certain chambermaid back at the Cliff House," reported Ronny.

"Really," exclaimed Dave. "Okay Dingman, details, and don't leave anything out."

"Remember back a month ago… I told you about this woman who walked out to the Cliff House to get a job and walked back and forth from work to the village every day," said Ronny.

"The real looker who wouldn't take a ride from you?" questioned Jacobs.

"The very same. Our shy Walter and this woman are now an item."

"Good for him," chimed in Dave.

"I hope so," added a sober Ronny.

"What? What's the problem?" asked Dave.

"I don't know. It's not even the fact that they look like the odd couple, this girl being drop-dead gorgeous and Walter being… Walter. But, it's more than that. No one knows jack shit about who this girl is or where she comes from. Then there's the fact that it was she who went after Walter. I mean, come on, give me a break!" exclaimed Ronny.

"Dingman, you're out of your mind!" roared Durette.

"No, Dingman may have a point… besides the one he keeps so cleverly hidden underneath his filthy cap. Did you ever consider what our buddy, Walter Plews, might be worth?" asked Chris before taking a quick draw from his beer. "The guy makes a good salary, drives around in his Corvette, which he paid cash for, and doesn't even pay any rent for his apartment. He hasn't been dating since that German broad dumped his ass ten years ago. The guy has to be really socking it away!"

"And how would mystery girl know all this?" asked Dave.

"Yeah, of course, the women at the Cliff House never talk among themselves about guys. You're right, Durette, how could I have been so stupid?" answered Jacobs in mock fashion.

"She's made him a different guy," injected Ronny. "He's been really upbeat lately. You'll see when he gets here."

It was a few minutes after six o'clock when the men looked up from the table and saw their friend darkening the doorway, an uncharacteristic broad grin covering his face. Plews waved to the bartender then meandered to the table.

"My apologies gentlemen, for again being the last to arrive." Walter slipped down into his chair and waited on a response.

"That's okay, Plews, we were just here trying to remember the last time you bought a round for the table. We couldn't remember the year but we do remember that Durette still had a full head of hair," wisecracked Jacobs.

"You know what?" came back Walter. "All kidding aside, the drinks are on me tonight. I'm in high spirits and what's wrong with sharing a spell of good fortune with friends," he declared. A cheer went up from the table as the men opened their menus and prepared for their meal together. For the following sixty minutes the four old friends shared stories, both professional and personal, from the last fortnight of their lives. This was the ritual, the glue that kept the foursome together over the years.

With their dinner dishes cleared away and deserts yet to arrive at the table, the discourse picked up among the four friends.

"So, Jacobs, how are things coming along with your sister and her ghost problem?" asked Ronny.

"Man, I really don't know what to make of that," he replied. "It's hard to tell if she's really got a problem or just flipping out?"

"You know, I'm glad someone said something about that. I told you last time how I had a story about ghosts and hauntings. There may be something to what she says. Any of you guys interested in something that happened to me a few years back?" The group replied in the affirmative and Dave Durette proceeded. "A few years after I got out of college I took a second job to keep the creditors away from the door. Elaine was still at home with the baby and we'd just learned that little Alex was on the way. I took a job working nights at a sporting goods store in Portsmouth. The first night I'm working and sitting with the assistant manager and he nonchalantly tells me that the store has a ghost but not to be alarmed. I laughed but he stayed serious and told me how I might be hearing the lockers rattling out back in the stockroom sometimes. He said they'd sometimes rattle when there was no one out there. He said that if it wasn't the rattling lockers then it might be the sound of keys jingling in another aisle... even when there was no one in the aisle or the storeroom. He's telling me this and I'm thinking that maybe I'm being set up for a practical joke. I worked there a couple of months, Christmas season came and went, and I had no problems. Then, in January, something odd happened. One of the other salesmen there, Phil Ackroyd, ups and quits, claiming that he can't deal with the strange crap going on at the store at night. I'm there when he's handing in his keys and he says he saw a figure walking out back, a shadowy figure that walked right through the wall. He says he needs the money but this is just too weird. At that point I saw the makings of a practical joke being set up for me. The next week I caught a couple of the closing shifts. My first night the manager left at six and left me to close at nine. Near the end of my shift I thought I heard the lockers rattling but when I stuck my head through the door it had stopped. The second night, well, that's when the proverbial shit hit the fan." Dave paused for a second and took a sip from his glass of beer. He had his friend's complete attention. "The second night went smooth as silk with no strange sounds or anything. Again, I'm alone to close the store. Just before leaving I realized that I really had to go to the bathroom. We're living in Epping at the time, a good thirty minutes away. So, given that it's been a quiet night, I go out back to the bathroom at the rear of the store. Anyway, I'm in the stall taking care of business when suddenly I hear the sound of jingling keys from somewhere close by. Guys, my hair stood on end. I said a quick prayer and stuck my head out of the stall. There was nothing visible but the piss poor lighting and the filthy floor so I ran to the sink to wash my hands."

"You took time to wash your hands!" exploded Jacobs. "He's got Freddie Krueger bearing down on his ass and he's taking time to wash his hands," repeated Chris in amazement.

"Once the good sisters beat it into you, it's beaten into you," wisecracked Ronny.

"May I continue?" asked Dave. The men laughed and gestured yes. "I turned from the sink, forget about drying my hands, and all of a sudden, between me and the door, a figure starts to materialize out of thin air. It's blocking me from getting out."

"Are you kidding me?" exclaimed Chris.

"What the hell did you do?" asked Walter, his eyes trained on his friend.

"I did the only thing I could think of doing under the circumstances. I ran through the goddamn thing and out of that building as fast as my two legs would carry me. Next day, I turned in my keys. I wasn't going to work one more night shift in that place."

"Holy crap," said Jacobs.

"What did it feel like, the ghost I mean?" asked Walter.

"A cold spot…like twenty degrees colder than the rest of the room. Now guys, you know me, analytical and scientific. The scientific community would have a field day with my account and these supposed events. They'd tear it to shreds. All I know is what I saw and did. So Chris, cut your sis some slack. There are things all around us that we haven't even scratched the surface on. Ghosts are one of them."

"Wow, Durette, I'm looking at you in a whole, new way," confessed Ronny. "Confused and demented," added Dingman while winking across the table at his other two buddies.

"Guys, you just don't make something like that up."

"I believe you, Dave," said Walter. "I definitely believe you."

Later in the evening, long after the dessert plates had been cleared away and while the four friends were nursing down their last brew, Jacobs turned to Walter.

"We hear you've made some headway with the shore road's mysterious walking girl. Anything in the way of erotic table scraps to share with your buddies?" asked Chris. The big man leaned back in his chair behind a broad grin.

"I've taken Felicia out a couple of times but there's nothing going on that couldn't be shown on the Family Channel. She's a nice girl and I'm not going to push anything. I mean… we're talking about going for the brass ring here."

"Felicia Moretti's definitely in the top one percent in the looks category. Our boy Walter is a lucky man," piped in Ronny.

"You know guys, there's a part of me that wouldn't mind if she was just a little less attractive. There's a lot of pressure associated with going out with a gal that men can't keep their eyes off," confessed Walter quietly.

"Every other man in Maine and about a third of the women in Ogunquit," cracked Jacobs, a reference to the town's sizeable gay population.

"Watch your back, Walter. You don't know where your competition might be coming from," warned Dave lightheartedly.

"She's really that hot?" mused Jacobs, his mind seemingly conjuring up an image to identify with his friend's romantic interest.

*W*alter sat alone in his office on a windy May afternoon. Outside his window a line of pine trees could be seen bending away from a robust, ocean breeze. He had not seen Felicia in two or three days and planned to call her that evening. At the moment his mind was fixated on the analysis work strewn across his desk. For the past week he had poured over personnel data involving a project associated with the company's workmen's compensation costs. As his analysis work grew nearer to completion, he sensed a reason for optimism. Raising his eyes in the direction of the clock, he spotted someone standing in the doorway to his office. It was Felicia.

"Is there any chance that I could catch a ride from you when you're done?" she asked seriously.

"I'll give you a lift right now," he exclaimed, jumping to his feet.

"No, I don't want you leaving work early on account of me. Besides, I wanted to find a quiet spot where I can take a load off my feet and do a little thinking," she responded. Plews looked back at the clock. It was after four-thirty.

"What if I work until six and then come and find you?"

"That'll be fine. I'll probably be somewhere over behind the 'Ledges' building. I shouldn't be too hard to find," she declared before turning and leaving the office. Walter watched as the woman's trim body vacated his office space, a slight limp visible in her movement. His eyes returned to the computer monitor at the corner of the desk. His friend's demeanor concerned him. She seemed troubled or, at minimum, distracted. A wind gust, blown up from the nearby Atlantic, prompted his eyes to shift toward the window. There he viewed the now familiar sight of the solitary spider conducting maintenance on her web. Her intricately engineered trap showed only scant success, the remains of two microscopic insects the only evidence of any good fortune. He had now been monitoring this particular insect's predatory exploits for over a month and developed an interest in her success, or in this case, apparent lack of it.

It was a few minutes before six o'clock when Walter walked from his office and made his way outside, strolling along the path tracing the rim of Bald Head Cliff. Reaching the end of the footpath, the man peered across the rocky terrain in search of Felicia. She was nowhere within sight. He proceeded forward, descending a series of rocky steps toward the ocean. His path brought him downward between columns of basalt and quartz. Fifty yards away the ocean water lapped aggressively against the shoreline, the sound a constant reminder of the sea's dominant role over all other elements of nature in this place. He continued his descent until he reached a deep, fault line in the rock. Pausing to contemplate his next move, a brownish chasm now blocking his progress, he looked across and spotted Felicia. She was turned from his position and not conscious of his presence. He called to her and she turned.

"Are you ready to go home?" Plews hollered. The brown-haired girl gestured to him to join her. Walter found a perfectly flat outcropping of rock rimming a side wall, leading him away from an immediate drop into the flume. Then, he eased his bulk down into the depression and, after gaining his balance on a wet, smooth stone, climbed the far side of the chasm. Moderately out of breath, the man joined his female friend on a flat wedge of rock.

"I've never come this far down before," she confessed, hooking her arm under his and drawing the man to her. Walter looked out over a vista of the Maine coastline, framed on one side by the shoulder of Bald Head Cliff. In the far distance, Nubble Light flashed its automated warning.

"Do you know that millions and millions of years ago this rock we're sitting on was part of a volcano?" he asked.

"What!"

"I have it from a reliable source," he reassured her while crossing his heart. She rolled her eyes in disbelief and resumed staring southward along the jagged coastline. "What are you thinking about?" She glanced up at him and drew in a deep, contemplative breath.

"I knew everything was just going too good. Why do things have to always get so screwed up and cause problems," she reasoned aloud.

"Okay, what's causing you all this grief and aggravation? Out with it." She focused her brown eyes on his and gestured him to rise to his feet.

"Walk me back to your car and I'll get you up to speed on everything," she answered, clasping his hand and moving them both in the direction of the parking lot.

Felicia Moretti's limp was plainly visible over the two hundred yard walk to Walter's Corvette. The vehicle had pulled out of the driveway and onto the shore road before the woman opened the conversation.

"Did you know that it was three point nine miles from the front door of the Cliff House to my front door?" she asked the man.

"I'm not sure I should believe you. After all, you didn't believe me when I told you about that volcano thing back on the cliff." She laughed and tweaked his ear. "You know, someone else did that to me a lot a long time ago," he confessed.

"Did what?"

"Grab my ear."

"Someone nice?"

"Extremely." Felicia reached out and pushed his shoulder.

"Well now you've got someone who's not so nice doing it to you." He shot the woman a fleeting glance and returned his eyes to the winding roadway. "I'm already worried about tomorrow morning and the walk to work," she admitted, her voice growing more serious.

"I'll pick you up. Don't give it a second thought," directed Walter.

"I can't have you driving all the way to my apartment every morning whenever I get an ache or pain. There's no way."

"Come on, it's no big deal," he reassured her.

"No, Walter, you know how independent I am and now there's just a growing pile of problems cropping up on my plate these days. It's a little over-whelming." The huge man shook his head in frustration. "Now I know I made you a promise just a couple of weeks ago about being around for a while but things are already starting to go wrong. My ankle's as sore as hell. I got a crappy night's sleep last night worrying about the apartment."

"What's wrong with the apartment?"

"I can't be laying all my problems on you. We're supposed to be just friends, and, you know, share a few laughs together," she explained.

"Real friends are there in good times and bad. Talk to me here," he insisted. The car pulled to a stop and prepared to join Route 1A. She stared straight ahead through the windshield.

"If you're up to it, you could come upstairs and I'll make us a cup of tea," she suggested behind a pouty smile.

"What if Gary's home?"

"He's probably not… and that's partly why I'm not sleeping well these days."

Walter watched from the couch as Felicia hobbled into the kitchen. Seconds later the clanging racket from the adjoining room told him that his hostess was at work preparing their beverages.

"Walter, I'm going to duck into my bedroom and put on something a little more comfortable. If the kettle starts to whistle before I'm back, then turn off the burner," she instructed. The man acknowledged her directions and settled back onto the couch. He glanced around the spacious living room in search of a magazine. It appeared none had survived since his last visit.

Walter rose from the couch at the first sound of boiling water but immediately noticed Felicia back in the kitchen and dropped back onto the furniture. It only took seconds before the woman appeared carrying a tray and service. She had shed her jeans and blouse, her body now wrapped in a silk bathrobe.

"You're okay with my change into something more casual?" she asked, her inflection fashioning the question rhetorical.

"No complaints from this corner," he answered while watching her pour the tea. Her guest's beverage poured and served, she claimed one corner of the couch, stretching out her exposed legs and crossing her ankles atop his huge thigh. Walter felt himself grow rigid, a shockwave of sexual tension crackling through his body. Recovering quickly, he forced his eyes up from Felicia's milky, smooth legs.

"Okay, kid, let's get these problems of yours completely out on the table."

"Well, the first one we've already gone over. With my ankle acting up it's going to be increasingly problematic getting to work everyday. I've already told you that I'm not about to let you come down here to get me every morning. You're not a chauffer service. My second problem involves Gary. I've not seen hide nor hair of the guy in a week and a half. He hasn't even called. I have no way of knowing where he is or when he's coming back."

"Is his stuff, clothes and things, still here?"

"Yes, most of it. But Walter, in about two weeks I've got a rent payment due and there is no way in hell that I can come up with all of it. What if he's moved in with someone else and just not told me about it? It's me who's on the line here. I can't bring in another roommate given that the lease is in Gary's name and Gary's name only. Oh, and I certainly can't move closer to work. It's kind of an expensive neighborhood up there closer to the Cliff House. I'm screwed here," she exclaimed. Walter reached down and took her hand.

"I want you to just relax and drive any notion of moving on out of your head."

"Walter, that's not realistic." He lifted the index finger of his free hand to her lips.

"If June first comes around and Gary is still among the missing, I'll cover his half of the rent. So, no more worrying about next month's rent. Okay?" She stared silently into his face and nodded yes. This weekend, if your ankle is still giving you any trouble, and my guess is it still will be, then we go out and find you a dependable used car."

"That won't work."

"Why not?"

"My credit is shit and I haven't been working long enough at this job to get anyone to give me a loan," she answered.

"That's totally immaterial. We'll pay cash for the car. I'll put up the money."

"You mean the car will be yours?"

"Absolutely not. It goes in your name. I'll help you with the registration and insurance, too. You pay me back when you can. I'm not going to ask for anything in writing. I trust you, Felicia." She looked deep into his eyes and let out an extended sigh. "Now can we put an end to any talk from you about problems and moving on?"

"Are you sure you want to do this?" she asked.

"More than anything." She leaned forward and pressed her lips to his. Walter sat in a state of complete helplessness while Felicia crawled onto his lap. His mind fixated on the exposed flesh of her legs, he tried and failed to blurt out a rational thought. Breaking her lips from his own, she ran her mouth across his face. Reaching Walter's exposed neck, she pressed her teeth down and into his skin. The action of her mouth, the repetitive draw and release, soon had his skin raw and reddened. Her erotic aggression played on for three or four minutes before she pulled back from his overheated body. Temporarily paralyzed by the sensual onslaught, the large man cleared his head and reached for her. Pulling back to the far end of the couch, she extended her legs, bringing her locked ankles back to their original position atop his thigh.

"Walter, rub my sore ankle… please," she implored in a childish tone. He sighed and complied with her wishes.

Darkness had fully descended on the village of York Beach when Felicia escorted Walter to the front door of the apartment. He paused in the doorway, his head dropping onto her shoulder. A second later his face was burrowing into the silken fabric of the bathrobe.

"I can smell you in the fiber of the robe," he mumbled.

"You're sure?"

"Yes." She smirked and raised her eyes in jest.

"The robe is Gary's," she added laughingly.

"If you've got a gun in the house, then for god's sake use it on me... and I mean right now," he blurted out. He turned and slowly descended the outside stairs. Walter turned back to her on the landing.

"Do you have any idea how important a part of my life you've become?" he asked. She shook her head in the negative.

"Good night, Walter, and thank you so very much," she called down to him. The slender woman stood motionless in the doorway and waited on his good-bye.

"I bless the day you moved here from only God-knows-where," he cried out. Withholding a response, she turned from him and disappeared behind the door.

9

Ronny Dingman lifted his eyes from the half-empty glass resting on the table in front of him. He had arrived at the pub early on this Wednesday. Across the room a pair of familiar young men were engaged in a competitive game of pool. Their elevated skill level had prompted a small crowd of spectators to gather around the table. Outside the Union Bluff Hotel sheets of rainfall driven by thirty-mile-per-hour winds buffeted this neck of land called York Beach. Dingman thought to himself how it was a good time to be indoors, while his eyes focused on the beads of water making contact with the window only feet from the table. He had secured the group's table of choice through his early arrival. With the prime tourist season rapidly approaching, he knew that this could be the last time the foursome would lay claim to the table until the fall. Two hours earlier he had phoned Dave Durette and asked his friend to join him earlier than their customary five-thirty. It was a few minutes before five o'clock when Dingman was abruptly pulled from a semi-trance by a headlock applied from the rear by his friend of a dozen years.

"Thanks for giving me an excuse to abandon work early," cracked Durette, plopping himself in the chair to the left of Dingman. "What about the other two bozos?"

"They'll be along… regular time I imagine." Leaning back, Durette motioned to the bartender for a glass of his usual beer.

"So… what's up?" Dave asked, curious to know why he had been called to the pub early.

"Well, at the risk of sounding like some kind of mother hen, I wanted a chance to talk to you about Walter. I'm afraid Chris might not take what I'm about to tell you seriously. I have a little more confidence in your maturity, Dave." Durette's face grew more serious and he gestured to his friend to continue.

"You remember that whole buzz about Walter taking out that really attractive girl, the one that walks to and from work about ten miles every day?"

"Yeah, the real looker."

"Right, well, last week she did this whole song and dance about pulling a muscle or hurting a foot… some load of crap… and she starts hinting to Walter that she's thinking about moving on because getting to and from work would be so much of a hassle. Anyway, after laying this whole sob story on Walt, she got him to go out and buy her a car... cash on the barrel. He says she can pay him back whenever she can... no paperwork, no note, no nothing."

"How do you know all this?" asked Dave.

"Straight from the horse's mouth, from Walter. Except, when Walter fills me in on the details it's like he's completely blind to what seems to be happening."

"Have you considered the possibility that the guy is completely ga-ga over this girl?" questioned Dave.

"I have no doubt he's head over heels for her but I'm thinking that this little broad has some ulterior motive and our friend is being set up for the kill." Dave paused and took a sip of his beer.

"We're talking about very dangerous territory here. I mean... if Walter is gonzo for this girl, the last thing he wants to hear is how his friends think she may be using him. You're talking about jeopardizing the whole friendship. I don't know, Ronny. I don't know?"

"So, as his friends, are we just supposed to sit back and watch this broad use him? Is that what you're saying?"

"First, we don't know for sure she's even using him. Second, it may be too early to stick our noses into his affairs. Why don't we just monitor this whole situation a little longer. For all we know they could be history a month from now and then we can speak up and give him advice."

"I don't know," came back Ronny, clearly not convinced.

"Buddy, you asked for my advice and there you have it. You can do what you want, when you want. I just value my man Walter's friendship too much to put a strain on it for this," reasoned Durette. Dingman folded his hands behind the back of his head and stared over at his friend. "When in doubt, zip it," reasoned the older man.

Chris Jacobs and Walter Plews appeared in the door to the pub simultaneously on this evening. They had met in the parking lot and made a mad dash together to the front door. Both showed the effects of the continuing downpour outside but only Jacobs took time to spruce up in the men's room before joining the group.

"You guys been here long?" asked Walter while picking up a menu.

"Not too long," answered Ronny.

"Hell of a night... hell of a night," repeated Walter, his eyes dancing over the familiar menu.

"You buying the drinks again tonight, Walt?" questioned Chris sarcastically while arriving back at the table.

"Not tonight, guys. My checking account's taken a real body shot this week. I'll be needing a few weeks to recover," answered Plews. Dave shot Ronny a subtle glance and held his tongue.

"Well, I'm coming off of a crap week... a crap week embedded in a crap month," acknowledged Chris before tossing his menu on the table.

"Out with it, Jacobs. That's what we're here for... to wallow in each other's misery," declared Dingman. The handsome salesman shook his head in disgust and proceeded.

"How many years have I been talking about getting the top spot in the sales department?"

"Since Jesus was a boy," barked Durette.

"That's right... almost from day one at that rat hole of an office. I've been kissing Scholinger's fat, incompetent ass for seven years now so I could someday step into his job. Unfortunately for me, it's taken that classless buffoon seven, long years to move up and out. Last week it happened. Headquarters finally found a position that that clown might actually be able to function at and they transferred him to Boston. A week ago the rumor around the office was that Scholinger's position was either going to be offered to me or Heather Prescott."

"Isn't that the young broad with the MBA they brought in a couple of months ago?" Dave asked.

"The same. Late yesterday the announcement came down. It didn't matter that my sales numbers were almost double hers. It didn't matter that I've sucked up to that puke, Scholinger for the past seven years. No, all that mattered was the fact that I had to stand there with a disingenuous smile plastered across my face while Ms. Prescott, the twenty-five year old Ms. Prescott, was introduced to the office as the new sales manager."

"Sorry, buddy, I know how much you wanted that promotion," muttered Walter.

"Today she called me into her office, behind closed doors. I mean, there was no beating around the bush. She tells me how the morale in the office is priority number one, and if she even gets so much as a hint of me badmouthing her or the company then I'm history. So here she was, clearly out to get me but disguising it behind this pretense of doing it for the company. The message was coded but quite clear... free spirits will not be tolerated. Only bootlickers need apply. God, she sat there so smug and superior."

"Who the hell is this little broad? Does the little witch have compromising photographs of upper management or something?" barked out Ronny.

"Last night lying in bed I started mulling over this whole nightmare. Lying there it dawned on me that seven years ago when I was hired, Heather Prescott was eighteen years old! I can actually picture her sitting in front of the mirror squeezing her pimples and worrying about what dress to wear to the senior prom. Seven years ago she was in high school and now I'm taking orders from her. What the hell happened to my life? I'm answering to someone named Heather," groaned Jacobs. There was a pitiful quality in his tone of voice that caused subdued laughter around the table. Seconds later a powerful gust of wind propelled an empty corrugated box by the window and up the street.

"God, I love living and working by the sea. It's on nights like this, when you never know what will blow in from the ocean, that I truly appreciate my place on the planet," announced Dave, lifting his glass to his friends.

The unabated storm outside the pub window provided the perfect backdrop for an extended evening of food and drink. The conversation eventually settled on a topic of particular sensitivity. In no particular order, each man took center stage and spoke fondly of their first love. All sat quietly and respectfully as one, then another, shared intimate details of the young females who had left permanent memories, impressions, and scars on these middle-aged and soon-to-be middle-aged men. Walter, in particular, found himself immersed in the detailed accounts of his friend's youthful romantic escapades. He was last to tell the tale of his first love, Melinda Klaus. Melinda's was the first and only name to ring familiar with the group. The heavy set man recounted the first time he had set eyes on the woman, and then recounted memories from a weekend spent in a log cabin in the White Mountains with her. Purposely, he avoided any mention of the two days stranded in the mysterious ice house in northern Maine. That was an event he shared in common with Melinda and Melinda alone. The four men sat in quiet recollection as Walter's account of his memorable weekend came to an end, each of them embracing these shadows from their past. It was the elder statesman of the group who would cut through the quiet.

"I would not want the Mrs. to know this, and I ask that whatever is said at this table remain between us." His friends all answered yes. "I want to go on record as saying that I would gladly surrender the last year of my life in order to go back and spend one hour with Norma Finnegan," stated Dave with an air of reverence, a tribute to his sixteen-year-old first love.

"Shall we all join our buddy in this pledge," added Jacobs. The four men touched glasses over the center of the table and consumed the remaining contents of their drinks.

"Now, in case the powers that be in the next world were not listening too closely, let me restate my position. I did not pledge my soul or anything, just the last year of my life for Norma Finnegan," repeated Dave, his words coming out slightly slurred.

"We get it, holy man. God gets it too," wisecracked Chris, patting Durette's back in reassurance. While the four reached for their wallets to begin settling the tab, Ronny decided to breath new life into the discussion.

"You know, Dave, when you take a minute to think it over, it really isn't any big deal giving up a year of your life… when it's the last year of your life. I mean, you're probably going to be strapped in an iron lung by then anyway… and who gives a shit if you lose that year. You're really not giving up all that much for your precious Norma Flanagan."

"Finnegan."

"Sorry, Finnegan."

"Okay, Dingman, then I'll change it to a year of your miserable life. Happy?" wisecracked Dave. The foursome gazed down at the tab and slapped cash onto the table, no doubt leaving the waitress a healthy gratuity, whether intentionally or not. The band of brothers meandered out into the lobby together where they gazed out into the dark, stormy night. It was Dave who noticed that Walter appeared to be showing the effects of the evening's drinking more than the other three.

"Walter, buddy, why don't you go back inside and ask Larry for some coffee? Seriously," suggested Dave. Walter stared down at his friend.

"Yeah, Walt, and I'll keep you company if you want. The battle ax can wait another twenty minutes for me," added Ronny. Walter waved off his friend's offer and meandered back into the bar where he ordered a cup of black coffee. He was borderline sober but figured that caution, under the circumstances, was advisable. He sat at the end of the bar, a stranger to all but the bartender. He was alone in a crowd of people and, understandably, his thoughts conjured up the image of Felicia Moretti. He envisioned her face earlier that week when he hand- ed her the set of keys to her new, pre-owned vehicle. The urge to see that face grew inside him, an almost intolerable desire to be near her. The realization that Felicia was less than a quarter of a mile away took hold of him. He could walk to her, right now, through the rain and wind and anything else the ugly side of nature could find to keep him from her door. Walter had the bartender transfer his coffee to a Styrofoam cup and made his way to the front door. Freeman Street was only a hundred yards away. Walter simply needed to rest his eyes on her. Clearing the front door he was met with a sheet of torrential rain, sending him staggering into the roadway. He turned his body from the teeth of the wind and plodded in the direction of Freeman Street. Within seconds he felt the rivulet of rainwater from the road saturate his shoes and socks.

Walter stood motionless by the side of the road, looking up at what he hoped was Felicia's apartment building. The structure, as well as most of the street, was in darkness. He climbed the faintly familiar set of stairs while rain droplets blurred his vision. Reaching the second floor of the building, he drew in a deep breath and knocked assertively on the door. Before long a light flipped on from an interior room and he heard footsteps approaching the door.

"Felicia?" he asked.

"Walter, is that you?"

"In the soaking flesh," he answered, his voice exhibiting a sense of relief. The door swung inward and the tall brunette stared at him from the shadows.

"What in the name of God are you doing here?"

"I know it's going to sound absolutely insane… and perhaps I am certifiable, but I had to just see you tonight. Nothing more… just set my eyes on you," he explained.

"Come inside out of the rain," she ordered. He stepped inside the darkened but familiar living room. "You just had to see me! What kind of juvenile shit is that?"

"I met the guys for drinks tonight, down at the Union Bluff, and we got to talking about first loves and romantic experiences."

"I'm not your first love or any love, Walter."

"I know. But it turned into a long evening and I did have more to drink than usual… and all the talk about first girlfriends and innocent love sort of got to me." Felicia switched on the overhead light.

"And who did you talk about? Who did you tell them was your first love?" Walter lowered his head shyly.

"Melinda." The woman looked intently at him, then smiled. Crossing the room, she tweaked his ear and marched into the kitchen.

"I'll make us some coffee. I'll use Gary's expensive, special blend." Walter scanned the living room for a place to sit. His clothes were saturated, causing him to refrain from depositing himself on anything in the room.

"Any sign of Gary?" he called out.

"Nothing. Not a call or anything."

Felicia Moretti rejoined her friend in the living room carrying an assortment of linens and blankets. Entering the room, she found the man leaning timidly against the wooden frame of the door.

"These are for you. I'll not have you driving back to Wells at less than a hundred percent, particularly on a night like this. You can take the couch. It's a fold-out. It's way too short for you but if you lie at a forty-five degree angle, it should suffice for one night."

"Are you sure?" he asked tentatively.

"I'm sure," she replied, narrowing her eyes and feigning displeasure. "Let me get us some coffee."

The two friends sat and talked for the next thirty minutes. Felicia spoke enthusiastically about her Honda Civic and her plan to repay Walter every cent it had cost him. Walter, huddled inside a pair of dry blankets and spread out on the couch, repeated over and over the absence of any timetable on the repayment of the loan. Secretly, he viewed the debt as an obstacle to the woman's leaving. He perceived, whether correctly or not, a basic honesty in this enigmatic woman.

After clearing the coffee cups and having turned out the lights, Felicia stood in the doorway to the hall, her long, slender profile visible in muted light.

"Try to get something loosely resembling sleep tonight," she jested to her guest. There was no immediate answer from the darkness in the room. "Goodnight Walter." Again, her words were followed by silence. She turned and walked toward her bedroom.

"The day is going to come when you meet someone... someone you really care for... and I'm afraid it's going to tear me apart," he blurted out. Again, his words were followed by a short period of silence.

"You can't let yourself worry about that. It will not happen. Not that. You have my word on it." There was a small measure of comfort in her words and tone but also a hint of unstated possibilities. Seconds later came the sound of the woman's bedroom door closing.

10

*W*alter gazed hypnotically at the monitor of his computer before casting a glance through the window of his office. The end of May was approaching and the surrounding foliage was in full bloom. He separated his arms and let out with a prolonged yawn. It was Friday and the extended Memorial Day weekend was upon him. From outside his window came the clatter of human activity. Leaning sideways, he strained to pick up on the source of this mental interruption and saw a detail of two men working their way in his direction along the outside of the building. Following a moment's hesitation, he sprang to his feet and scrambled outside. The workers were two windows away from his when he approached them.

"Special request gentlemen, if you don't mind?" asked Walter amiably. "I've developed a sort of paternal feeling for the spider in my window. She puts a lot of work into that web and I'd hate to see her sent back to square one. God knows she catches little enough as it is. Could you just skip on by my window when you get to it? If Ronny Dingman gives you any grief over it, you can refer him to me. We're drinking buddies and I'm sure there'll be no problem. It's not like any of our guests are going to be happening by this end of the building." The young men laughed at the special request but assured the man they would honor his wishes. Walter returned to his office and stared out at the long, thin spider, debating within himself the rationale behind his concern. His reflection was short-lived. The telephone rang, bringing him back to the here and now.

"Business office, Walter Plews speaking."

"Hey, Walter, got a minute?" It was Felicia.

"Sure. It's just me here at the moment."

"I'm going to be taking my thirty minute lunch in a couple of minutes and I'd love to have some company. I brought enough food for two," she informed him.

"Where will you be?"

"I'm going down to behind the cliff… to the ledge beyond the flume. I sort of think of that as our special place," she answered. "I really need to talk something through. I need to make a decision… and quickly."

"What time?"

"I was thinking like, right now."

"It's a little early for lunch by my standards but what the heck. I'll be there in five minutes," he promised before hanging up the phone.

Walter made his way down the layered rock, carefully descending from level to level until the deep crevice in the formation came into sight. Along with negotiating layer upon layer of weathered rock, he balanced a half-filled cup of coffee in one hand. He knew enough to approach and cross the chasm with caution. In the next second he spotted Felicia seated on the far side of the gully, flowers held in one hand. She gestured to him to join her. The husky man carefully climbed down into the depression in the rock, the coffee cup clutched in one hand limiting his progress. Following a brief hesitation while he searched for a route out of the depression, he awkwardly pulled himself upward and finally joined his friend on the flattened ledge at the far side.

"No matter how many times I come out here, it's always a little tricky," he confessed, settling in beside the woman. She extended him a warm smile and handed him her flowers.

"A cup of coffee, there's always that cup of coffee. For your office," she stated. The petals were white and yellow and probably grew wild somewhere nearby. He lifted the blossoms to his nose, inhaling their pleasant fragrance. Wasting no time, the brunette lifted a brown bag from the ground and proceeded to extract items from it. Within seconds she had passed him a sandwich wrapped in wax paper, a few celery sticks, and a banana.

"You know, you really didn't have to do all this for me," he explained, pulling a celery stick from inside a plastic bag.

"I needed a sounding board and where I come from… you always feed your sounding board," she declared.

"And where was it you came from?" Walter asked. She answered with a playful jab to his ribs.

"It's getting close to the end of the month and I still haven't heard from Gary." Sensing a degree of stress in her voice, he interrupted the woman.

"I told you, Felicia, I'll cover the cost of Gary's half of the rent and utilities. I don't want you worrying your gorgeous, little head over that. No strings attached," he said. She leaned sideways, hooking her arm around his.

"I know what you've promised, Walter, and it's really, really appreciated. But I just cannot accept that sort of assistance from you. It's just too… too much money," she stated with clear determination.

"There are no strings," he restated, his tone exhibiting an inkling of desperation.

"I know that… you wonderful, wonderful man." She reached up, plucking at his ear. Walter responded with a long sigh, his massive body drooping forward.

"So what does this mean, I mean for you?"

"As much as I love it here, it's time to go. All of the low cost housing has been gobbled up by now by the college kids. I'm pretty much screwed." She rested her head on his shoulder, an acknowledgement of the affection she felt for her friend. Reaching into the man's lap, she grabbed half of his ham and cheese sandwich and brought it up to his mouth. He listlessly opened his mouth, accepting her offering. She gazed intently at his face while he stared trancelike out to the open ocean. Thirty feet away, seawater sloshed noisily at the mouth of the flume. Her words had effected an incredible change in his disposition and physical appearance. It was as if the air and the spirit of the man had been released from his massive body.

"I know that this comes as a disappointment to you. You have to know that I will miss you terribly, too. Walter, you mean more to me than just a friend. But, and this is very important, I cannot accept rent and utilities money from you. I just can't. There's something about the money that makes it wrong and dirty. I'll give you back your Honda, too. Just let me hold onto it until I go. Please." A few seconds passed before Plews shifted his eyes away from the blue seawater and trained them on his friend.

"So, it's really only the money that's making you make this decision?" She nodded her head in the affirmative and bit halfheartedly on a celery stick.

"So if it didn't cost me any money and you had a nice place to stay, you wouldn't go?"

"No, why would I want to?" He reached for the slender brunette. His large hands took her by the shoulders and turned her to him.

"Come and stay with me up in Wells. You can have your pick of the bedrooms, except, of course, when my aunt comes this summer. We can drive in to work together… or not. You keep your car. Hell, with everything you save on rent you'll be able to pay me back even faster than you wanted to. What do you say Felicia? Is it a deal?" he asked excitedly. Her face brightened.

"Are you sure you could put up with me at work *and* at home?"

"Given the size of my aunt's house, we might just run into each other on occasion," he jested. Felicia looked on as the vitality miraculously returned to her friend. His face brightened along with every other element of his body language.

"I'll get my landlord up to speed about everything that's happening. He probably has a security deposit of Gary's. I won't have much to move." Felicia Moretti looked hard into the face of Walter Plews. "Oh, Walter, let me get a closer look at that," she said. "Lean back." The man complied with her wishes.

"What is it? What's wrong?" She looped her long, slender body over his, mounting his massive chest like a horse.

"Okay, Walt, open your mouth and say ahh," she ordered. After a short deliberation he followed her command.

"Ahhhh," he said. She responded by lodging the end of her banana into his mouth. Her good-natured attack was accompanied by an outburst of laughter. "You seem to have an unhealthy willingness to accept cylinder-shaped objects into your mouth," she exclaimed while continuing to hold the ripened banana to his mouth. "Is there some secret from your personal life that you maybe want to share with me?" The big man let out with a contented laugh as the weight of his friend's body and the fragrance of her perfume aroused his senses. Biting off a portion of the banana, he smiled up into her exquisite face. Walter strongly suspected that he had just been the victim of this woman's manipulation. He knew that, in all likelihood, she had set out this day to close the distance between them and establish residence within his four walls. The proposal was his but the orchestrated events leading up to it were unquestionably fashioned by her.

"Walter, I'm going to have to get back to work in a few minutes. I'm not like you. I'm on the clock." She eased herself up from atop the man and seated herself beside him. Forty feet beneath them and out of sight, the ocean crashed against the side of the rocky wall of Bald Head Cliff.

"Memorial Day weekend's here. The tourists will be on us in a matter of hours. Things are going to be pretty hectic right through to Columbus Day," he announced.

"Having any second thoughts yet about having a roommate?" He reached his arms around Felicia, pulling her body against his own.

"I am so incredibly psyched about the prospect of having you under my roof," he confessed. "You've made me so damn happy." Felicia reacted by jumping to her feet.

"I've got to go. Don't forget your flowers... or your coffee cup... and pick up the banana peel," she barked. He glanced up at her thoughtfully, a sweet smile etched on his face.

"What's with it with you and flowers?"

"That question will answer itself someday, you just have to trust me on that." With that said she reached down and cuffed his ear. This gesture had become their mutual sign of endearment over the last month. Walter cleared the rocky ledge of all traces of their lunch and escorted his female friend back to the complex. They parted by the rear of the main building, each knowing that in a few days their lives would be drawn into tighter orbits.

Five hours had passed since Felicia Moretti had decided to accept his offer and move into the Sand Castle with Walter Plews. He found his mind in a state of total distraction on this afternoon, unable to remain focused on any task for more that a few minutes. It was just before five o'clock when he wandered out of the office and outside onto the grounds of the complex. He was quick to notice the parking lot filling up with vehicles, many displaying out-of-state license plates. Sipping from a cup of coffee, he meandered away from the buildings and in the general direction of the shore road a quarter-mile to the west. Two or three minutes into his walk he noticed someone working on a downed ground-lighting fixture, a piece of company property that had fallen victim to the bumper of a car the previous day. On closer scrutiny, Walter saw it was Ronny Dingman kneeling over the damaged equipment. He approached his friend without speaking until he was within a few feet of the man.

"Okay, Dingman, upper management's sent me out to honcho this little project to a rapid conclusion. Damn it man, three weeks and no end in sight!" Walter wisecracked. Ronny turned from his work.

"I feel like the kid from *The Breakfast Club,* the one who starts crying because he pulled on the elephant's trunk and the light wouldn't go on. I've been working on this goddamn thing for over an hour and I still can't figure out why I'm not getting any illumination."

"Anthony Michael Hall."

"What? Is that the idiot who drove over this thing?"

"No, that's the actor in the movie who cried because he was flunking shop class."

"Thanks, Walter. You've been a big help." The big man chuckled and sat down beside his friend. "So what brings you out of your comfy office and into the world of the gainfully employed?"

"It's turned into one of those days when something happens and you're not able to focus on your work for the rest of the day."

"Yeah, like you find out that the girl you took to the junior prom just became a grandmother... and suddenly you feel like the grandfather from *The Waltons*," answered Ronny.

"Is the girl you took to the prom a grandmother now?"

"No, but Dave's is. Don't you remember him telling us that a couple of years ago?"

"No, can't say that I do. He must have vented that on one of those nights I joined you guys late. Actually, my distraction isn't from anything negative, quite the contrary." Dingman paused and glanced over at his friend, beckoning Walter to share his circumstances with him.

"I asked Felicia to give up her apartment and come stay up at the house in Wells with me... and she's agreed," confessed Walter, leaving out the details of negotiation. Ronny stared silently into the face of his buddy for a moment, clearly processing the ramifications of this revelation.

"Congratulations, buddy," he said, albeit with curbed enthusiasm. A few awkward seconds passed with no words exchanged. Finally, Dingman pushed aside his tools and took a seat beside his friend. Plews drew in a deep breath.

"Ronny, I'm absolutely crazy about this girl. I mean, in the little over a month I've known her, she's all but taken possession of me. It's wonderful and it's scary at the same time."

"She's a beautiful woman, Walter, and it sounds like she's got her hooks in you. Hey, there are worse things that could happen." The two men smiled as each pondered Walter's state of affairs.

"If it were just her looks then I could maybe rein in my feelings a little bit. But Ronny, it's more than her looks. It's also the way she acts and talks and plays with my head. She is so much like Melinda. I don't think I noticed it at first. It's like she's metamorphosized into her over time."

"Have you told her about Melinda?"

"A little... but not all that much."

"She may be picking up on little things, here and there, and copying them to make you like her more," suggested Ronny.

"Well, whatever she's doing, it's working," admitted Walter. Dingman lifted himself from the ground with a groan and stood over his friend.

"Buddy, we've been friends for a while now and I think of you as a brother. I hope you feel the same way towards me." Ronny had now broken all eye contact, staring intently back toward the Cliff House.

"Of course I do."

"And anything I say to you is meant in your best interest. With that in mind I want to go on record as suggesting you be real careful around this woman. I mean, she's already gotten a car out of you..."

"That's a loan, Ronny."

"She's gotten herself a car loan out of you and she's about to take up residence in your house. It may be all above board and innocent… and then it may not be. Be very careful, buddy. With her looks, this woman could pretty much have any guy she wants. She's chosen you. You may be the luckiest guy in the world… and then you may not be. You're going to have to get to know her a little better before that determination can be made. However, given that this magnificent creature is about to move in with you, it shouldn't be long before that determination, and a few others of a more carnal nature, can be made. For that, you are a lucky man… I think." Ronny reached down and offered Walter a hand. He accepted and awkwardly returned to his feet. With that accomplished, the two men exchanged bear hugs, and Dingman returned to his project.

Walter plodded slowly back toward the main building and his office. Glancing back over his shoulder in the direction of the employee parking area, he observed that Felicia's Honda was missing from the cluster of cars on the backside of the property. A half-dozen vehicles motored by him in the span of the next two minutes, a reminder that Memorial Day and the unofficial start of summer was upon southern Maine.

11

*W*alter extended his arm, allowing the cuff of his shirt to recede and expose the face of his watch. It was after seven o'clock and the bright, afternoon light was just now surrendering to evening. At the moment, he occupied one of two Adirondack chairs situated between the front of the house and the man-made stone wall that constituted the boundary between the Atlantic Ocean and individual private property on Wells Beach. This was moving day for Felicia Moretti and she had given Walter an estimated arrival time of six o'clock. Over the past hour he had jumped to his feet on more than a half-dozen occasions, reacting to the sound of a car's engine on the roadway leading up to the Sand Castle. Now, mired in a state of nervous frustration, he raised himself up from the chair and made his way down the flight of cement stairs to the packed, ocean sand. The ocean water was perhaps a hundred yards in the distance, the sea having receded to near low tide over the last six hours. Walking eastward over the nearly deserted beach, he reached the water's edge. The ocean water lapped listlessly a few feet from his position while he stared toward a horizon shrouded in clouds. He had not seen Felicia earlier at work on this day and in true, Walter Plews fashion, set out to torture himself with visions of a change of plans at her end. Again, his eyes shifted downward to his watch. It was nearly twenty-five minutes past seven. A nervous, stressful knot pressed against the wall of his stomach. His eyes panned northward toward the main beach then back to the house. There, standing atop the ocean wall was the figure of Felicia Moretti. He turned and quickstepped his way in the direction of the house, the nervous energy trapped in the pit of his stomach dissipating as he walked.

"I was beginning to wonder if you had a change of heart," he called out as he grew nearer to the house.

"There's always more to pack than you anticipate," responded the woman. "Any chance of getting a little help unloading?"

"You bet," he called back. Reaching the cement stairway, he scrambled to the top with a surge of renewed energy, no doubt motivated by the woman's arrival. Walter followed his friend to the parking area at the rear of the house where the Honda rested, the back of the car crammed with loose clothing and boxes. It took nearly a dozen trips up the stairs by each of them to empty the vehicle of the woman's belongings. Walter instructed Felicia to drop everything in the sun-room on the main floor, it being only a few steps from the side door.

Felicia dropped off the last moving box onto the floor beside a wide, comfortable looking chair and collapsed backwards onto it.

"Do you have anything cold and wet in the house?" she asked.

"I think so. Let me check downstairs," he answered, then hurried from the room. Felicia used her friend's absence to closely inspect the sunroom. It was a sprawling, elongated room furnished with an assortment of simple chairs suited for a vacation home, most surrounding a spacious, round table. The view outside the extended series of windows took in one hundred and eighty degrees of open ocean along with the Maine coastline from Crescent Beach on the south to the Wells Harbor jetty to the north. She walked to the row of windows at the eastern end of the building, taking in the waters of the Atlantic Ocean, her line-of-sight void of any evidence of mankind except for the sails of a solitary craft nearly a mile off shore. Her trance was broken by Walter's return, a bottle of orange soda in one hand.

"It's all I had," he confessed, joining her at the far end of the sunroom.

"One of my favorite flavors," she answered. "I swear, everything is just perfect… and I have you, Walter Plews, to thank for it." The large man beamed with appreciation from the woman's words.

"I probably should've said something earlier before we lugged all your stuff upstairs but I was hoping you might move in close to me downstairs in my living area. We'd have all the comforts of home." The woman shifted her eyes away from the shoreline and back to her friend.

"I'll follow you," she replied thoughtfully. Lying his hand gently on her shoulder, Walter ushered Felicia through the kitchen and out onto the porch. From there he guided her down the stairs to the entrance to his apartment. Withholding comment, the woman was directed through a spacious combination living room/dining room with a large television set positioned in the far corner. Along this far wall were three windows that brought in light and laid claim to a peek at the nearby Atlantic Ocean. Connected to this dominating room was a hallway, off of which were a full-sized bathroom and two bedrooms, one standard size and the other enormous. After standing at length in the doorway of the larger bedroom, Felecia turned back to her friend and benefactor.

"May I see the rest of the house, the bedrooms I mean?" Walter nodded and signaled for her to follow him. The two circled the building in silence, re-entered the main house, and climbed the stairs to an upper floor. Walter was having difficulty trying to disguise his disappointment from Felicia's reaction to his apartment. From the top of the paneled stairwell he introduced his guest to a series of five bedrooms. The man watched with keen interest as the woman's mood brightened on this portion of the tour. The entire exercise reached a climax when she stepped inside the fifth bedroom, a spacious, square room, tastefully furnished and laid out with two windows, one looking directly out to sea and the other facing southward. The southerly facing window came with a view of Moody Point and sections of Ogunquit. From the near wall extended a queen-sized bed. A few steps into the room, Felicia turned back to Walter. She stared up at the man as tears formed in the corner of her eyes. She stepped deliberately back to him in the doorway, burying her face in the fabric of his shirt.

"This room is so beautiful and wonderful. Is there any way you could let me stay here? Walter, I can't begin to tell you how happy it would make me," she whispered through joyful weeping. Within seconds he felt the moisture of her tears penetrating his shirt.

"This is Aunt Delores's room," he responded apologetically. Her response was non-verbal. It consisted of a sequence of deep breaths, the warmth from her mouth penetrating his shirt. Walter stood perfectly still while his friend of less than two months wrapped her arms around him, imploring him to grant her this one request. "I had also hoped to have you somewhere in the house a little closer to me." There was silence for a few moments.

"There's no reason you couldn't move upstairs with me. There's that wonderful room across the hall. Your aunt hasn't ever said you couldn't stay up here, has she?"

"No, she never came out and said I couldn't. Of course, I've been staying down where I am forever. She might think it odd."

"What are you saying, Walter?" Felicia asked, making no effort to disguise her disappointment.

"Listen, if you want this room then you can have this room. We'll have to move you out when my aunt arrives in July, but that's only for a couple of weeks. I'll stay put where I am for the time being." She lifted her face from his shirt, a smile breaking through the moisture left behind by her tears.

"You are such a wonderful man," she declared before raising herself onto the tips of her toes and kissing him tenderly on the lips. He stood planted in the doorway while she performed her magic on his senses, the proximity of her body heating his blood. Hesitantly, he returned her affection by draping his arms around her. The feel of her sculpted body sent sexual images rushing through his thoughts. He withheld any mention of the disappointment he felt. She had shown no resistance to his declaration of staying two floors below in the apartment.

Walter and Felicia spent the remaining forty-five minutes of daylight moving her belongings up the narrow flight of stairs and into the corner bedroom. On Felicia's insistence they were to share a light meal later by candlelight in the dining room, a simple spread to be pulled together by the woman in the main kitchen. For his part, the fatigued man watched from an easy chair in front of the television as his energized houseguest flitted between the kitchen and dining room preparing the food and setting the table. He marveled at her ability to appear completely at home in this house after less than two hours. He sat quietly in the shadows before an expansive picture window, his eyes avoiding the network programming across the room in favor of the darting silhouette of Felicia Moretti. He was already questioning his decision to remain in the down-stairs apartment, asking himself why he had not jumped at his friend's proposition of taking the bedroom located only a few steps from her own. Dismissing his own second-guessing, he embraced the moment. After all, she was here with him, he thought. This woman who, only two months earlier, was literally just a beautiful flight of fancy moving gracefully over the rocky ledges of the Cliff House… unreachable, untouchable, unattainable. Who could have ever even conceived of this woman being here, in this place, with him?

"Dinner is ready," she called from the adjoining room, bringing Walter out of his thought pattern and back to the moment at hand. He looked up to see her lighting the two candles placed on the far end of the formal table, the candlelight striking her face and enhancing her beauty. From this day forward she would be an undeniable part of his life, he thought.

12

*R*onny Dingman's truck decelerated into the village intersection before pulling a sharp left onto Beach Street. The man at the wheel did not need a calendar to know that June had arrived at York Beach. The roadway was already lined with parked vehicles, a testament to the return of summer residents and a smattering of off-season tourists. Dingman directed his pickup into an empty parking space a short distance from the entrance to the Union Bluff Hotel and grabbed his wallet from the glove compartment. It was Wednesday night, he was running a little behind schedule, and he longed for the company of his friends. Clearing the front door, he made eye contact with an attractive, young woman behind the front desk, shot her a congenial smile, and headed through the doorway into the pub. A glance to his right told him that the group's table of choice had been commandeered by a family of vaguely familiar summer people. Ronny stuck his head into the side room and searched in vain for a friendly face. Coming up empty, he pulled an about-face and moved toward the far side of the pub.

"Dingman, to your left," called out a voice from close by. He looked down to see Dave Durette and Chris Jacobs occupying one of a handful of booths lining the back wall. Ronny smirked in acknowledgement and deposited himself next to Durette.

"You're late," complained Dave.

"Got in a jawing match with the old lady. Sorry to leave you stranded here alone with Jacobs."

"Actually, Jacobs made for good company... a couple of horror stories from his office and suddenly my job and life didn't seem so bad," explained Dave behind his wry smile.

"Okay, I want to be updated... and don't spare me anything," responded Ronny. "No, first let me guess. This wouldn't have anything to do with that new boss of yours, would it?" Jacobs grimaced and shot a frigid glance across the table. The acknowledgement brought forth a roar of laughter from both of his friends.

"I've already told the story once," said Chris.

"Our buddy's boss happened to glance into his office and catch him with porn on the computer monitor," blurted out Dave.

"Not the youthful and lovely Heather?" quizzed Ronny lightheartedly.

"The same," confessed Chris.

"How the hell did you let that happen? Why didn't you just close the screen before she got an eyeful?"

"She picked up on it in a mirror on the wall."

"Ah, of course, pretty boy Jacobs and mirrors… inseparable," added Ronny. "What did she do?"

"She came in, closed the door, and ripped me a new asshole. She's written me up and put it in my personnel file. She's going to have this thing to hang over my head from this point on." Picking up on the tone of his voice, Ronny and Dave backed away from their needling, and the atmosphere at the table grew more sympathetic. The change in mood caused a temporary lull in the conversation. It was Chris who took the initiative and broke the silence.

"So, can we expect Walter tonight or is he too good for us now?" asked Chris of Ronny.

"Walter will be here in his own good time."

"And how is his love life coming along? Is he making any inroads with that living doll chambermaid?" queried Dave.

"Inroads is putting it mildly. She's moved in with him. She's living up in that big house on Wells Beach with him," reported Dingman as his first beer of the evening arrived at the table.

"Are you kidding me!" erupted Jacobs, his mouth half-filled with brew.

"No, I'm not kidding you. God, it seems like only yesterday when she got that Honda out of him and now she's in his house and, I'm assuming, living rent-free."

"I thought he only guaranteed the loan," came back Dave.

"No, idiot, he bought the car for her. She owes *him* the money. Our boy is totally on the hook for that money."

"You know, maybe, just maybe, this girl actually cares for our boy and you're worrying over nothing," reasoned Dave. Ronny turned to his friend, his face shrouded in skepticism.

"There could be a way of finding out exactly how sincere this little broad really is," offered Jacobs, his words capturing the other men's absolute attention. "What if I should meet up with her and put her to the test. You know, ask her out."

"Jacobs, don't go there. Don't use these circumstances as an excuse to go after your buddy's girl," snapped Ronny.

"What a humanitarian!" wisecracked Dave, laughing aloud before lifting his glass of beer to his mouth. "Jacobs, you remind me of those two women in *The Man of La Mancha* who sing about having Don Quixote put away but claim they're only thinking of him. You've heard Dingman and Plews talk about this gorgeous broad and you want a crack at her. Admit it."

"Well thanks for the goddamn vote of confidence," answered Chris.

"Jacobs, you're so freaking transparent," said Ronny, reaching across the table and giving his friend a good-natured shove.

The three men were engaged in an enjoyable discussion involving the movie, *Pulp Fiction,* when Dave peered across the room and spotted Walter standing in front of the bar.

"Hey, Plews, they're keeping us out of sight of the tourists tonight," called out Durette, capturing Walter and another half-dozen patron's attention. The big man ambled over to the booth and slid in beside Chris.

"I was beginning to think you guys had found another watering hole," confessed Walter, settling into his spot at the table and giving Chris a sociable pat on the back.

"Someone hail down a waitress so we can order some food. Once again, Walter's tardiness has me lightheaded from hunger," complained Dave.

"You know, with all this *Pulp Fiction* talk I'm sort of in the mood for a hamburger royale with cheese," wisecracked Ronny.

"You guys were talking about *Pulp Fiction* before I got here?" asked Walter.

"Yeah, it kept our minds off of starving to death because big Walter wasn't here yet and we couldn't order anything solid," explained Dave.

"Yeah, Walter, I was telling the guys that the movie wasn't anything special except when Samuel Jackson or John Travolta were on screen," added Chris. Walter, who fancied himself as something of an expert on motion pictures, grimaced.

"There was a heck of a lot more to that film than Jackson, Travolta, and the royale with cheese scene. That entire movie was laced with great dialogue and the complex time line was brilliant," chirped Walter.

"Someone call Cannes and ask them to mail us a beret for the cultured giant here in our midst," said Dave while rolling his eyes and searching out a waitress. Within seconds the four friends were pouring over the familiar menus amidst the hum of socialization within the pub.

With their dinner meals ordered, the men sat back and prepared for an evening of unwinding. It was Chris who introduced the first major topic for discussion.

"So, Walter, my friend, what is this I hear about you and a certain tall, brunette knockout? Is it true you have managed to lure this gorgeous creature into your home? And in almost record time, I might add." Plews shot Ronny an uncomfortable glance and shrugged.

"It's no big deal. She's living at the house but she's a full, two stories above me," he admitted.

"How the hell did that come about?" Dave asked. Walter rolled his eyes and shook his head as if in disbelief.

"You won't believe this but she suggested that I move upstairs and take the bedroom just down the hall. I declined before thinking it through. I think in the back of my head I was worrying about all the effort with moving my stuff upstairs." In unison, his friends let out with a loud moan.

"Sweet Jesus, Walter, she invited you upstairs. What the hell do you need, a road map?" Chris asked.

"God forgive me for saying this, but it almost reminds me of that episode on *Seinfeld* when the girl invites George upstairs for coffee… and he declines because the caffeine might keep him awake all night," wisecracked Durette. The booth exploded into laughter with Walter joining his friends in the outburst.

"Oh, man, it really was a George Costanza moment when you think about it," he confessed good-naturedly.

When the food arrived the table conversation grew more subdued, something akin to soft, background music. For the next thirty minutes the banter was made up of single sentence comments on sports, current events, and any tidbits of gossip that anyone thought might be of general interest. However, shortly after the dessert orders went in, it was Chris who re-energized the foursome. Ronny Dingman had just commented on his friend's somewhat quiet deportment this particular evening. It triggered a response from the usually boisterous salesman.

"You know, someday, years from now, when I take a critical look back on my life, it will be during this period in my life when I identify that I began losing my looks," confessed Chris.

"Please tell me I just didn't hear those words from someone at this table and it's simply audio bleeding into the pub from a soap opera in the next room," bellowed Dave. "For god's sake, you're letting that little broad from work screw with your head," he added.

"What are you two talking about?" asked Walter.

"Shall I tell them?" Dave asked. Jacobs nodded his consent.

"Before you two guys got here, our buddy confided in me that he asked Heather from work out… and got turned down. That, if we are to believe him, marked the first time in his life that he'd been rejected by a woman." The explanation caused Dingman to erupt into laughter.

"First of all, I think he's full of crap. But on the slightest chance he isn't, then I say, welcome to the club… and trust me Jacobs, it's a big, freaking club." Walter, always the supportive friend, chimed in.

"Chris, buddy, she probably realizes that if she lets her guard down in any way, she'll be putty in your hands. You're looking at it the wrong way."

"Yeah, pretty boy, don't let this get you down. Take Dingman here. Rejection's all he knows," stated Dave while digging an elbow into his friend's ribs.

"Hell, if my old lady had rejected me twenty years ago, I'd be a happy man today," added Ronny.

The confession by Chris Jacobs to what was his support group did not represent a first time experience for the men. The four friends felt no hesitancy sharing personal matters with each other, and often did. It was what kept them close and strong. At this junction in time, Chris Jacobs was staring down the barrel of the first stage of his own mid-life crisis. His friends all knew it even if Chris did not.

13

Felicia Moretti and Walter Plews shared the living space, in separate quarters, under the roof of the Sand Castle for the first twenty-three days of June in the spring and summer of 1995. From day one of her residency, she occupied the southerly exposed, corner bedroom of the second floor. To date, Walter returned to his basement apartment each evening at bedtime. The arrangement saw Felicia preparing dinner three or four times per week. Twice a week, Walter would bring home fast food, a pizza or burgers, and the two would sit in front of the television set on the main floor. On some evenings, she invited Walter to join her for a walk up the beach to the jetty at the entrance to Wells Harbor. Without exception, he accepted. Over this time he felt himself grow more and more fond of his female friend. The vehicle he purchased for her more than a month earlier was now an important element in her life. They never drove to work together, choosing to keep their professional and personal lives totally separate. Under their verbal agreement, Felicia should have made her first loan payment to Walter in repayment for the car two weeks earlier. As of Friday, June twenty-third, she had avoided any mention of the obligation to Walter while he could not bring himself to confront her with it for fear of fallout.

Walter let out a moan as he eased himself onto the front seat of his car and the concentration of heat accumulated within the vehicle. After starting the engine, he fiddled with the air conditioner dial, hoping for relief from the inferno that was the cabin of his Corvette. It had been a steamy, hot day, the sun beating down on southern Maine through a blanket of heavy, humid air. Turning right onto the shore road, he motored northward over a winding and curling roadway that would bring him by Perkins Cove and ultimately into the heart of Ogunquit. With tourist season and summer heat upon the region, he anticipated a snarl of traffic between him and Route 1. Five minutes passed and his worst fears were realized, a quarter-mile backup between him and the perpetually congested intersection in Ogunquit Village.

It was nearly seven o'clock when Walter waved through a visibly shaken female motorist from Rhode Island, cleared the heart of Ogunquit, and rolled up Route 1 into Wells. 'No Vacancy' signs graced motel frontage on both sides of the road on this Friday night as the summer season unofficially roared in. Annoyed by the antics of a carload of teenagers packed into a convertible directly in front of him, Walter directed his sports car out of the caravan of traffic that made up the north lane of Route 1 and headed eastward toward Moody Beach. He reasoned the snail's pace of traveling the avenues down along the Atlantic Ocean was preferable to the noise and vexation awaiting him on the main road. On this night the street aligning the oceanfront houses of Moody was cluttered with scantily dressed individuals, each one seeking out relief from the heat and the humidity. He rolled his vehicle slowly in the direction of home, his eyes darting in the direction of any shapely women that materialized out of the sweltering mist. Finally, after clearing the knob of land that is Moody Point, he passed the dozens of people loitering in the humidity atop the seawall at Fisherman's Cove and made his way toward the Sand Castle. He approached the house and spotted Felicia's Honda at the far end of the parking area. He had neither seen nor spoken to her all day. He pulled his car up to the back of the building and stepped from the comfort of his air-conditioned vehicle. Even here, less than a hundred yards from the cold Atlantic, the oppressive air enveloped him. Walter was relieved that Felicia was home. Over the past day and a half he had been entertaining unsettling thoughts. He was beginning to think their relationship was becoming strained and, perhaps, there was someone else in her life. He opened the basement door to his apartment and stepped inside. It was cooler here than outside. Nevertheless, he flipped the switch and started the air conditioner.

A few minutes after arriving home, Walter paused and listened for the sound of footsteps on the floorboards above. After a few moments spent frozen in his tracks the big man ambled out of the apartment and climbed the stairs up to the porch. Reaching the entrance to the kitchen, he tried the door. It was locked. After peeking through the kitchen window and observing no sign of Felicia, he fished his keys from a front pocket and entered the building. The interior of the house was oppressively warm and altogether quiet.

"Felicia," he called out, making his way through the house toward the stair-well. "Felicia." With no response to his calls, Walter reached the flight of stairs and climbed to the second story. With each step the temperature rose until he reached the second floor landing, perspiration beading on his forehead and running down the side of his face. "Felicia," he called out again. His only response was the continued silence. Walter followed the hallway around the house until he reached the woman's room. The door to her bedroom was partially open. "Felicia." The lack of a response emboldened him to push in the wooden door. It swung in, exposing a bed littered with various articles of clothing. Across the room the curtains on both open windows hung limply toward the floor. Walter walked to the bed and looked down on the items strewn over it. His eyes passed over an assortment of blouses, belts and skirts, laid out as if considered for wearing in combination with another article. His eyes continued to scan the sur-face of the bed until they paused on the familiar sight of her worn, denim jeans. He paused, staring down on this lifeless configuration of fabric. Walter reached down and plucked them from the bed. Then, following only an abbreviated inner struggle, he brought the crotch of Felicia's jeans to his face and breathed in the faint, blended odor of denim, laundry detergent, and Felicia Moretti. He stood motionless, a sense of lightheadedness descending on him as Felicia's scent took possession of his thought process. It held him captive, frozen in place, for over a minute before he regained a measure of composure and laid the jeans back on the bed. It was at this precise moment that a feeling of sickness came upon him. It was spawned by the realization that Felicia was gone from him at this moment and even, perhaps, with another man. He turned from the bed and retreated downstairs and out of the house, returning to his familiar, basement apartment.

Walter sat motionless at the end of his couch while the news anchor punched out story upon story of crime, bloodshed, car fatalities, and of another Clinton Administration scandal. The big man let out a sigh of relief as the weather girl was brought on to advise Maine on matters of a meteorological nature. His spirit trampled, he considered calling Ronny or Dave for words of encouragement. Felicia's disappearance on this evening had virtually laid waste to his psychological state. He had not called his two friends earlier for fear of upsetting their wives. He had even contemplated calling Chris but assumed he would be out on a date, this being Friday night. The weather girl on Channel 13 delivered her forecast in the form of good and bad news. The good news was that the hot, humid air was about to lift. The bad news was it would be lifted by a series of violent thunderstorms caused by a cold front moving down from Canada. Walter pulled himself up from the couch, crossed the living room, and turned off the television. The quiet lent itself to thoughtful reflection, and that meant thoughts of Felicia. He listened for the sound of her footsteps upstairs. There were none to be heard.

With the sound of the air conditioner droning into the room, Walter fell back onto the couch. His mood was one of agonizing disappointment. He was sure his relationship with Felicia was about to change. He thought of the money spent to purchase her Honda and the words of caution spoken by Ronny a few weeks earlier on the grounds of the Cliff House. He did not want to believe she was using him but the evidence to support this was beginning to mount. A painful knot of disappointment invaded his nervous system, attaching itself to the pit of his stomach. He held out little hope of seeing Felicia before morning. Falling sideways and stretching his body over the length of the couch, he closed his eyes and conjured up images of his first night with Melinda Klaus at the ice house.

Walter silently stared down at the darting light from the fireplace as it reflected across Melinda's face. Her eyes were closed and she appeared to be on the verge of nodding off to sleep. An hour earlier they had made love within the confines of her sleeping bag, laid out only a few feet from the open fire. Outside the windows to the living room, the ice continued to pelt down on the house and all along the northern coast of Maine. Walter was now positioned outside the sleeping bag, his body covered in blankets but still spooning the frame of Melinda Klaus. Above her objections he had left the warm confine of the bag, knowing he needed to tend to the fire overnight and not wanting to disturb her each time he needed to add wood. The combination of heat from the exposed flame and the thermal qualities of three blankets had managed to keep him sufficiently warm. His eyes were slipping shut when Melinda abruptly rolled over, bringing her face within inches of his own. The movement jolted him into a state of full consciousness. Gazing intently into her sleeping face, he spotted the slightest trace of the blueberry pie they had eaten earlier in the evening above her mouth. In a show of his continuing affection, he ran his tongue over her face and erased it. Her eyes popped open.

"There was the teeniest smudge of blueberry above your lip and I felt compelled to lick it off," he confessed.

"That means I get the extra piece of pie tomorrow," she clowned.

"Too late, I finished it all while you were out," he answered. Her eyes widened. "Gotcha!" Melinda smiled warmly at him.

"You were wonderful, Walter. You really were."

"What? My driving? Sure kid, turn your car over to Walter Plews and let him lead you out of the civilized world," he bragged sarcastically.

"Your lovemaking." He grinned sheepishly. "I'm not exactly an expert. It was only my third time. But it was the most wonderful experience of my life," confessed Melinda.

"It was my first, but it was easy... loving you as much as I do," he said, his eyes moving away from hers. Seconds later he turned back to her and observed an expression of astonishment written over her face. Lifting his hand from under the blankets, he brushed back a single tear from under her eye.

"No man, outside of my father, has ever spoken those words to me," she admitted. Walter, visibly flustered, dropped his eyes to the floor and began easing himself away from her. "And I love you, Walter, with all my heart."

The sound of pounding at the door brought Walter out of a deep sleep. He opened his eyes and looked around the room. He was alone. Glancing into the kitchen area, he saw the clock read just beyond twelve-thirty. He rose from the couch and stumbled toward the back of the house. Through the window portion of the door he was able to make out the darkened figure of a woman. Rubbing the sleepiness from his eyes, he made his way to the door and pulled it open. Outside, standing amidst gusting winds and practically hidden in the shadows, was Felicia. She appeared dressed in nothing more than a sheer negligee.

"Walter, the weather bureau just issued a severe thunderstorm and high wind warning for York County, particularly for Sanford, Wells and Ogunquit. I was hoping I could ride it out with you." Momentarily speechless, he stood frozen in the door. Felicia stepped forward, allowing her friend to see her more clearly in the artificial light. She appeared to have just climbed out of bed, standing barefoot in the doorway, dressed only in a negligee that clung seductively to her body. "These sort of things really freak me out," she confessed, an element of desperation coming through in her voice.

"Felicia, of course, come in," he answered, at last mentally sorting out the unexpected arrival at his door.

Making her way into his living area, she climbed onto his couch, curling her legs beneath her. Walter walked to the refrigerator.

"Can I offer you something cold?" She waived him off, opting to sit quietly at the end of the couch and stare thoughtfully in his direction. He removed a can of ginger ale from the fridge and joined her in the living room. Her mood and general behavior seemed unusual to him, perhaps from her apparent fear of electrical storms. He quickly realized that he would have to initiate any conversation.

"I missed seeing you tonight. I didn't know you had plans to go out somewhere," he said.

"I didn't. I just acted on the spur of the moment."

"Well, you must have had some kind of a plan. I noticed you went out in someone else's car," stated Walter.

"You're assuming I was out driving around somewhere."

"Well, I mean, I think that's a pretty safe assumption, isn't it?" She stared soberly across the sofa in his direction until the intensity of her gaze prompted him to turn away.

"Are you suggesting that I don't have the right to keep anyone else's company without your permission?"

"Absolutely not! Listen, I'm sorry if it sounded like I was interrogating you. Why don't we just drop the subject?" She turned from him without responding. "I can turn the television back on until the storm passes?" She shook her head in the negative.

"I was out walking for a good part of the night. I had a lot of things to mull over and I think best when I'm walking on the beach. I'm sorry if you worried about me." From outside, the sound of distant thunder could be heard over the constant whir of the air conditioner. The faint crackle of thunder caused Felicia's eyes to widen. She rose from the couch and walked to the window. Her movement across the room commanded Walter's complete attention as the thin fabric covering her torso bore witness to the magnificent lines of her feminine body. She quietly peered out into the darkness, then turned back to him.

"Were you up in my bedroom earlier tonight?" she asked.

"I went up to see if you were home... and to make sure you were all right," he answered defensively.

"You went into my room when I wasn't there?"

"For a second, just to make sure you weren't lying there sick or something."

"And did you touch anything?" He hesitated, unwilling to tell the truth while fearful of being trapped in a lie.

"I may have..."

"Did you go through my underwear drawer? Don't lie to me, Walter!"

"No, absolutely not. I swear on the grave of my sainted mother," he cried out. Felicia responded with a hearty laugh, crossing the room and depositing herself onto his lap.

"I don't know. You have this guilty look about you that makes me wonder what exactly you did in my room. But as long as you stayed out of my panty drawer then I think I can cut you a break this one time."

"Trust me. I didn't open a single drawer," he swore solemnly, covering his heart with his right hand. Her face softened as she sat astride her friend. Walter's breathing became labored, no doubt from the close proximity of Felicia Moretti's soft flesh to his.

"What are you thinking about at this precise moment? I want the truth."

"I was wondering if you had any underwear on beneath what you're wearing?"

"It's practically see through. Can't you tell?"

"I didn't want to stare." She leaned into him, bringing her mouth up to his ear.

"Nothing… absolutely nothing," she whispered seductively.

Outside the walls of his apartment, the sky released a torrent of rain just before the air exploded with crashing thunder. Felicia arched her back while seated atop Walter.

"Take me upstairs to my bedroom. We'll make love through the storm." Beneath her, he was lodged in something akin to a semi-hypnotic state, his mental faculties prisoner to the force of his female friend. The weight of her perfected, feminine body on his own, the aggressive nature of her bedroom interrogation, the sexually explicit manner of dress, all of these had left him void of free will and resistance. He raised himself from the couch, lifting her with him. She made no effort to dismount him, choosing instead to wrap her extremities around his arms and torso. Pausing momentarily at the door to his apartment, he flicked off the lights and stepped out into the onslaught of torrential rain. Felicia shouted wildly as the two were immediately saturated in the downpour. Through difficulty catching his breath, Walter slogged through a rivulet of streaming rainwater to the side of the building where he climbed the stairs to the first floor porch.

"Oh shit, I think my keys are back downstairs," he moaned as they approached the door leading into the kitchen.

"Never mind, I left it open," called out Felicia just before a clap of thunder exploded through the air around them. Walter pushed in the door and delivered the two of them from the howling wind. "Upstairs, my lord," commanded the woman, not willing to untwine herself from him. He let out a groan but followed her directions and made his way to the stairwell and, eventually, the second floor.

Walter carried Felicia over the threshold and into the bedroom in the traditional bride-groom manner, depositing her gently in the middle of the queen-size bed. In the darkness outside the windows, rainwater continued to cascade to earth, only visible when the sky lit up prior to a clap of thunder. Incredibly, the floor was dry by both windows, the storm cell speeding in from the northwest. Walter gazed down on Felicia longingly through the damp, humid air of the room, her beauty continuing to intoxicate him. She, in turn, stared up at him seductively before slowly removing her negligee. His eyes followed her every movement as she peeled off the sheer garment in slow motion. Then, from her position seated naked on the bed beneath him, she fell back onto the pillow. He felt himself growing erect. Her body, stretched out and spanning the length of the bed, glistened from a subtle layer of perspiration created by the heat. Her eyes were dark, intense, and riveted on him. Through his own arousal a nagging thought entered his mind. If he should disrobe and share a bed with this magnificent creature, how would she react to his body? Would she be repulsed by his overweight condition?

"You may be the most beautiful and perfect woman on earth," he blurted out. She smiled up at him.

"Would you mind rubbing your hands over me before we make love?" she asked. "It relaxes me and always makes intercourse so much more enjoyable if I'm relaxed."

"It would be my pleasure," he answered, taking a seat on the edge of the mattress.

"There's oil in the left, top, bureau drawer. One of the drawers you swear you didn't rummage through earlier." Walter snickered before rising to his feet and fetching the rubbing ointment. Within seconds he was back on the bed, pouring oil into the palms of his hands. She took the cue and nonchalantly rolled onto her stomach, exposing the back of her naked body to Walter for the first time. He sighed aloud, complimenting the woman. Felicia visibly arched her back as his hands made contact with her warm flesh. She breathed deeply, the side of her face resting on one pillow, while his hands moved down both sides of her back. A crackle of thunder broke above them in the heavens but neither responded to it.

"You've done this before," she commented after nearly two minutes without a word.

"Melinda enjoyed massages. She told me what she liked a lot and what she didn't like so much."

"From everything you've told me about that relationship, I'd say she was a lucky girl."

"We were both lucky... and then our luck ran out," he mumbled, then reached down and reapplied ointment to his hands. Felicia lifted her head from the pillow and glanced back at him. Her eyes probed his face.

"I'm a creature of habit, Walter. I have a set routine prior to making love. You do know we're going to make love, right?" He laughed apprehensively. "I have a set routine and I like to stick to it. Following four hours of stimulating massage, I slither up your body from beneath you and eventually we become one."

"How much of that time will I be getting the massage?" Walter asked.

"Oh, you mean you're expecting to receive as well as give?"

"Well... yeah," he answered in a dumbfounded manner.

"Okay, then four hours and five minutes into the massage, I turn and slither up your body..." He burst into laughter, bringing his face down into the long, brown hair matted on her shoulders. His mouth found bare skin through the swirl of hair and he delicately showered kisses over her shoulder.

His head reeling from the proximity of her naked body, Walter sat up and resumed rubbing his hands over the length of her torso. Following a period spent kneading her neck and shoulder muscles he was prompted to move the massage downward to the bottom half of her body. Her legs curled and ankles locked, he ran his folded knuckles along the arches of her feet, a procedure that elicited a contented groan from the woman. He continued, exerting pressure on both arches and along the balls of her feet. He read her silence and blissful expression to mean total acceptance. He noticed her toes were long and gracefully curled.

"Your feet remind me of the ones on Roman statues in museums. They're perfect, like the rest of you," he said.

"Connect the dots, Plews. I'm Italian. I think my name gives that away. Who do you think modeled for those statues?" Walter laughed aloud while continuing to manipulate the young woman's feet. He gazed to the head of the bed and closely observed her face in profile. This humanoid, this technically perfect female with whom he shared this bed, was perfectly beautiful. It gave him incredible joy and satisfaction to be able to give her pleasure, pleasure reflected in the dreamlike expression on her face. Her beauty, in profile, both stimulated and exhilarated him. His head grew light as blood pumped feverishly throughout his body. Moving his eyes from her superb face, he followed the magnificent line of her body and came to rest on her buttocks. From outside the window, the sound of distant thunder wafted into the room followed by the repetitive tapping of water dripping from the eaves of the house. Lightheaded, his body stimulated by the rising temperature of his blood, he leaned forward and kissed the soft flesh of her backside, gently at first, then with increasing intensity. She gradually raised her head and peered back at him. What she saw was a man possessed with passion, abandoned by all elements of his personal self-restraint and propriety. She turned the trunk of her body ninety degrees and reached down to him. Unable to grab him by the hair, she grasped for an ear. A moment later she grabbed his ear and took control of his head.

"You've literally taken possession of me, Felicia. I have no self-control. I love you with a passion beyond words," proclaimed Walter, his breathing altered by his current state of arousal. Her eyes softened as she rolled onto her back. His pupils were glazed and unfocused. Lifting her legs over his shoulders, she manipulated his head into position for oral sex. She was met with no resistance. A rush of cool, night air blew in the bedroom curtains while the electrically charged weather cell beyond the confines of the four walls moved eastward out over the Atlantic Ocean. Inside the darkened bedroom, Walter responded to the subtle commands of Felicia Moretti's body, her limbs manipulating and dictating his every movement, her scent and taste neutralizing the powerful man's physical strength.

The two lovers lay spread out on the bed, their bodies naked and moist from passion. Walter, his arm draped over the woman's shoulder, stared down on her. The room harbored a chill, the bi-product of the Canadian cold front now covering southern Maine.

"I hope I wasn't too rough on you," whispered Felicia playfully.

"You are not a woman to be trifled with, particularly in bed," he answered.

"No, seriously Walter, you did enjoy yourself, right?"

"Are you kidding? It was beyond great. You're incredible."

"It's just that, I don't know, a lot of our time was spent on pleasing and pleasuring me," she acknowledged. He craned his neck and planted a kiss on the top of her head.

"All that time I spent on the bottom half of the bed was time spent in heaven." She chuckled.

"Heaven, huh? Okay, if you say so. Does this mean I can go on being selfish whenever we become passionate?"

"You have my permission." He followed his words by reaching down and pulling a portion of the bed covers over his exposed body.

"You only covered yourself," she said.

"Are you cold?"

"Not really."

"Then I see no reason to do that. Your body is the thing that fantasies are made of." She turned and looked up at him, her brown eyes probing his face.

"Can you remember everything you said an hour ago?"

"Just because I was utterly and completely under your power, it doesn't mean I can't recall what I said or did," he answered.

"You said that you loved me." Walter grew silent. "Did you mean it?"

"Yes, completely."

"And it wasn't just your penis talking?"

"No, it was my mind and my soul talking?"

"More than you loved Melinda?"

"I can't speak about love as an expert. I've only felt it twice in my life, romantically anyway. I don't have any kind of volume control on it. For me, it's always been the same... completely. I can't say I loved Melinda more than you, or vice versa. You both made me glad to be alive... and to be a man." She lifted her body from the mattress and mounted him.

"Please, Felicia, I'm spent," he confessed.

"Mr. Walter Plews, that was the perfect answer." She cradled his head between her hands and tenderly pressed her lips to his. "And as far as that thing about being spent, you're spent when I say you're spent. Am I making myself clear?"

14

The pending arrival of Delores Plews prompted a flurry of activity at the Sand Castle during the waning days of June. Her stay would begin on July 1st when Walter would pick her up at Logan Airport and end fifteen days later on a Sunday when she flew back to San Francisco. The transfer of Felicia's belongings from the corner bedroom down to Walter's apartment was accomplished two days before the expected appearance of his elderly great-aunt. It was mutually decided that Felicia would take possession of the unused and larger bedroom. Walter was not sure of his aunt's reaction to a strange woman living in the house. By housing Felicia in a separate bedroom, he played to Aunt Delores's Victorian values. Following her arrival at the house on Saturday, all contact between Delores Plews and Felicia was kept at a minimum. That would change on July 4th when Walter and Felicia joined Delores and two family friends for dinner in the sunroom of the house.

The Fourth of July was a workday for Felicia Moretti. Anticipating a four o'clock release from work, she asked Walter to join her on the ledge beyond the flume for some quiet, private time. At three-thirty, he left the company of his aunt and motored his car southward to the Cliff House. As expected, he found the parking lot crowded with cars, forcing him to leave his vehicle a distance from the main building.

After sticking his head inside his office and checking his calls, he made his way down the pathway toward the ledge where, presumably, Felicia awaited him. It was a glorious day, the sky pale blue and the water turbulent with whitecaps. He reached the succession of rocky steps leading down to the chasm and spotted Felicia seated on the ledge, her eyes staring down into the depression below. Arriving at the stretch of natural sidewalk rimming the north wall, he cautiously stepped along the trajectory of flattened rock, conscious of the churning, ocean water thirty feet below. A few seconds passed and he was scrambling up the ledge on the far side.

"Beautiful, isn't it?" she asked, reaching down and assisting him up the last few steps of his climb.

"Beautiful, but you've got to watch your step out here." She led him across a short stretch of uneven ledge to a familiar, stone surface. There rested a paper plate covered by an assortment of cookies.

"You're too good to me," he said. Reaching down to the ground, she produced a metal thermos.

"Ice cold milk to go with our cookies," she announced.

"This could ruin our appetites for tonight but what the heck," he declared, reaching down and taking an oatmeal raisin cookie.

"If you want to know the truth, I'm nervous as hell about tonight," sighed Felicia.

"Don't get uptight about it. It's no big deal," he reassured her.

"Your aunt has barely said two words to me since she arrived three days ago. I don't think she approves having me in the house. Thank God she doesn't know I've been sleeping in her bedroom for the past month."

"Everything's going to be fine. Twelve more days and she'll be back in San Francisco."

"And what about these people she's having over for dinner? What are they like? Are they her age?"

"No. The Desmonds are old friends and go back a ways, but they're much younger. They're pretty close to my age. Donna, the wife, was just a little kid when Aunt Delores and her grandparents were friends. She'd come and spend summers next door. She literally grew up here, during the summer anyway. I know Donna better than I know her husband."

"Did you and Donna play together growing up?"

"Not too much; I didn't spend much time up here. Aunt Delores was not a particularly close relative and, also, I was just her nephew."

"What's the husband's name?"

"Don." Felicia did a double take.

"Don and Donna?"

"Yes, Don and Donna Desmond." She giggled and snapped up another cookie. "Hey, it could be a lot worse. What if Don had married a girl named Dawn?"

"Okay, Walter, now you're just boring me. Tell me how I should dress tonight."

"I'm guessing Donna will be dressed in something fashionable, but casual. Aunt Delores, no doubt, will be dressed in a hand-me-down from Susan B. Anthony."

Delores Plews scheduled dinner for seven-thirty on this evening in the sunroom. It was an expansive room on the ocean side of the house that, generations before, was part of the grand house's wraparound porch. No doubt, Delores decided to use it rather than the dining room to impress her guests by catching the final hour of sunlight on the blue water of the Atlantic. It was seven-fifteen when Walter and Felicia made their way up the stairs from below and entered the main living quarters. He followed Felicia through the kitchen and into the sunroom, their arrival interrupting the quiet conversation. Don Desmond rose to his feet.

"Here is Walter and his female houseguest," proclaimed Delores as the pair made their way across the room.

"Donna, Don, this is my friend, Felicia Moretti. Felicia, this is Don and Donna Desmond." Felicia smiled down on Donna and extended a hand. The woman was prettier than she anticipated with sparkling, blue eyes and an engaging smile. She made note of the woman's perfectly fitting slacks and deduced that her Bermuda shorts were a little too casual for the occasion. She turned to Mr. Desmond and swapped pleasantries. A few feet away Walter and Mrs. Desmond exchanged the briefest of hugs and settled back into their chairs.

Midway through the meal, Walter was struck with a recollection of a day from his childhood in the company of Donna.

"I can't believe this is all coming back to me after all these years," he announced to the table. "Aunt Delores, you had invited Donna's grandmother over to the house to join you and my parents in watching a home movie. I remember the projector was set up in the dining room and all the shades and curtains were drawn. Donna and I wanted no part of that and we went outside. Is any of this ringing a bell, Donna?" The woman stared blankly at Plews for a moment, then broke out in a wide grin.

"Baseball cards," she cried out. A look of relief came over her husband's face.

"Right, baseball cards. I had brought this big stack of baseball cards with me. To my surprise, Donna had some cards, too. I don't know if they were hers or belonged to a brother, but she had cards. Anyway, she lets me look at her stack of cards and, lo and behold, she has a Tony Conigliaro card, which I didn't have but really, really wanted. So, sneaky me, I challenged her to shoot cards with me, you know, scale them against the wall." Walter glanced across the table and saw Donna laughing quietly under her breath. "To make a long story short, an hour and a half later, she's got my entire stack and I'm practically in tears."

"Walter, I think I cheated."

"What?"

"I may have cheated you. I remember that I had this card that was covered in wax, which made it slide better and made it heavier," she confessed.

"It sounds like you owe Walter an apology and some baseball cards," chimed in Don. Walter smiled at the couple.

"No, not really. You see, that night when I went to leave the Sand Castle, I remember picking up my jacket from the couch and finding my cards stuffed in the pockets."

"Did she give you the Conigliaro card?" Don asked while affectionately draping an arm over his wife's shoulder.

"No, no Conigliaro card," answered Walter wistfully.

Appetizer to dessert the dinner covered nearly two hours. Happily, the Desmonds largely entertained the table, recounting stories of European vacations and of an especially romantic trip to Ireland where Don proposed. Walter shared the story of his first encounter with Felicia, vividly describing the falling cosmos from the rocks overhead and his early intimidation in the company of this beautiful woman. Delores Plews sat quietly throughout much of the evening, judiciously sizing up the woman sharing her nephew's apartment and perhaps even his bed. No doubt, Felicia picked up on the sophisticated scrutiny, her eyes darting apprehensively toward her hostess from time to time over the course of the evening. The gathering was drawn to a conclusion over brandy. It was after ten o'clock when the Desmonds thanked Delores Plews for her hospitality, bid Walter and Felicia a good evening, and excused themselves.

The sound of the Desmond's vehicle exiting the yard broke the silence of the sunroom as Walter, Felicia and Delores Plews sipped the last vestiges of brandy from their glasses. A single candle dimly illuminated the room. Outside, barely thirty feet away, wave action pounded against the property's sea wall, providing only the slightest hint of a vibration throughout the house. Delores lifted her brandy glass to her mouth. Even in the muted light the shaking of her hand was visible. She turned to Felicia.

"Dear, I'm afraid I know so little about you. I cannot even remember your last name," she stated deliberately.

"It's Moretti," answered Felicia.

"Moretti. And what nationality would that be?"

"It's Italian." The woman glanced over her glass disapprovingly.

"I know you work with Walter…but in what capacity?" Felicia became visibly annoyed.

"I'm sure what I do for a living is of no interest to anyone, Delores, let alone someone as sophisticated and well-traveled as yourself. Now, I'm afraid I'm going to have to excuse myself. You see, I had to get up early this morning and work today. It has left me practically out on my feet." Felicia rose from her chair. "Thank you again for the wonderful meal and the interesting conversation, Delores. Walter, feel free to spend a little more time with your aunt. I'll let myself into the apartment." With that said, she turned and walked from the room.

"I won't be too long, Felicia," he called out to her. Turning back to his aunt, he flashed a timid smile.

"Your lady friend is as bold as brass. She also doesn't know her place."

"Aunt Delores… I am very, very fond of her."

"I find her presence in this house very troublesome."

"You wouldn't if you knew her better." The elderly woman shook her head and swallowed the last of her brandy.

"You don't have a very good track record when it comes to women. I can't forget what that German trollop did to you not so long ago."

"Melinda wasn't a trollop and it was ten long years ago. Aunt Delores, I practically have no track record when it comes to women. Besides, it's too late in this instance. I love her madly and there's nothing I wouldn't do for her." Delores Plews had heard enough. She sprang awkwardly to her feet, dismissed her nephew with an irritable hand gesture, and shuffled from the room.

15

*W*alter sat and watched as his computer monitor began shutting down. It was Wednesday night and in a few minutes he would be joining his friends for drinks at the Union Bluff. His workday was drawing to a close. Less than twenty-four hours had passed since the uncomfortable dinner with Aunt Delores and the negative impact from that evening was still with him. That morning he had learned that Felicia would not be returning to the apartment directly after work. She and two other women from the hospitality staff had scheduled an informal evening out. He threw up his arms and let out with an elongated yawn. While stacking folders on the corner of the desk, his eyes picked up on microscopic movement from the other side of the window. The familiar brown and black spider was back at work, repairing damage done to her web by the wind, rain and any windblown, oversized foreign objects. He paused, remembering the moment he first set eyes on this tiny creature. It was back in April, a short time after the Cliff House re-opened for the season. His mind played with the notion that this was not even the same, exact spider he first noticed three months earlier.

Following a period of utter futility, Walter found a parking space near the playground and made the long trek along Short Sands Beach to the Union Bluff Hotel. He entered the pub, slightly out of breath and in need of a cold beverage. Miraculously, in spite of the army of tourists in the region, his friends had managed to commandeer their favorite table. He joined them in the side room to the pub, slapping Ronny on the back and playfully disheveling Chris's hair before claiming his chair.

"It appears someone's in a good mood. Welcome to the table of doom and gloom, Plews. Glad you could make it," said Dave. Walter took on a confused expression and shot a glance at his three friends.

"What's up?" he asked.

"Well, for starters, there's a rumor making the rounds at work that we're about to be bought out by Chilton-Weatherly out of Washington... Spokane, Washington. Chilton-Weatherly has a long history of buying up small companies, running upper and middle management through a meat grinder, and moving what's left of the company to the west coast," stated Durette.

"It might be nothing, Dave," said Walter. "You know the rumor mill."

"I'm getting my information from some pretty, damn good sources." A second later the waitress was hovering over Walter. He ordered a beer and took a menu from her.

"What percentage of your wages do they give you at the unemployment office?" questioned Chris to the table.

"Oh, there's a nice, positive attitude, Jacobs. You've already got our man sacked and out the door."

"Put a lid on it, Plews. I wasn't talking about Durette. I was talking about myself. Maybe if you got here on time, just once, you wouldn't have to be brought up to speed every week," sniped Chris.

"Okay, Jacobs, so what's your problem?"

"That incident a couple of weeks ago… with the porn on my computer. Heather, that little ball-buster, sent a memo on it down to headquarters in Boston." Walter shook his head.

"There're not going to let you go. You've got the top sales numbers in the office," reassured Dave.

"You never know… not with those corporate pricks," snapped Chris.

The four friends placed their food orders and settled in for an evening of socialization. Walter's beer arrived at the table and he immediately downed a third of it.

"Well, guys, I don't know how you all spent your Fourth of July, but you can count your lucky stars you didn't have to spend it staring across the table from one, Delores Plews."

"Damn, even her name sounds crusty and old," injected Chris. "Try to picture an adorable baby girl lying in a crib—staring up and laughing—named Delores Plews!" The observation brought on a chorus of laughs.

"Anyway, her and Felicia didn't hit it off at dinner last night. Felicia actually got up and walked out. Thankfully, it was right at the end."

"Hey, Walt, does your aunty know that Felicia's been sleeping in her bed?" Ronny asked.

"God, no! She'd freak out."

"And while we're on the subject of Felicia and beds, Walter, come clean, have you made it with her yet? Come on, buddy, we're friends and all adults here," reasoned Chris. Walter's eyes darted around the table and saw he had everyone's absolute attention.

"She and I have grown real close but she's a very moral and conservative girl," answered Walter in a lowered tone.

"In other words, our man has tripped over the bag rounding first and is sprawled out in shallow right field with his dick in his hand," joked Jacobs. The men laughed politely but spared Walter any further needling. Walter Plews was quite Victorian in matters of intimacy with the opposite sex. He still viewed a woman's good reputation as something to be preserved at all cost, even if it meant being the butt of a few jokes.

"You know, Walt, last week on NPR there was…"

"Oh great, now we've got to listen to Jacobs tell us what the left wing pukes on public radio have to say on the subject," growled Dave. Please,

Jacobs, I beg of you. Spare us that liberal crap before our food arrives. Some of us have weak stomachs."

"You know, Durette, if you listened once in a while you might learn something," countered Chris.

"Yeah, I'd learn what the Democratic National Committee wants me to learn. But you know what really fries my ass?"

"We really don't want to know but I'll bet we're going to find out anyway," reasoned Jacobs.

"Those liberal clowns are getting my hard-earned tax dollars to spread their biased propaganda."

"And what's with all the English accents? What do I care what some upper class, London yuppie thinks about what we do here?" Walter asked.

"You've noticed that too, huh? Yeah Jacobs, what's with all the foreigners they try to shove down our throats? What, when they run out of American lefties, do they cross the Atlantic and hire on the English ones? I guess it's a matter of hiring anything but a conservative."

"Conservatives need not apply," added Ronny, dryly.

"It sounds like you clowns listen a lot more than you own up to," sniped Chris.

"The ball and chain and I were up in northern New Hampshire on vacation a couple of years ago. Christ, NPR was all we were getting on the radio. Man, it was like this subtle form of torture with all those lifeless voices and smug comments. They got this show from Wisconsin or Minnesota or somewhere, and they crack these god-awful jokes and play stupid music… and it sounds like there's a live audience," recalled Ronny.

"Prairie Home Companion… it's called the Prairie Home Companion," explained Walter.

"Lucky for me, I wasn't traveling with my gun in the car because I would have asked Helen to blow my brains out… and I'm pretty sure she would have taken me up on it," continued Ronny.

"Lucky for you, unlucky for us," chimed in Dave.

"Hey, there are times I have to listen to Rush Limbaugh and you don't hear me complaining," added Chris.

"No, but then again, he's not sucking tax dollars out of your wallet for the privilege of screaming back at the radio," Dave added.

"It always comes back to money, Durette. With you conservatives, it's always about the money," concluded Chris just as the waitress arrived with the four meals.

It was after nine o'clock and the social activity within the four walls of the pub was in full swing. The dinner plates from their meals had long been removed and the four men were growing nostalgic over the television programs and the starlets on them from decades earlier.

"I'm not sure you guys are old enough to remember this, but for me it was Anne Francis. God, as a young kid I had this terrible crush on her on a show called *Honey West*," confessed Dave.

"Is she the one with the beauty mark over her mouth?" Ronny asked.

"Yeah, you got it." The topic of conversation awakened something in Walter who jumped into the discussion.

"With me it was Jennifer O'Neil in the *Summer of 42*. I know it's not a television show but nothing or no one ever blew me away like her in that movie. Man, that scene when the kid carries her groceries home for her and gets invited in for coffee. I mean, when he winds up standing there while she climbs the ladder wearing those semi-revealing shorts…sweet Jesus." Concluding his recollection, he focused his eyes back on his three friends and found each of them transfixed by something above and behind him. He turned and looked up.

"Maybe I should spend a little time with the group on Wednesday nights. It might prove to be a learning experience," declared Felicia. Standing directly behind Walter, she placed her hands down on his shoulders and beamed a smile at the three men.

"Felicia, what are you doing here? I thought you were out with the girls tonight."

"I was. We had dinner right after work and then took in a movie. We called it a night right after the movie and, well, I was just a few steps down the street and thought I'd surprise you." Following a few moments when everyone appeared frozen in place, Chris jumped to his feet and borrowed an unused chair from the next table. He slid the chair between himself and Walter. "I promise I won't stay long. I know how you men value your time bonding." The four friends responded with polite laughter.

"Well, Felicia, why don't I do the honors and introduce everyone. Directly across the table is the elder statesman of the table, Dave Durette. To my immediate right is a face you probably recognize. Ronny Dingman heads up all the maintenance functions at the Cliff House. The fellow at your right elbow is Chris Jacobs. Gentleman, this is Felicia Moretti, the young woman who has pretty much swept me off my feet over the last couple of months. So now you all have a face to put with the name," concluded Walter.

"And a face with every naughty story," added the woman through a burst of laughter.

"Okay, Plews, how much of our personal lives, our hearts and souls, have you gone home and shared with the lovely Miss Moretti?" Dave asked.

"Only the stuff you wouldn't turn beet red over if it showed up on the evening news," reassured Walter.

"Felicia, if I may speak in complete candor, the reports by Walter and Ronny on your physical beauty have not done you justice," exclaimed Chris, placing his hand over hers. She smiled and discreetly slipped her hand from atop the table.

"At the moment I'd say I'm benefiting from dim light and the enhancing effect of a few beers. But what I'm really quite concerned about is a certain someone's fondness for Jennifer O'Neil." She lifted her arm over Walter's shoulder and brought her face in close proximity to his. "If I remember correctly from renting that film, having been too young to go see it in the theater, Ms. O'Neil has blue eyes, freckles sprinkled over her nose, and one of those killer Irish smiles. We're talking about a woman who is poles apart from Mr. Plews current girlfriend," she chided. Her comment brought a chorus of playful groans from the men.

"Jennifer O'Neil has nothing on you," insisted Chris, leaning his body against the woman. His actions caused her to spring to her feet.

"Well, for fear of overstaying my welcome, I'll wish you gentlemen a good night. This is a guy's night out and I'm an intruder. I was just curious and wanted to meet you fellows, knowing how fond Walt is of you... and be sure there were no Veronica Lake or Barbara Stanwyck look-a-likes draped over the table." She planted a kiss on the top of Walter's head and flashed the table a radiant smile.

"No, stay Felicia," implored Jacobs.

"You told her about our actress fantasies?" cried out Dave.

"No, not really," answered Walter.

"Oh, which one of you was the one who wanted to carry Vivien Leigh up the stairs to the bedroom?"

"You did tell her, Plews... you traitor."

16

Walter glanced across the front seat of the car at his great-aunt while the Corvette rolled away from the Sand Castle. She was staring sideways at the imposing house, an unfamiliar expression frozen on her sharp, Yankee features. He remained silent, content to simply observe this one moment in the woman's long, regimented life. There was both a vulnerability and a sobriety in her facial appearance, prompting him to wonder if she was, at this moment, battling with thoughts of her own mortality. Was she considering the very real possibility that she would never set eyes on the house again? Or was she reliving the details of some romantic encounter from the distant past and remembering a lover who, long ago, left this world, obliging her to live out the ensuing days and years comforted solely by waning memories of his tenderness and passion.

"It must be hard to leave the place behind knowing it'll be a whole year before you see it again," observed Walter. She turned in his direction and he noted the dreadful sadness present in her eyes. "Aunt Delores, it's not like you can't break tradition and come back more than once a year." Her nephew's words brought the glimmer of a smile to her face. They motored down the road and away from the Sand Castle and the beach at Wells. "What were you thinking about back there at the house?"

"Just the sentimental thoughts of a crazy, old woman."

"Share them with me. It's a pretty long drive down to Logan and I'm sure there's nothing decent on the radio."

"It's just something you do a little too much when you get up there in years," she explained. "You start thinking long and hard about the people who came before you and that you long to be reunited with."

"You don't have to be old to do that," he reassured her.

"No, but it helps. Walter, if you must know I was thinking about your great-grandparents and some of the others in the generation before mine. My mind was reliving the details of a dozen cloudy memories. It's what I do most during my visits here every summer... and it's both heartwarming and sad. Oh, and I was thinking about your parents."

"I miss mom and dad. Not a day passes that I don't think about them," he confessed.

"And when I really want to torture myself, I think about Danny Riley." Her words filled the vehicle and hung in the air around them. Walter waited for his aunt to further explain herself but she opted to remain silent.

"Danny Riley? I'm afraid I don't know who he is."

"No, it was a long time before you were born. Danny was a boy who lived in the area… a local. His father fished for a living and was moving Danny along the same career path. We met at a bonfire on the beach one summer night and quickly paired off from the rest of the crowd. I know I wasn't the prettiest girl in the world, but Danny didn't seem to notice. We were inseparable that summer and I accumulated story after story to bring back to Boston that September and share with the girls at my school. My God… weren't they jealous." She smiled sweetly at her nephew, something she had not done over the previous two weeks.

"Don't stop there, Aunt Delores. Then what happened?" She searched his face for sincerity and found it within his pale, blue eyes.

"The following summer the family returned to the Sand Castle and to everybody's surprise, even mine, Danny came to the house asking for me, first thing. My father asked me not to keep company with him but I did anyway. Every free minute he had away from the boat and fishing, he was with me. On a number of occasions I had him over to the house. I would have him come by when my parents weren't home. I was getting older by then and things were getting more serious. At summer's end, Danny couldn't stand the prospect of my returning home. However, I still had a year of high school left. He asked me to go steady, offered to move to Boston and get a job there, and even hinted at becoming engaged. My father appealed to the more practical side of me. He told me I could do much better than this young fisherman… and after a great deal of consideration, I agreed. On the morning we left Maine and returned to Boston, I put an end to my relationship with Danny. It was on the back porch. Some of the family's luggage was already sitting out there that morning when I told him. That's what I was thinking about when we were pulling out of the yard a few minutes ago."

"And did you ever see him again?" Walter asked.

"In passing, over the next couple of summers. In a town as small as Wells, it's almost unavoidable. He was always civil." Walter stole a glance at his aunt across the front seat of the car. She was looking straight ahead but her eyes did not seem focused on the road. "The better prospect my father spoke about never materialized and I wound up fixated on a career instead of marriage."

"Any regrets?" The old woman focused her eyes back on her nephew.

"A year after graduating from college I was working for an insurance company in Hartford. I was already making very good money, particularly for a woman. That summer I returned to Wells for an extended vacation with my folks. I had also decided to contact Danny, as crazy as that sounds."

"It doesn't sound crazy at all," added Walter.

"I had missed him and I wanted him to know that. Unfortunately, two months before I arrived he married a girl from Kennebunk. I heard through the grapevine that he had impregnated the woman. Back in my time, that meant something."

"I'm sorry to hear that… and I'm sorry for being so nosy."

"Don't be sorry. It's been almost twenty years since Danny passed away. He had a heart attack sometime between Christmas and New Year's... in 1977, if I remember correctly." With her story recounted, the woman threw her head back and gradually closed her eyes.

Sunday traffic was light as Walter motored southward on Route 95 toward Boston and Logan Airport. The weather was warm and clear with a light breeze, ideal for flying. It was he who broke through the quiet, following ten minutes of silence.

"Aunt Delores, thank you for sharing that personal information with me a few minutes ago. It means a lot. I think I feel closer to you now than I ever have before." The gray-haired woman peered over her reading glasses at Walter.

"Walter, I am about to reveal to you what an incredible, old fool I really am." She rolled back her head and shifted her eyes toward the heavens, a grin etched on her face. "Remember those evenings when I put on a shawl and went for walks up and down the beach? If you recall, I insisted on going out for those walks alone. Well nephew, I did so with the insane hope that one of the figures that approached me from out of the fog and the darkness would be Danny. You see, when my time comes, I'm hoping the Lord will send Danny to bring me home. Now *is that* or *is that not* the ramblings of a crazy, old woman?" He shook his head in total disagreement.

"Aunt Delores, I'd say that's about the most level-headed thing I've heard you say all month." The old woman broke into laughter.

The Boston skyline was within sight when Delores Plews unexpectedly moved the conversation away from the trivial and toward matters of more importance.

"Walter, before we get to the terminal, I want to advise you on a couple of matters. First, on my death, you will inherit full ownership of the Sand Castle from my estate. Secondly, over fifty percent of my cash and equity holdings, between eight and nine million dollars, will be passed on to you. All of this is spelled out in my will."

"Thank you, Aunt Delores. Hopefully that will be a long, long time from now."

"I also want to apologize for that comment I made about that young woman you dated years ago who passed away. I had no right to refer to her as a trollop. I didn't even know the girl. Lastly, I must add my two cents regarding the woman you are currently keeping company with. I'm asking you to be very careful around this woman. I strongly advise you not to share the information on my estate with her. I have long prided myself in having the ability to correctly size up people. This young woman, the Italian, is very hard to read. So, accept my counsel and be careful. My first impulse was to insist that she move out of the house, but I have reconsidered. Am I making myself perfectly clear?"

"Yes, Aunt Delores, I will be careful," he promised.

Walter escorted his great-aunt through the luggage check-in process and pre-pared for final good-byes. Around them, travelers flitted through the terminal like ants to and from a nest.

"I hope you'll seriously consider my suggestion and not wait until next summer for your next visit," he said, looking down on the woman and pressing his hand onto hers. She smiled up at him.

"You'll be the first to know," she answered, then beckoned him to lean forward. He complied and received a soft kiss on the cheek. "It was a very enjoyable stay and I'm glad to see you so happy." Walter stepped forward and respectfully embraced his aunt. On separation, he noticed what appeared to be a trace of tears in her eyes. "Nephew, take good care of our house and perhaps you'll see me again before next summer." With that said, the woman turned and walked in the direction of her gate.

17

Walter's trip home from Boston to southern Maine was made in just under an hour. He was marveling at his good fortune this day until he joined Route 1 and found the bottleneck in the village at Ogunquit. There he entered the back of a line stretching southward nearly a mile. He was anxious to return home and rejoin Felicia on her day off from work. When he left the house that morning she was already up, sitting in the apartment living room, dressed in nothing but a flimsy robe, a cup of tea balanced in her lap and her long legs draped over the coffee table. However, on this July day, the final leg of Walter's journey home to the Sand Castle was extended thirty minutes while traffic maneuvered through the gridlocked center of Ogunquit.

With the town of Ogunquit growing smaller in his rear view mirror, Walter felt his spirits soar. He stayed on Route 1 and drove due north until arriving at Mile Road where he banked a right hand turn and proceeded in the direction of the Atlantic Ocean and the Sand Castle. Reaching the barren marshlands, his eyes took in the extended finger of land that was Wells Beach and the line of ocean-side houses that overpopulated the sandy sliver of land mass. His eyes scanned the unbroken row of rooftops until he was able to locate the distinctive outline of the house's chimney. Inside his chest his heart raced uncontrollably. It was there he would find Felicia and following two long weeks they would be alone, he thought.

After threading his way through pedestrian and vehicular traffic in and around the main beach, Walter made his way the short distance back to the Sand Castle. Entering the back yard he noticed that Felicia's Honda had not moved and remained parked in the far corner of the lot. He got out of the car and made his way into the apartment. Surprised to find the living room and kitchen in meticulous order, he proceeded down the hallway and into the woman's bedroom. His heart sank when he entered. All evidence of her occupancy from the prior two weeks had been removed. Hurriedly, in a mild state of panic, he walked from the apartment and made his way upstairs into the main house.

"Felicia," he called out from the kitchen. His voice echoed through three floors of rooms. There was no immediate answer. "Felicia," he called out again, his voice exhibiting more than a hint of desperation. He raced from the kitchen, through the dining and living rooms, and up the narrow stairwell to the second floor. At the top of the stairs, he pushed on the bathroom door in hope of finding it locked. The door swung open to an empty room. Ignoring the series of second floor bedrooms, he marched down the hall to Felicia's bedroom of choice. Pushing in the door, he found her seated in front of the window, her feet balanced on the edge of the sill and a cup of tea nestled in her lap.

"I knew you'd find me eventually," she said calmly without looking up from her chair.

"Didn't you hear me calling for you?"

"I heard you."

"Then why didn't you answer me?" She shrugged her shoulders and drew a sip from her cup. Walter ambled into the room and deposited his nearly three hundred pounds to rest on the edge of the bed. "So I guess you've decided to come back upstairs."

"Brilliant deduction, Sherlock." Her words brought a pained expression to his face. "Look, Walter, I'm sorry for being such a crab. It's nothing personal. It's a woman's thing. We get into our moods." He reached over and tussled her hair. She lifted herself from the chair, carefully placed her cup of tea on the windowsill and dropped herself onto his lap. The big man's expression brightened and he reached his arms around her.

"Walter, I want you to move upstairs with me. Take the room just down the hall." He deliberately lowered his face down into her brown hair.

"Consider it done."

"We'll sleep together tonight to celebrate Aunt Delores' return to California," she purred.

"You want a massage that badly?" joked Walter.

"No, I want you lying beside me in bed that badly… and the massage." He laughed and planted an innocent kiss on her cheek.

The oceanfront homes were casting lengthened shadows across the packed sand as Walter and Felicia lay side by side in the bedroom. For five hours they shared the bed and their Sunday, drifting in and out of ecstasy while, less than fifty feet away and outside their windows, tourists played and frolicked at the edge of the foaming Atlantic Ocean.

"I just realized that I've barely had a bite to eat today, and the day is almost over," exclaimed Felicia, raising herself from the bed and propping up her head with one arm.

"I'll go downstairs and see what's in the fridge," answered Walter, slowly lifting himself from the mattress.

"No, I don't want any crappy leftovers."

"I know we have fresh haddock in the house and my aunt bought strawberries and cream a couple of days ago. I can whip together a nice haddock dinner and top it off with homemade strawberry shortcake. What do you say my little Italian doll?" She wrinkled her nose and frowned.

"I was thinking a little more along the line of lobster. However, the strawberry shortcake will do just fine for dessert." He lifted his weight from the bed and crossed the room to retrieve his clothes.

"I can't believe I'm going out for lobster at this hour," he lamented as he dressed himself.

"That's funny, because I can," she responded. He looked back at her. Lying naked on the bed, her eyes were trained on him.

"And why's that?"

"Because you love me, you've told me that you love me, and you'll do anything for me," she said confidently. Walter stood frozen in place, his eyes locked on hers. "Correct me if I'm wrong." Withholding comment, it was he who broke eye contact and made his way from the bedroom.

18

*W*alter stole a quick glance down at his watch then refocused his attention back to the computer screen. It was Wednesday and he only had until Friday morning to finalize the company's interim financial statements for the period ending July 31, 1995. It was also his night to meet the guys at the Union Bluff Hotel. Nearly a month had passed since their last meeting. Their normal night out two weeks earlier was cancelled due to conflicting vacations. Both Dave Durette and Chris Jacobs were on the road and unavailable, taking time away from their jobs and the region. He had just adjusted the last number on the company's statement of revenues and expenses when the telephone on his desk rang.

"Plews," he answered into the phone.

"Walt, I'm leaving for the pub right now. Do you want to drive down together?" asked Ronny Dingman.

"No, Ronny, go ahead without me. I promise I won't be long. I'm at a good breaking off point and I promise not to keep you guys waiting."

"I'm taking you at your word, Walter. No keeping us waiting for an hour."

"Ronny, I promise. I'm out of here in five minutes." He placed the phone back on its cradle and scanned the numbers. Revenue for the year was up and the month of July had a great deal to do with it, he thought.

Walter walked from the office, made his way outside into the heavy, humid air, and continued toward his car. It was after five-thirty, meaning the worst the hot, August sun had to offer had passed. Nevertheless, the three-minute walk to his vehicle caused perspiration to dampen his shirt before he was halfway to the car. Reaching his vehicle, he was delighted to find a dozen or so flowers tucked under the windshield wiper. They were cosmos, the familiar blossoms Felicia often surprised him with, yellow and white petals on long stems. He removed them from his windshield, tossing them on the passenger seat beside him.

Ronny Dingman cleared the door to the pub and stepped into a sea of people. The eternal optimist, he glanced over to the group's table of choice and saw a party of perfect strangers occupying it. Wandering further into the room he scanned the bar before glancing over in the direction of the pool table. It was there in the far corner of the establishment where he spotted Dave and Chris hunkered down at a table. He approached his two friends undetected, then burst upon them by dropping his hands down on Dave Durette's broad shoulders.

"We're going to have to talk a little louder tonight over all this noise, so the old feller here can still hear us," heckled Ronny before sliding into the chair between his friends.

"It makes you appreciate those evenings in February when it's ten below outside and we can have any table in the house," answered Dave. Ronny nodded in agreement, dropped his weight onto a chair, and glanced around the room for the nearest waitress.

"By the way, Dingman, before you arrived, Dave and I were discussing Walter's little Italian squeeze. Damn, when you and Walter talked about her all those times I didn't picture anything quite that fine. Now your concern about her motives makes a lot more sense," remarked Chris.

"Yeah, you can't help but wonder about what's going on up in that pretty head of hers," added Dave "Though, she seemed like a nice girl for that short time she spent with us."

"Broads can turn that sweetness act on and off like a faucet," said Chris.

"Why do you say that? Was Heather sweet to you before she took over your office and your life?" needled Ronny. The wisecrack drew a round of laughs, launching the table into its familiar lighthearted exchanges over the course of the evening.

"Just one more observation on the lovely Felicia Moretti and I'll forever hold my peace," said Dave. "That girl has the features of an angel, soft and kittenish... except for the eyes. There is something predatory in those dark eyes. And gentlemen, the eyes are the windows to the soul."

Thanks to Walter's early arrival on this evening the men finished their meals and were left to sip on their brews by eight o'clock. The banter subsided to a hush when Dave Durette began to speak in a more serious tone.

"I don't know if any of you guys read about it in the paper, probably not, but we did get bought out by Chilton-Weatherly a couple of weeks ago. They brought in a couple of empty suits from the west coast to make the announcement and to make it official." Dave looked up from his glass and saw the concerned expressions registered on the faces of his friends. "Their CEO and the company lawyer addressed all of us and fielded questions. On the plus side, we were reassured that they had no plans to cut payroll or to move us out of New Hampshire. On the minus side, this is probably the same corporate horse shit they fed the last three companies they bought out."

"You guys are making money, aren't you?" questioned Walter.

"Yeah, enough to pay some pretty nice profit-sharing checks for the last seven years. Hell, we stayed in the black right through the recession and didn't have to lay anyone off," reasoned Dave.

"They're businessmen, they have to know they've got a good thing," said Walter, hoping to encourage his buddy.

"They're corporate weasels. They probably think they can do better. Just the fact that they brought some scumbag lawyer along doesn't bode well," injected Jacobs.

"Any chance Heather might be looking for some new blood in the sales department?" joked Dave, the question directed to Chris.

"I wouldn't wish that backstabbing, little witch on my worst enemy," responded Chris before lifting his glass and drawing in a mouthful of beer. Dave Durette's report on the purchase of his company caused the table banter to grow more subdued.

Eventually, the mood at the table was lifted by Dave himself. He broke the quiet with a statement that piqued everyone's curiosity.

"Last week I was sent up to Berlin, New Hampshire on business. We have a small manufacturing facility up there. I lived there in the White Mountains some years ago, before I was married. The new guys sent me up to function as an internal auditor."

"You know what they say about internal auditors: they're sent in after the battle is lost to bayonet the wounded," cracked Jacobs.

"Well, in this case, that's not too far from the truth. They sent me up there to critically review the operation and write a detailed report. I was up there for two and a half days. I finished up at around noontime on the third day and, instead of coming straight down Route 16 and home, I took a detour. Back in the seventies when I was young, carefree and had hair, I lived and worked in Lancaster. It's a small town a little less than an hour away from Berlin. Anyway, two of the best years of my life were spent living up there. Why is it that the best years of your life always seem to be from your youth? I digress. Well, I intentionally hopped on Route 2 and drove toward Lancaster. You see, all those years ago I went out with a gal from up in the mountains. She was young, pretty, and deeply moral… a good, Christian girl. We became a regular item," recalled Dave, his eyes focusing on everything but his companion's faces. His three friends had grown utterly quiet. "I didn't have a hell of a lot of money and Janette was still in high school. What I did have was a car and we would go for drives out of town and find quiet, scenic places where we'd stop and spend time together away from the rest of the human race. There was this one place in particular, a grassy lot of land with some kind of monument on it. It sat at the edge of Route 2 in Jefferson and overlooked a beautiful valley. We would go there and talk and cuddle, and eventually make out. Anyway, last week with my extra time, I went back there. Jesus, it hadn't changed a bit. It was the same rusting chain-link fence and grassy hillside. I climbed up to the monument and sat. I sat there thinking about everything that had happened in my life, and all the people who had come in and out of it while cars drove by me a hundred feet away like I wasn't even there."

"And what about Janette?" Walter asked respectfully. Dave looked up from his glass of beer.

"That's who I thought about the most. I have a strong suspicion she still lives up north in Coos County. I wondered if she ever drives by this spot and glances up at the monument… and thinks of me. It was a gorgeous day so I stayed there for close to an hour. Maybe I even stayed because of the one chance in a million Janette might drive by and see me up there," he admitted.

"Well, are we going to hear the rest of the story or are you going to just keep us hanging," sniped Chris.

Dave peered across the table as if considering the pros and cons of providing any additional information. "We went out for a couple of years and then I got distracted. There were other women, my education, and a million other distractions. I woke up one morning and I was no longer in love. It happens all the time, but I made a goddamn mess of the breakup. I think, over the years, I was able to push it to the back of my mind and, eventually, completely from my memory. I did, until I went back to that little park by the side of the road. God, I must sound like a real strap with all this sentimental crap. I think it's because of the shit at work with the Chilton-Weatherly buyout."

"No, I think it's because you're halfway normal and have a heart," added Ronny quietly. Walter glanced around the table and wondered if Chris or Ronny had such a place or such a person in their past. His memory brought back the image of the ice house in northern Maine. Unfortunately for him, there was no way to go back and revisit the place where he and Melinda bonded and rode out the ice storm in 1985. He looked across the table at Dave and considered how lucky he was. Dave knew the exact location of his hallowed ground. The bizarre circumstances surrounding Walter's adventure, the blinding storm on arrival, and the unusually thick fog on their hasty departure, had so complicated pinpointing the location that he had long ago abandoned any hope of finding it.

Shortly before nine o'clock, the four men rose from the table and marched out the front door of the Union Bluff Hotel. Ronny went out of his way to accompany Walter back to his car. Reaching his vehicle, Walter turned to his friend.

"You're not expecting a goodnight kiss or anything, I hope," he joked while swinging the car door open. Dingman answered with an awkward laugh.

"I was hoping maybe we could talk, just you and me, a little later in the week. How about after work one night?" asked Ronny.

"Sure, of course. Is everything okay?"

"No, not really. I'm having some trouble on the home front. Helen and I seem to be drifting apart. I'm not sure what the hell is happening but it would really help to talk it through with someone I trust." Walter slapped his friend on the back.

"You name the time, place, and date. I'll be there."

19

It was late afternoon at Wells Beach on an idyllic, August day when Walter rolled his car to a halt behind the Sand Castle. As expected, Felicia's Honda sat parked in the shady far corner of the back yard. He hopped from behind the wheel and walked quickly up the back stairs and into the house, eventually making his way into the sunroom. There, strewn across the table, were two or three days of mail. He lumbered to the far side of the room and began perusing the assortment of statements and advertising junk. Shortly thereafter his attention was garnered by the sight of Felicia lounging on the cement patio at the front of the house. She was spread out on a hammock and attired in a revealing, two-piece bathing suit. He stared down on her, his eyes taking in each and every detail of her contoured body. He presumed her eyes were closed behind a pair of oversized sunglasses. He moved to the next window and continued to take in the visual that was Felicia Moretti, his repositioning subtly changing the angles and lines of her physique. He stood in the window above her for the better part of a minute, gazing down on her in a trancelike state.

"Take a picture, it'll last longer," she mumbled up to him. Her words brought from him an embarrassed laugh.

"I was hoping your eyes were closed behind those Foster-Grants," he confessed.

"It's not like it's the first time you saw anything on exhibit here."

"No, but all the other times I was much, much closer. I'm not sure I fully appreciated my roommate until I got this aerial view of her," explained Walter.

"So that's what you think of me as... your roommate." She looked up at him and saw his face grow serious.

"I think it would be presumptuous of me to think of you as anything more, as much as I would love to."

"That's funny, I was under the impression you loved me."

"I do love you," he answered, albeit feebly. Felicia lifted herself from the hammock and marched toward the eastern entrance to the house, the contact of her bare feet on the cement walkway sounding her advance toward the building. Walter stood frozen in his tracks as he listened to her clear the door and proceed toward him in the sunroom. Stepping inside the doorway to the room, she stopped and stared in his direction.

"I've got a ton of things weighing on my mind right now, Walter. Do you have a few minutes to listen?"

"Oh, Jesus, kid, I always have time for you. You know that."

Felicia proceeded into the room, walking up to Walter and warmly kissing him on the mouth. She immediately claimed a chair and beckoned to him to join her. Seconds after depositing himself beside her, she hoisted her feet onto his lap, the full extent of her long legs left exposed above the surface of the table. The unspoken directive being clear to the man, he began massaging her arches, his eyes darting between the woman's beautiful facial features and her extended, tan legs.

"By now you're aware of my problem with depression," she muttered. He shrugged his shoulders in response. "I've been wrestling with my demons for a few days now and I'm not pulling out of it."

"Come on, kid, come clean. You know you can tell me anything. There's nothing that can't be worked out," he encouraged while her eyes bore into his own.

"I'm an absolute failure. I'm uneducated with no money and no career. I'm a failure because I'm borderline stupid with no money in the world and no world-ly possessions." She punctuated her statement by closing her eyes and letting out with a sigh.

"Three months ago you had nothing. Now you have your own car, a place to live that most people would kill for… and you have me," he reasoned. Reopening her eyes, she stared across the table at him.

"I only have that because you were generous enough to give me that."

"So what can we do to take care of the problem?" he asked.

"I think it's best if I just pull up stakes and move on. I can give my notice at work tomorrow or at the end of the week. The Honda should and will stay with you. I haven't made a single payment on it to you. That's not right either." Walter inhaled deeply, her words visibly undermining his mental state. "We had this discussion before. Remember, it was at the Maine Diner. I sang that song to you."

"I figured we were past all that talk."

"We'll sing in the sunshine, we'll laugh every day, we'll sing in the sunshine, then I'll be on my way," she sang out in tune.

"I think things between us have progressed a little since back in May," he insisted.

"Things may have progressed in your mind but I certainly haven't progressed any."

"Felicia, tell me what you want."

"You don't want to hear what I want or need."

"Tell me."

"I'm going to come off sounding like some selfish, little bitch if I do that," she answered.

"I just want you to stay here with me… and to be happy," he confessed. She fidgeted in her chair, raising her eyes to the ceiling in mock disgust.

"I want money in the bank so I don't have to worry about what could happen to me next month, or next year. I want things like antiques and investments, things you can always sell if you should need more money. If I had these things I wouldn't be getting all depressed about being stupid, uneducated, and a failure. So Walter, as you can see, I'm a selfish, little bitch."

The sunroom was quiet following Felicia's disclosures. Walter sat thoughtfully, halfheartedly massaging her feet and seemingly deep in thought. Returning her legs to beneath the table, she appeared ready to exit the room.

"Please, kid, hear me out. I don't like discussing my financial situation but, if you must know, I have nearly four hundred thousand dollars sitting in various savings accounts right now. I mean, I'm not even forty years old, got a pretty good job, and nearly no expenses. It's not that hard to save money under these conditions, particularly when you've had nothing resembling a social life until recently. I also have a pretty substantial collection of rare coins, stamps and autographs. That's worth a hundred grand, at minimum. On top of this, my aunt made it known to me that, upon her death, I'd be coming into another three to four million dollars from her estate plus the Sand Castle. So, you see, I'm sitting on a pretty nice nest egg here."

"I hope you're not suggesting what I think you're suggesting," muttered Felicia. A confused expression broke over Walter's face. "You're not suggesting that I marry my way into this money, are you?" The man's mouth dropped open in astonishment.

"No, that's not at all what I was getting to," he answered defensively. She sprang from her chair and circled behind him, placing her hands comfortably upon his wide shoulders.

"I am so sorry about making that crack. Walter, I care for you more than I'm able to say. There are things I just can't come out and share with you. I think it's fair to say I love you but, right now, it's a different kind of love. What I can say is that there is no other man on earth I want to be with." He reached back, placing his hand over hers.

"Felicia, I absolutely can't bear the thought of losing you. Please promise me that you won't make any decisions on giving your notice at work or moving out of the Sand Castle until we've had a long talk and I've laid out a new arrangement. I'll just need a few days. Please, promise me there'll be no decisions on your part until we talk." She stepped out from behind him, beckoning Walter to pull his chair back from the table. He complied, and she promptly deposited herself onto his lap. Their faces were inches apart as her brown eyes searched the details of his face. She smiled and tweaked his ear.

"How can I say no to someone as sweet and lovable as you?" she purred before resting her head on his shoulder and breathing warmly on his neck.

They remained seated in the sunroom for ten minutes, the proximity of their bodies allowing him to pick up on her heartbeat, evidence of the life force enclosed within her human form. He held her tighter than usual, her presence in his life more tenuous since their earlier conversation. She appeared sleepy, her arm draped lazily over his shoulder and her head now cradled on his chest. The warmth from her scantily clad body, the cadence of her breathing and the feel of her limbs draped over him brought on an emotional revelation.

"I need you more than my next breath and I love you more than I have ever loved anyone or anything that came before you," he confessed. His admission was followed by a deafening silence from within the room. Seconds passed before Felicia reacted by lifting herself from the chair and standing over him.

"Why don't we go upstairs and spend some personal time together in my room?" she suggested.

"We haven't had dinner yet," responded Walter.

"I am your dinner," she answered brashly. "I think we're on the brink of lifting our relationship to the next level. Now if you think a baloney sandwich or a bowl of soup is more important than that, then Mr. Plews, perhaps you're not the man I should be spending all of my personal time with." Walter vaulted from the chair and followed Felicia to the stairwell. Stopping at the bottom step, she whirled around and proceeded to remove the top and bottom portions of her suit. She handed the two articles of clothing to him and took in the dumbfounded expression on his face.

"Okay, Walter, I'll give you the option: you can follow or precede me." He smiled down on her without making eye contact.

"Precede."

"Precede! You want to precede me up the stairs!" exploded Felicia through a rush of laughter. "And here I was thinking you loved my ass." He shook his head and waved her off.

"No, I wanted *you* to precede *me*. Isn't that what you asked?"

"You can follow or precede me, that's what I asked. Incredibly, you decided to precede me," she stated, shaking her head in farcical disbelief. Mildly embarrassed, he chuckled and planted a kiss on the top of her head. "Is there any chance you might be having second thoughts about joining me upstairs? I've been known to leave marks on men and then there's that whole pleasure/pain place I've been known to take a guy. Are you still up for an evening in the far bedroom with that awful Moretti woman?" Still clutching onto her bathing suit, Walter deliberately dropped to his knees. He took hold of her torso, rotated her one hundred and eighty degrees, and showered kisses on both sides of her firm buttocks.

"Beautiful, funny, intelligent… what chance does someone like me have up against you?" he asked.

"None, Walter, you have no chance."

20

*W*alter turned the ignition key in the car, switched on the windshield wipers, and pointed his vehicle in the general direction of Route 95. A day earlier, he had requested an impromptu day off from work and was now headed south to Lowell, Massachusetts to spend a day with his uncle. Allen Hurd was the younger brother of Walter's late mother. He was a retired investment councilor who had never married and now lived comfortably in a spacious garrison near the crest of Christian Hill. The house sat overlooking a small park and most of the historic city. Walter had grown up on stories about his Uncle Allen from his mother. The former Betty Hurd had habitually pointed to her baby brother as a model for her son to pattern himself after. Hurd was a man who had set goals for himself at an early age and never let anyone or anything sidetrack him from his educational and career objectives. In addition, Walter always remembered his uncle as a wise man with a warm, kind manner about him. When contacted by his nephew twenty-four hours earlier, Mr. Hurd had not hesitated to invite his closest blood relative down for a visit to his home.

Walter relied on his memory of the city of Lowell to find Christian Hill and his uncle's home but became frustrated when his route into the city delivered him across town from his destination. For the better part of the next thirty minutes he motored helplessly through a grid work of streets until a faded recollection from his youth summoned him across the Bridge Street Bridge and into the Centralville section of the city. With the silent, dark waters of the Merrimack River in his wake, he stared up at a manifestation of time and people from his past. One hundred yards in front of him stood an imposing four-story building that dwarfed all other structures in the immediate neighborhood. Capped by a steeple imprinted with the inscription 'United, 1882,' this structure brought to mind abstract memories of trips with his mother to his Uncle Allen's house. The massive, eggshell-colored edifice stood at the foot of Third Street at the base of Christian Hill. He turned his car ninety degrees to the right and proceeded up the steep incline to elevated ground.

Stepping out of the car, he was met by a refreshing breeze. His trip southward from Maine had rid him of the precipitation that was predicted to linger along the coast the better part of the day. He approached the house and found his uncle standing in the doorway. Allen Hurd was a man of sixty-five years with white hair and strong, gray eyes. Walter was ushered into a majestically carpeted living room where he was offered a cold beverage. Literally within seconds, the two men were reminiscing over stories from family gatherings from almost thirty years earlier. For Walter, many of the stories were familiar with details unintentionally embellished over the passage of time. However, his interest was always piqued when his uncle recounted anecdotes that involved his mother as a girl. It seems he was eternally interested in the personal history of the woman who brought him into the world and was the primary architect of his own development.

The two men had shared each other's company for well over an hour when Walter introduced the subject that prompted the visit.

"Uncle Allen, I really needed to speak to you and run some circumstances by you that are very important to me and that I have to make a decision on in the next forty-eight hours or so." Hurd's expression turned more serious. He gestured to his nephew to continue. "A few months ago I met a woman who I quickly grew very fond of."

"Are you fond of her or do you love her?"

"I love her. I utterly and completely love her. I am already living with her and we have a semi-regular sexual relationship. However, she is somewhat of a free spirit and most definitely a rolling stone. From day one she hinted that our time together would be limited and that she would be moving along in the not-too-distant future. A few days ago the timetable became crystal clear: she was about to give her notice at work and bid farewell to me and to southern Maine. As she explained it, she was suffering from a bad case of depression from lack of self-esteem. Her complete lack of any personal wealth and therefore, independence, had caused her to take action."

"Is she pressing you for a marriage proposal?"

"No, she already knows I would marry her in an instant. It is she that balks at the mention of marriage."

"Then I'm a little confused," admitted the uncle.

"She's looking for some kind of financial independence from me. She knows what I'm worth and what my prospects are."

"And how does she know that?"

"I told her... in complete detail." Hurd raised his eyebrows and flashed his nephew a look of surprise. "I love this woman... intensely... and I have to lay out a financial plan to make her happy and keep her from pulling up stakes."

"How trustworthy is this woman?"

"I trust her, but I'm not sure the rational side of me is operating on any matters dealing with Felicia," he admitted. His uncle took a sip from his iced tea and stared back across the room at Walter. "I am seriously considering putting a lot of my money and valuables at risk. I have a fairly good idea what your advice is going to be. I know what *my* advice to a friend would be. But I love this woman and the thought of her walking out of my life scares the hell out of me," confided Walter.

For the next half hour, Walter fielded questions from his uncle regarding his personal finances. His uncle also pursued questioning of a more personal nature.

He probed into the details behind how the couple had met, on how money was spent on evenings out together, and of the existence of any other men in her life. At the end of this question and answer period, Walter was asked to accompany his uncle upstairs to the second floor.

Arriving at the top of the stairwell, Walter was escorted into a darkly paneled room that was clearly his uncle's library. Along the far wall extended a row of windows that looked out over the better part of the city of Lowell. From this point near the crest of Christian Hill could be seen the meandering course of the Merrimack River along with the spine-like expansion of mill buildings extended along its banks. Beyond this relic of the nineteenth century's industrial revolution stood the *Sun Building,* a towering benchmark at the city's epicenter.

"What a fantastic room," exclaimed Walter, walking across the maroon-carpeted floor to the wall of windows. His uncle joined him a moment later and the two peered out over the city.

"I bought this house many years ago for the distinct purpose of building this room and furnishing it as a study and library." Walter glanced behind him and noticed a mahogany desk positioned in the far corner, a green-shaded banker's lamp adorning this magnificent piece of furniture. They stood together by the windows. Hurd now stared with interest at his nephew while Walter's eyes searched out specific landmarks in the distance. "Now nephew, would you like to hear why I really bought this house?" The inquiry brought the younger man's attention back to within the four walls.

"You had a reason beyond the obvious?" Hurd smiled and faced out the window.

"I want you to look beyond the park here, to the row of houses at the far side. At about the halfway point you'll see a bluish single family. Have you spotted the house I'm talking about?"

"Yes. It's halfway down the row of homes. Most of the other houses are for two families. Right?"

"That's the one. Inside that house lives Mr. and Mrs. Herbert Twyman. Mrs. Twyman is the former Kathleen Creegan. She is my Felicia." Walter looked over at his uncle.

"I don't understand," he confessed.

"We were sweethearts through three years of high school. Kathleen went to work right after graduating from Lowell High. I, of course, went on to college. She waited for me through four years of college and then for two more years while I surrendered body and soul to the firm. Eventually she confronted me with an ultimatum: commit to our relationship through a proposal, or set her free. The rest is my life's history. I chose my career and future earnings over the love of my life. That leaves me here in my golden years, needing to be content with stolen glances at the woman I should have committed to forty years ago."

"Uncle Allen, why are you telling me this?"

"You came looking for objective advice and perspective. I'm afraid I'm the last person to give it to you. Nephew, give this girl what she wants and needs. That's my advice."

Walter started the Corvette and slowly rolled it out of his uncle's yard. He had spent over four hours with Allen Hurd, far longer than he had anticipated. He drove slowly alongside the small park then coasted down Third Street, away from his uncle's home and from the line of windows from where his Uncle Allen watched over his own Felicia Moretti. Descending the steep incline of Christian Hill, Walter's mind wandered back to his mother's lectures on her baby brother's career path and the prudent insight shown by such a young man. He wondered how his mother would respond today to the particulars clouding the life of Allen Hurd and the self-orchestrated circumstances that brought him to this point. Walter avoided downtown Lowell in his retreat from the city, choosing instead to follow the Merrimack River eastward on the first leg of his journey back to Maine. He had come to the city in search of sage advice to counterbalance the strong inclinations of his mind and body. To his amazement, he left with a distinct course of action. He knew he must do everything within his power to keep Felicia in his life.

21

*W*alter reached across the bed, making contact with the alarm clock button and silencing the electronic wail that filled the room. He yawned and rolled his considerable weight up from the mattress, his feet touching down on the throw rug by the side of the bed. Outside his window the languid, August sun slowly rose up over a calm Atlantic Ocean. Remembering why he had set his alarm clock to this early hour, he stumbled out into the hallway and made his way downstairs to the kitchen. Within two minutes a pot of coffee was brewing and Walter was standing beneath the restorative waters of his morning shower.

Reaching down and placing a mug on the hallway floor, Walter freed his right hand and turned the knob of the bedroom door. It swung in gradually, exposing a room cluttered in summer clothing and a woman stretched out beneath a pale, green sheet. Felicia's body was turned from him, her face directed toward the nearest window and the cool, morning breeze that fluttered the curtains. Wasting no time, he dropped to his knees by the side of the bed and nudged the woman with a mug. When this failed to stir her, he repeated the exercise. The second contact on her back proved successful. She rolled her body in his direction and half-opened her eyes.

"Walter, what time is it?" she muttered.

"Six-thirty. I've brought you up some coffee."

"I'm not due at work until nine-thirty. Go… away."

"I wanted to talk to you about that matter from earlier in the week," he explained. She glanced up at him through eyes heavy from sleep.

"Not here… not now."

"If not now, when?"

"After work, I'll come by your office and we'll go out to our spot," she answered lazily. He looked on while Felicia began slipping off to sleep.

"I made you coffee. It's going to go to waste."

"Leave it down in the kitchen. I'll put it in the microwave when I get up," she answered, not bothering to open her eyes.

"I can't begin to tell you how beautiful you are when you sleep," he whispered down to her.

"That's not the half of it, I'm naked under the sheet." The room grew silent except for the listless lapping of the wave action from outside the windows.

"I've already taken a shower… and besides, I've brushed my teeth," admitted Walter sheepishly. His words caused Felicia to open one eye and stare across the bed to him. A moment later she began giggling.

"Boy, that came out sounding stupid," confessed Walter.

"Very stupid," she added.

"Very, very stupid."

"Preposterously stupid," she continued, slipping one leg out from under the bedding and looping it over his shoulder. He froze, then scrambled for a flat surface to place the mugs down upon. Felicia reached up and pressed her lips to his. "I love you, Walter. Now, get to work. I'll come by for you after I finish my shift."

It was a Friday afternoon and the parking lot at the Cliff House was already filling up with an assortment of late model cars of weekend guests. Walter sat absorbed at his desk, working on a new set of ratios aimed at measuring the contribution of returning guests to the complex's profitability. He expected to hear from Felicia at any moment. All day his heart had raced in anticipation of their meeting. His phone rang and he instantly picked it up. At the other end of the telephone line a female voice launched into a series of questions regarding the company's supply of toner. He sat back and politely allowed the woman to laud the benefits of her particular supply house while his eyes scanned the room and beyond. After focusing on the adjacent tree line, his attention was grabbed by the flutter of movement in the window. Leaning forward in his chair he eyed the early stages of a life and death struggle between an oversized flying insect, some variation of the wasp family, and the familiar black and brown spider residing in the corner of his window. The wasp, easily four times the size of the spider, struggled wildly at the center of the web, one wing snagged in the silken lines of its adversary. Walter strained his eyes, immediately engrossed in the drama while a female voice spoke into his ear from the telephone receiver. Anxious to rid himself of the solicitation call, he agreed to meet with the saleswoman the following week and ended the distraction.

Walter pushed his chair to within a foot of the window and resumed his observation. The wasp continued to struggle to free itself while the spider cautiously approached her oversized foe. On each approach by the spider the wasp would step up its counterattack, spinning wildly in the hope of breaking the strands of silk holding it captive. He watched the ebb and flow of attack and counterattack with piqued interest. This spider, or one of its offspring, had appeared in his window months earlier in April. On one occasion he had saved the web from total destruction, stopping a maintenance team from obliterating it during a routine cleaning detail. Walter tore his eyes from the battle and checked the clock. It was after four-thirty and still he had received no word from Felicia.

The life and death struggle in the window had now extended over ten minutes in duration. Just when it appeared the wasp would break his wing free of its silken knot the spider attacked its second wing and wrapped it repeatedly in band after band of adhesive silk. Again, the wasp battled violently in return. However, with the additional strands of silk encircling him, its motion and potential for any offense against its adversary was greatly reduced. Behind a thin layer of glass, Walter Plews sat immersed in the violent, miniaturized drama just inches from his desk. This was nature in the raw and the penalty for defeat would be severe and horrific, he thought to himself.

Following an abbreviated action to the edge of the web to examine the plight of a microscopic fly just snagged in her silken trap, the brown and black spider returned to her oversized prey and proceeded to add spiral after spiral of gummy silk around the victim. Still very much alive, the wasp thrashed within the confines of its limited mobility while the sleek, emboldened spider maneuvered feverishly around her quarry, restricting more and more movement with every pass over the wasp's significantly disabled body. Walter glanced around the office and saw that the coffee pot light was still on. He lumbered across the room and poured himself a cup. Returning to his chair and the dark contest outside his window, he refocused his eyes on the web. The spider was now perched atop the immobilized body of her victim. She appeared to be probing the flying insect's solid outer layer for points of vulnerability. Walter sat back in his chair and considered the plight of the hapless victim ensnared outside. He wondered if this lowly insect had any premonition of the long, torturous fate awaiting it. Unable to look away from the drama, he watched as the immobilized wasp was aggressively rolled through the strands of the web. Incredibly, after nearly twenty minutes of the spider's relentless immobilization tactics, a single limb of the wasp twitched in a futile effort to escape.

"So, so sorry for running late," apologized Felicia from across the room. He looked away from the window to see Felicia standing in the doorway, her slender arms and legs outlined against a sun-drenched outer room. "I have to drop off a set of security keys at the front desk. Why don't you give me a couple of minutes, then meet me on the ledge beyond the flume." Walter flashed her a smile and nodded yes. "It's my lucky spot. Only good things have happened to me out there... maybe because it's always been you I've met when I went there," she explained. She lingered in the doorway for an additional second, knowing he would be unable to look away until she made her retreat. "See you in ten."

Sitting alone in the quiet office, Walter Plews stared out into the next room long after Felicia left the building. He considered her cheery disposition and the positive reference she made to their relationship and their experiences out on the ledge. He could not imagine any reason for her to turn down his offer and abandon her life with him. In spite of this, his stomach churned with anticipation. The idea of this woman moving away from the Sand Castle and out of his life was unbearable. He sat transfixed in the room, his eyes staring blankly at the far wall. At last, voices from outside the building jolted him out of his daydream. Regaining a measure of composure, he glanced outside his window. The spider was positioned atop the immobilized wasp, the larger insect barely visible under countless strands of adhesive silk, its life force the property of its unyielding and merciless conqueror.

There was a fresh breeze along the immediate coastline that caused Walter to exercise caution while circling the natural walkway of smooth stone above the chasm. Felicia had already arrived at their predetermined destination. She sat facing south, her brown hair blowing horizontally. Instinctively, she turned and saw Walter cautiously making his way around the crevice in the cliff.

"You could make it a little easier on yourself and leave the coffee cup back in the office," she called out over the sound of the surf pounding against the rocky, coastal wall.

"The caffeine helps keep me awake in your company," he wisecracked back. Reaching a series of natural steps, he climbed upward, utilizing his free hand for leverage, and joined the woman on her perch above the ocean. He dropped his massive frame beside Felicia who promptly hooked her arm around his own.

"It's our spot, Walter. Only good things can happen in this place," she proclaimed. He leaned toward her, his face coming down on the top of her head. Inhaling the lingering scent of her shampoo, he paused within the moment. He was with the woman he loved.

"I've given your feelings and situation, or should I say our situation, a great deal of thought and consideration. I've decided to put your name on my personal checking account and on my savings accounts. In addition to that, your name will be added to, and you will have complete access to, my safe deposit box. So, as of early next week, you will have approximately four hundred thousand dollars in the Maine Colonial Savings Bank and two other institutions, and collectibles worth over another hundred grand in Maine Colonial's vault in the basement," he explained. She stared out to sea for a moment, evidently immersed in thought.

"And I won't have to come to you for permission or a signature if I should want to take as much or as little of it out as I want?"

"No. We will both have equal access to everything. The money will be just as much yours as it is mine," he reassured her. She turned her face to him, delivering a broad smile.

"I do love you, Walter, even if it doesn't seem so at times."

"And all this talk about giving your notice and moving away from Wells is all behind us?"

"It's ancient history," she declared. He reached around the woman and pulled her to him just as a brisk gust of wind ascended from the ocean below. Felicia shivered in response to the chilly breeze. He offered her a sip from his cup of coffee.

"Hey, it's the second half of August, the time of year you can expect to get the first hint of autumn." Felicia reached between the rocks and produced a modest bouquet of yellow and white flowers.

"For the man I love," she stated in a resounding fashion. He closed his eyes and tightened his embrace. "We'll go home and throw together something easy for dinner. Then we'll go to bed early. You'll sleep with me tonight and every night. Do you think you can stand having me that close, Walter?"

"Felicia, I am now the happiest and luckiest man in the world," he called out, his voice reverberating above the ocean and against the nearby wall of Bald Head Cliff.

22

*W*alter clicked off the power to his computer and organized the paperwork stacked upon his desk. Another long day of work had been put to rest, he thought. The month of August was nearly over. Evenings at the Sand Castle now found a chill entering the house after sundown. He winced, realizing he was running late for his bi-weekly meeting with his friends. Forty-eight hours earlier he and Ronny Dingman had met for a sandwich after work. It was at this time that he learned that Ronny's wife had moved out of the house. Apparently, Helen Dingman had been having an ongoing affair with her employer, a doctor, for close to two years. In the last month both decided to leave their spouses and set up house in Rye, New Hampshire in the doctor's summer home. To the best of his knowledge, he was the only person Ronny had entrusted with this information. As he maneuvered his way across the complex to the car, Walter wondered if his friend would share these events with Dave and Chris later in the evening.

Arriving at the intersection at Short Sands, Walter turned the vehicle onto Beach Street and miraculously found an available parking spot a short way up the road. His spirits lifted by his good fortune, he locked the car while the sound of bowling pins striking each other and the nearby building wall filled the air. The big man hurried his way up the street and entered the front door of Union Bluff Hotel. Entering the pub, he spotted his friends at a table directly in front of a window.

"Plews, you're nearly a freakin' hour late," growled Durette after glancing at his watch.

"Sorry again, guys," apologized Walter.

"Sorry isn't good enough. I'm proposing that from now on we set a specific meeting time and everyone or anyone who arrives after that time covers the cost of the first round of beers," stated Dave.

"I second it," piped in Chris. The two men shifted their eyes to Ronny.

"Sorry, Walter, but they make a good point. We've been sitting here starving," conceded Ronny. Finally, Walter nodded his head in agreement.

"I agree," said Walter. "Maybe it'll get me off my ass and out the door on Wednesdays." A waitress approached the table and the men pounced on her with dinner and drink orders.

Their waitress on this evening was a particularly attractive woman with black hair and dazzling blue eyes. By virtue of his late arrival, Walter sat with his back to the window. Conversely, his three friends were all able to view the pedestrian traffic from the beach through the wall of glass behind him. For this reason Walter quickly noticed, on more than one occasion, the loss of any sustained eye contact with his buddies whenever an attractive female passed by on the sidewalk outside the hotel. It was Ronny who finally directed the conversation away from the Red Sox and Patriots.

"So Dave, what's happening at work? Anything positive at all happening after the buyout?"

"They've already announced they're closing the Berlin facility... and they used my report as part of the justification for it."

"What? You didn't say you recommended anything like that, did you?" asked a flabbergasted Walter.

"Of course not. I mean, my report just had some recommendations on how to tighten up operations. It was stuff the staff up there could have implemented themselves in a couple of weeks. It was no big deal. Those west coast bastards were just looking for a way to divert responsibility from themselves," explained Dave.

"So where do you think all of this is leading?" questioned Ronny. Durette looked back at his friend, thoughtfully.

"I remember watching a documentary once about some of these Jewish concentration camp prisoners who used to dig the graves for other prisoners and then fill them in after the slaughter had taken place. These were strong guys with strong backs who knew the Nazis would keep them alive as long as there were others to bury."

"Pretty sick stuff," added Jacobs.

"Well, I feel like I'm sort of in the same situation as those Jewish gravediggers... except the consequences are a lot less dire. I'll probably have a job until most everyone else has been given the ax," theorized Dave.

"Update your resume," suggested Chris.

"Sorry for throwing the wet blanket over the table," added Dave. "So if someone could just move the conversation on to a more positive subject, I'm sure it would be appreciated."

"Today I received an anonymous note from someone in the office. It said I was going to get terminated on Friday," announced Chris.

"What? Are you kidding?" called out Ronny from across the table.

"No, the nightmare that has been my life over the past three months just keeps rolling on."

"Who do you think might have left it... and do you think it's true?" Walter asked.

"Heather could have blown the whistle on me, and the main office is just following through on it. Maybe a secretary caught sight of the memo and she's giving me an early warning," answered Chris.

"Some jerk in the office might just be screwing with your head," suggested Dave.

"I'm telling you guys, if it's true and Heather's behind it, I'm not going to get much in the line of a severance package. Shit, I'm living close enough to the edge as it is. My lease at the apartment is up in a couple of months but I still have a nasty car payment every month and my credit card balance is up there. If I can't find something quick and have to depend on an unemployment check to keep me going, I could be living out of my car by Thanksgiving," confessed the man.

"Chris, you'll be fine," consoled Walter. "Worst case scenario: you take over my apartment in the basement of the Sand Castle until you're back on your feet." Jacobs shot his friend a look of overwhelmed appreciation.

"Thanks, buddy, that's nice to know. Hopefully, it won't come to that."

Walter glanced across at Ronny and subtly rolled his eyes as the table grew uncomfortably quiet. The four friends were still waiting on their meals when Chris reached over and took hold of Dave's forearm.

"Look at what is standing in the window behind Walter," he half whispered. Durette and Dingman glanced up and focused on the form of a tall and tan young woman engaged in a conversation on the sidewalk outside the building. Dressed in a white bikini, the college-aged girl seemed embroiled in a negotiation with another female. Overcome by curiosity, Walter began turning in his chair.

"Don't turn around, Walter. She'll see you and know we're talking about her and move," Chris insisted.

"She's the freakin' girl from Ipanema," observed Dave, referencing the hit record from the sixties.

"God, she's magnificent," muttered Ronny, his mouth hung open in awe.

"Give me a break here," chided Walter as he turned slowly in his chair.

"Don't spook her, Plews," warned Chris. A second later a shadow crossed the table. Their waitress had arrived with their meals.

"Which one of you ordered..." asked the black-haired woman before stopping in mid sentence. "Merciful mother of God, will you look at that in the window!" she sang out. "That's enough to send me back to school for lesbian classes," she joked, her eyes glued on the girl outside on the sidewalk.

"Okay, that's it," exclaimed Walter, rotating himself in his chair and glancing up at the young woman behind him. His movement caught the eye of the beautiful girl outside and she made eye contact with him. Immediately recognizing the developments behind the glass, the gorgeous, young woman gestured her companion away from the window and further down the sidewalk out of view.

"Plews, you suck," spat out Jacobs good-naturedly.

"Wow, I love guys, I've always loved guys, but that's enough to bring a girl over to the other side," confessed the waitress. The woman's words brought a round of laughs from the table.

"Are you new here?" asked Chris of the attractive woman.

"No, but I almost never work on Wednesday nights." The handsome salesman stared up at the woman, his eyes flitting between the features of her pretty face. She smiled back while placing the dinner plates in front of the party of four.

"I'd love to know your name," he declared while his meal was being placed before him.

"Susan."

"I'm Chris. In two days I could be unemployed. In two months I could be living in my friend's basement." Susan put down the last plate of food on the table and looked back at Jacobs.

"Wow, Chris, you really know how to turn a girl's head. Enjoy," she called out to the four men before making her way back to the kitchen.

Walter sat contented in his chair. As always, an evening in the company of his three friends had gone well. Internally, he questioned his decision not to share the details of his new, financial relationship with Felicia with his friends. Both Chris and Dave had been brutally honest regarding their employment situations. However, Walter knew that, on the surface, it appeared he had been manipulated by Felicia and had no desire to have to defend his actions. Besides, across the table, Ronny went the entire evening without mentioning his wife's abandonment of their marriage.

Their waitress, Susan, returned as each man was contributing his share of the tab into the kitty.

"We're going to split up and try to hunt down that gorgeous Amazon that was standing in the window an hour ago," proclaimed Ronny. "Want to join us?" The comment brought a broad smile to the woman's face.

"Actually, I'm going to give you males one more year to prove you're worth my affection and attention. If you don't show me something in the next twelve months, then you're history and I'm going over to the other side," she threatened through mild laughter. She lifted the tab and currency before circling the table. Passing behind Chris, she reached downward and slipped a folded piece of paper into his shirt pocket.

"No doubt the phone number of the York Beach office of Vegetarians for a Greener America or some other crackpot organization," joked Dave in a loud voice.

"He'll just have to call and find out," answered Susan from behind a wink.

Walter made the trip home to Wells Beach through air damp with humidity. A series of thundershowers and locally high winds had been forecasted for the evening. The Sand Castle was ablaze in light as he motored up the road to the house. Climbing the set of stairs to the porch, he felt the dizzying effects of his evening of drinking. In the distance, claps of thunder could be heard echoing through the dark, cloud-covered sky. He pushed in the kitchen door and moved toward the front of the house. Every light in the sun and living rooms was illuminated. He walked quietly between the two massive rooms, expecting to spot Felicia cradled in a chair at any moment. He called out for her but there was no response. Following a few moments of indecision, he plodded up the stairwell to a darkened hallway and made his way around to the ocean side of the building.

All rooms on this floor were in darkness except Felicia's. He entered her bedroom to the sound of curtains flapping listlessly in and out of the windows. The room was littered with women's clothing. Walter made his way to the window directly overlooking the Atlantic and looked due east. The ocean was cloaked in darkness but the sandy beach could still be made out, thanks to the artificial light bleeding in from the row of oceanfront homes. He took hold of the fluttering curtains and peered down on the dimly lit, packed sand. It was there he picked up on the outline of a female standing at the edge of the advancing waves. It was Felicia. He stood transfixed, gazing down on the woman who possessed him, mind, body and soul. His mind awash in thoughts of her, he watched as a flash of distant lightning lit up her image standing on the sand below.

Descending the stairwell on his way out to join his female friend, he heard the sound of rain pelting down on the roof of the house. He shook his head in amusement, assuming he would reach the main floor and find her standing by the front door in saturated clothes. Clearing the bottom of the stairs, Walter rushed to the main entrance. There was no sign of her, only the sight of torrential rain, washing over the patio and front steps. He stepped out onto the covered porch while gallons of rainwater streamed down from the inclined roof above his head. Walter moved to the lip of the porch, straining to spot Felicia through the deluge. Incredibly, she was visible through the downpour. She had not moved from her position by the water's edge.

"Felicia," he called out over the sound of falling water. She did not react to his voice. He rambled down the stairs and out into the drenching rain. Making his way from the yard, he descended the right-of-way to the beach. Frantically, he bounded across the hard, packed sand toward the woman while she stood as motionless as a statue, her back to him and the long row of houses that constituted Wells Beach. "What in God's name are you doing?" he asked, reaching her and the foaming surf.

"Thinking… and enjoying nature," she replied. As if on cue, the air around them flashed with light.

"Come on kid, back to the house," he insisted before a crash of thunder exploded above their heads. "The storm is really closing in." She looked up at him. There was no evidence of fear or concern registered on her face.

"Do you love me, Walter?"

"You know perfectly well I do."

"And do you believe I would never do anything to harm or hurt you in any way?"

"Yes, I do. Now, can we go back to the house?" A sheet of rain-drenched wind blew up on them, forcing Walter to brush the water from his eyes.

"No, a few seconds more. There's going to come a day when your faith in me will be tested. I want you to remember this conversation and everything I'm telling you. This storm and these circumstances should help."

"How could I possibly forget?"

"It's just that you seemed to lose your faith in Melinda once she was gone."

"That was different."

"Different from what?" Walter threw his hands up in frustration. "Are you saying that you're going to leave me, too?"

"No, I'm just saying that the day may come when everything we have could be tested," she concluded.

"Why are you talking this way? Why are you trying to depress me?"

"I'm sorry if this comes off as depressing or melodramatic but I'm trying to get something across to you," she explained.

"Out here, in this mess?"

"Everyone and everything has to leave. If you really love someone then you forget about yourself and make it as easy as possible on the one you leave behind." She paused and allowed him to digest her words. Finally, she folded her arm through his and turned for the house. "Now, with both our bodies cleansed by water straight from the heavens, let's retreat to the bedroom." Walter clamped on to her, stopping the woman in her tracks.

"You are so incredibly unpredictable and strange. The things you say and the way you act sometimes drives me crazy," he exclaimed. He closed his eyes and sank to his knees, his arms tightly enfolding her. "But I love you so very much. I would gladly die here on the beach with you… because it's with you." She smiled down on him for a moment before motioning him back to his feet. He rose just as a wind gust blew over them from the north, sending Walter sprawling sideways onto the sand.

"God, I really do have a flair for the dramatic," quipped Felicia as she reached down to assist him.

By the time the two reached the house, the conversation had shifted to more mundane topics. Walter updated Felicia on Dave and Chris's employment problems and on Ronny Dingman's fractured marriage. However, after some internal debate, he decided not to mention the scantily clothed young woman in the window of the pub and the commotion her appearance had created at the table.

23

*W*alter reached across his desk and brought a cup of lukewarm coffee to his lips. His eyes were glued on the computer monitor. He was quite satisfied with what he saw. Based on the revenue numbers from August and the Labor Day weekend, it was clear the Cliff House had totally recovered from the lingering effects of the recent recession. He removed a pair of reading glasses and rubbed his eyes. For the past forty-eight hours he had extended himself preparing a number of financial reports. Now he sat tired and satisfied.

"Is there anything else, Walter?" called out Pamela LaBossiere from the next room while she prepared to leave for the day. Pamela spent a few hours in the department every week helping with payroll.

"No, Pam, we're fine," he answered. His words were followed by a few seconds of paper shuffling, then nothing. He took another mouthful of coffee and shifted his gaze to the window. A light breeze sent a ripple through the web outside. He focused his eyes on the elaborate silken pattern. On the far side of the mesh, the remains of the unfortunate wasp fluttered with the movement of the air, its lifeless carcass a trophy to the wily, patient spider sharing the window with Walter.

"I'm off for home," came a voice from the doorway. He turned to see Felicia approaching his desk. For you," she said, extending to him a fistful of white and yellow cosmos.

"My God, are these things never out of season?" he exclaimed. "Wait, I've got just the vase for them." He jumped to his feet and crossed the room.

"I have tomorrow off and I want you to take a day off and stay home with me," demanded Felicia. "We haven't been spending enough personal time together lately... and when I say personal I mean deeply personal. It's September and the weather is beautiful. Just you and me all day at the Sand Castle, what do you say?" Walter hesitated. "The Cliff House can get by without you for one day," she reasoned.

"Okay. How can I say no to an offer like that?" he confessed while placing his hand on the side of her face.

"If you'll pick up dinner on the way home tonight, I'll give you a wonderful rubdown after we clear the table." Her offer caused his eyes to widen.

"Are you sure? You know I love giving as well as receiving."

"Sold! I'll get the massage. Plews, he who hesitates is lost. I made the offer and you hesitated. So, if I'm following everything correctly, you pick up and pay for dinner and bring it home. After dinner, you rub me down for a couple of hours. Now, thank me for being such a wonderful and thoughtful girl." He crossed the room, vase and flowers in hand. Laying both down, he framed her face with his hands and pressed his lips to hers.

"I love you, Felicia Moretti."

"You'll love me even more by tomorrow night," she promised behind a coquettish smile.

"Impossible."

"I'll take a shower and make myself presentable before you get home," she said before turning for the door.

"No, no shower. I don't want to smell bath soap when I get home. I want to smell you," he stated seriously. His words brought a flurry of childish laughter from the woman.

"Poor, poor Walter. You do have it bad for me… very, very bad."

"I'm hopelessly in love with you," he admitted. His words brought a solemn expression back to her face.

"Yes, I know."

A chilly, ocean wind greeted Walter as he stepped from the car. The last hint of daylight hung in the air around him. In one hand he carried two seafood plates up the steps toward the extensive wraparound porch. Nudging in the door to the kitchen, he made his way through the darkened room toward the dining table on the ocean side of the house. His eyes were barely able to make out the outline of the table as he placed down the meal. It was only then that he noticed Felicia standing by the window, her back to the room, staring out at an ocean dressed in dusk.

"Whoa, thanks for the warning," he exclaimed. "What are you doing, trying out for *Dark Shadows?*"

"Sorry," she answered quietly.

"I got us a couple of combination plates. I got myself haddock and clams. For you, I got shrimp and scallops. Any complaints?" She moved out of the shadows and joined him by the table. She was wearing one of his loose fitting shirts and nothing else. His eyes quickly picked up on her state of dress and involuntarily shifted downward.

"You got fried clams for yourself?" she asked in a childlike manner.

"I'm not against sharing," declared Walter. "Maybe I should flip on a light?"

"No, no lights. Let me go into the kitchen and bring back a candle. We'll have a candlelight dinner." She circled the table and walked toward the adjoining room. His eyes followed her movement. She returned to the darkened sunroom, placed the candle at the center of the table, and lit it. Seconds later he removed the plates from the bag and distributed the food. He paused before taking his first bite and observed how the flickering light reflected off her face.

Ten minutes into the meal, Felicia had consumed nearly half her plate. Over that time, she had scarcely lifted her eyes from her food.

"May I ask you a question that might prove a little sensitive?" Walter asked.

"Will it piss me off and throw me into a bad mood?"

"No, it shouldn't."

"Go ahead, ask."

"I ran into someone in town yesterday. They mentioned in passing that you recently went down to the safe deposit department at the bank and spent some time looking over everything. Is that true?" She glanced up from her plate and stared at him coldly.

"And what if I did?"

"I don't know. I just thought it peculiar you didn't say anything to me about it."

"Why should I have to? Correct me if I'm wrong, but doesn't that stuff belong to both of us?"

"Yes, it's ours."

"Then why should I have to ask your permission to go look at it?"

"You don't! I just found it curious that you didn't ask me about anything or want to discuss some of the contents with me afterward."

"You never bothered telling me what was in there, so I decided to take a look for myself," she answered defensively.

"Felicia, you only had to ask. I would have loved to discuss it with you." She put down her utensils and folded her arms. "I don't like what your body language is saying."

"Wait until you see what it's saying upstairs an hour from now," she snapped back.

"Come on now, you're taking this the wrong way," he reasoned in a calm tone.

"You told me there was over a hundred thousand dollars worth of stuff in that deposit box. I find it hard to believe that those coins and stamps are worth that much."

"Did you happen to see some of the documents we have in there? We have papers signed by George Washington, John Adams and John Hancock. We have a hand-written letter written by Abraham Lincoln! Did you happen to notice that some of the coins in there were made of gold?"

"You don't trust me, do you?" she asked from across the table.

"I trust you completely. For God's sake, I love you!"

"Then, no more questions."

The couple resumed their meal. The first minute was spent in silence. Then, in a nonchalant manner, Felicia reached across the table and speared a fried clam from Walter's plate. He glanced over to her but her eyes were already back on her food. Following thirty more seconds of silence, her fork moved over the table again, stabbing a clam and delivering it directly into her mouth. This time their eyes locked, a smirk spread over her pretty face. He took a few moments to chew and swallow the food already in his mouth before he confidently extended his fork to Felicia's plate and stabbed a large scallop. Instantaneously, she snatched his hand at the wrist and thrust her own fork into the back of his hand, exerting enough pressure to hold it in place while not breaking the skin.

"Felicia, no," he stated firmly.

"Ask nicely," she instructed.

"I'm warning you," he replied. His words only brought a burst of laughter from the woman. She brought her face to within inches of his own and increased the pressure on his hand.

"Walter, I know what you want. I didn't shower tonight because you asked me not to. You want me to be a bad girl…a slightly sweaty, bad girl. Well, Walter, be careful what you wish for. Now, ask nicely."

"Please, Felicia, the hand," he responded. She lifted the fork from his hand and delivered a scallop into his mouth, her fingertips lingering seductively on his lower lip. He slumped back into his chair, her antics leaving him lightheaded.

"And to think we have all day tomorrow together," he muttered through a sigh.

"You will definitely need to take your heart pills tonight, Walter. I don't plan to let up on you. Just because you've made me a woman of some means, with my golden coins and president's autographs, doesn't mean I'm going to cut you even the slightest break. Put down your fork. We're going upstairs right now. Dinner's over." Hurriedly, Felicia removed her shirt and twirled it around his neck, tightening it until the pressure caused him to pull back from her. "You wanted to spend time with a bad girl and not your sweet Felicia."

"I didn't want you to shower because I love the way your flesh tastes… your flesh and everything else. It didn't have anything to do with you being a bad girl around me," he confessed while her shirt contracted around his windpipe. Standing in the nude above him, she leaned forward and tenderly bit down on his ear.

"Blow out the candle, Walter. We mustn't waste any more of our time together."

24

$\mathcal{W}$alter glanced outside his office window and was astonished by the splash of autumn color suddenly visible along the distant tree line. In a few days September would give way to October as 1995 sped its way toward becoming a part of Generation X's 'good old days.' He lifted his bulk from the desk and crossed the office to the coffee machine. Pouring himself a cup, he loitered in the far corner and pondered the events impacting his life. His friend, Chris Jacobs, was unemployed, the victim of a youthful manager's vendetta to rid the office of anyone who posed a threat to her authority. Another friend, Dave Durette, was currently in the early stages of interviewing for a job in New Jersey. The following week he would have to spend three days at an accounting software seminar in Newport, Rhode Island, and the prospect of spending seventy-two hours away from Felicia was bringing his spirits down. Abruptly, the room filled with the sound of the phone, bringing him out of his mental funk. He carried his cup of steaming coffee back to his desk.

"Accounting, Plews."

"It's beautiful outside. Why don't we have afternoon break together at our regular place?" It was Felicia.

"Great idea, maybe you can snap me out of my wicked case of the blahs."

"Bring coffee for two. I'll provide the snack," she instructed.

"It's a plan."

Walter closed the door to his office and made his way out of the building. He carried an oversized coffee cup filled nearly to the brim. He followed the trail across the top of Bald Head Cliff to the stratified succession of rocks leading down to the familiar ledge beyond the chasm. From fifty feet away his eyes picked up on Felicia, her hair blowing wildly in the invigorating currents of air careening in off the water. She stood facing in his direction but unaware of his approach, her eyes shifted downward to the seawater churning below in the chasm. Finally, she became aware of Walter's approach.

"Only one cup?" she called up.

"It's an extra large cup," he explained, making his way up the sharply chiseled rock to her position. With her lower lip bended into a comical pout, she began to whimper.

"I'll give you the whole cup," he cried out, causing her to explode into laughter.

"God, you're a softy," she replied affectionately. Felicia proceeded to reach down into a paper bag resting by her foot and produced a pair of huge oatmeal raisin cookies. "One of the girls baked them herself and brought them in. Given they're made with oatmeal, they're probably even slightly good for you." He took one of the cookies and, simultaneously, rested his head on her shoulder.

"It's been a lousy couple of days for me and I'm already dreading being away next week," he confessed.

"You're dreading Newport? Give me a break."

"It's Newport without you."

"It's Newport," asserted Felicia. He bit into his cookie and stared southward over the water. On this day the blue Atlantic Ocean was speckled with sparkling whitecaps.

Following a silent interlude, Felicia rose to her feet and stood directly in front of Walter. She took his hands and looked directly into his eyes.

"I want to propose something for next week that will help me out and also give us a little more time together before your Rhode Island trip." He gestured to her to continue while chewing on the cookie. "I'd like you to take next Tuesday off and spend the whole day with me. Tuesday's one of my scheduled days off next week. I'll drive you down to the hotel in Newport. I'm hoping to borrow the Corvette next week while you're gone so I can have some work done on the Honda."

"That's a long drive... down to Newport."

"I'll be in the car with you. It's more time together," she reasoned. He stared up at her, his mind visibly processing her proposition.

"And you'll come back on Friday and pick me up?"

"Yes. We'll work out the details on the phone when we talk that Thursday." He took in a deep breath and made a bewildered gesture. "Please, Walter, my car really needs this time in the shop."

"Okay, if you don't mind all that time on the road and behind the wheel, why not?" She finessed herself onto his lap, looping an arm over his shoulder and dropping a hand to his inner thigh.

"Next Monday night, the night before we drive to Newport, I am yours," she whispered into his ear.

"You are mine. What exactly does that mean?"

"It means I will do anything you ask me to do. Think of it as payment for letting me borrow your car." Walter nodded his head thoughtfully and smiled down at her. "You have almost a week to think about what you want."

"Anything?" he asked sheepishly.

"Anything," she answered decisively.

"You'll do anything I want?"

"How many definitions do you think there are to the word, *anything?* I'm saying... anything." Walter brought his lips down onto the top of her head, kissing and inhaling the fragrance from her brown hair.

"Only you could bring me out of my funk like this," he stated. She force-fed him the last remnants of her cookie and rose to her feet. She stretched out her arms and grimaced.

"Are you okay?" he asked.

"Not really. I've got this painful stiffness in both shoulders."

"Maybe I can rub you down with something warm tonight?"

"Yes. It's a date. Let's make it seven-thirty in the living room. I'll have a towel down on the floor. I'll set it up so I can watch *Jeopardy* while you're giving me my rub. I'll even pick up some seedless grapes on the way home so you can feed me during my treatment," gushed Felicia. Walter chuckled.

"Will you be wanting me to peel those grapes?" he questioned sarcastically.

"Don't be silly. That would make it seem like I was taking advantage of you," she replied before applying a hug and lifting him up to his feet.

Walter opened the door to his office and made his way to the desk. A blinking light atop his desk told him he had voice mail. Turning to the far wall, the clock indicated it was after three-thirty. He and Felicia had taken an unusually long afternoon break. He deposited himself into his chair, cradling the back of his head with the palms of his hand. His time with Felicia had brightened his spirits. By now he had come to realize that any time spent with Felicia Moretti brightened his spirits. He looked out the window and was amazed to see how low the sun was in the sky. It was autumn, he thought. There were now less sunlight hours than hours without sun. Beyond the window, the air was incredibly clear and free of humidity. Outside, the wind freshened, frantically blowing the strands of silk extended beyond the pane of glass. Walter noticed that the web was in a state of disrepair. Clearly, the spider with whom he had grown so familiar had abandoned it. He wondered if she had moved on or had simply perished? Still present, however, was the dried, lifeless carcass of the wasp, blowing hopelessly in the air currents. It remained, a grim tribute to the cunning and tenacious nature of the spider that had shared Walter's office window over the summer of 1995.

25

W alter sat at his desk, a stack of papers balanced on his lap. Close by on the floor sat a paper shredder. He was in the process of clearing all miscellaneous and sundry paper from the top of his desk. The procedure was simple: each slip of paper would face one of two fates. It would either be stacked in one neat pile for filing or be shredded immediately. By the end of the day and prior to his trip to Newport, his desktop would be free of all clutter. He had just sent the fifth consecutive sheet of paper through the grinding teeth of the shredder when Ronny Dingman appeared in the doorway to his office. Walter reached over and flicked off the machine.

"I just got off the phone with Chris. He's decided to move back to Albany," reported Ronny. Walter let out with a sigh of disappointment.

"How soon?" Walter asked.

"In a couple of weeks but no more than a month. The lease on his apartment is up and his family says he should have no problem getting work back there."

"Shit, it won't be the same without Chris," exclaimed Walter.

"Chris could be a real, pain-in-the-ass jerkoff… but he was *our* pain-in-the-ass jerkoff," reasoned Dingman. "Hell, with Helen gone I was actually considering asking him to fix me up with someone."

"Yeah, I hear he knows this girl named Deidre who's a real barrel of laughs," joked Walter.

"Ah yes, the charming Deidre. Maybe he could set me up before he goes," jested Ronny.

Ronny saw that his friend had a stack of work still facing him and shortened his visit. It was after six-thirty when Walter stepped back from his desk and work area and beheld the level of organization and tidiness he had brought to the office. Wearing a look of satisfaction, he stood in the doorway and took in the room a final time before closing the door behind him and leaving for home.

Bumper to bumper summer traffic on Route 1 was again only a horrible memory as Walter made his way back to Wells Beach from York. Halfway down Mile Road between Route 1 and the Atlantic Ocean he watched as the setting sun seemed to set ablaze particular windows on the houses lining the beach. The long, flattened grass in the marsh was beginning to take on its autumn colors, setting off the rich, blue fingers of water infiltrating the estuary. It was a wonderful and beautiful time to live in these parts, he thought. Two minutes later he pulled the Corvette up to the house.

After directing the vehicle to the fence at the far end of the back yard, he locked it for the night and made his way to the base of the porch steps. He glanced down and spied a yellow cosmo resting on the first step. After stooping to pick it up, he proceeded up the steps, plucking flowers from every other step until the trail of blossoms led him through the kitchen door, into the house, and ultimately to the living room. There, at the base of the stairway leading to the second floor were three flowers placed in the shape of an arrow, a sign directing him upstairs. He continued on, collecting the white and yellow flowers and following the trail of blossoms around the hall until he turned the final crook in the passageway. It was then he discovered Felicia lying on the floor. Stretched out and peacefully still, her eyes were closed while her head rested on a pink pillow wedged against her bedroom door. She was dressed only in a revealing, white negligee, the hem lifted to expose the tangle of blossoms surrounding her vagina. Walter stood in awe, temporarily immobilized by the vision of this woman before him.

"You did all this for me?" he asked. Her eyes casually opened at the sound of his voice, as if awakening from a hundred year sleep. There was something both mystical and erotic in her appearance. With her long hair flowing across the over-sized pillow, she fixed her eyes on him. "You have an incredible, incredible flair for the dramatic." His words produced no visible reaction from her. Thoughts raced through Walter's mind. Was this the same woman he routinely shared breakfast with only twelve hours earlier that day? Had some primal entity taken possession of her body and soul? Still, she did not speak, her eyes continuing to bore a hole in his composure. Finally, he lowered his body to the floor, placing down the handful of flowers and dropping his weight to his knees.

"I told you, Walter, I will do anything for you tonight," she uttered, her voice calm and controlled. An instant later his breathing heightened and became audible, the rising temperature of his blood setting off this physical reaction. He leaned forward, his open mouth coming in contact with the soft flesh of her inner thigh. The fragrance from the flower petals scattered beneath her torso mixed with the carnal scent of her body sending him into a state of debilitating euphoria. His hungry mouth moved further up her leg.

"My love, you needn't think of me," she assured him.

"It's not just for you. It's for both of us. Later, in bed, I'll share what I'd like with you," he answered, his mouth penetrating the warm, moist cleft in her torso. Felicia drew in a deep, satisfied breath, looping her legs over his shoulders. Walter, his thought process overwhelmed by this blissful gesture, probed his tongue over, along, and throughout the erotic chambers and most private regions of Felicia Moretti. His senses consumed by the magnificent taste and scent and feel of this woman's body, he abruptly felt his own body hurdling toward ejaculation. He hesitated and pulled his head back.

"Felicia, you have me as hard as a rock already. I'm afraid of expending myself way too quickly." She reached down and brought his mouth back to her.

"Dearest, we have all night… and all of tomorrow morning. Trust me, you won't be done for the night. I'll bring you back, again and again," assured the woman. Comforted by her words, Walter followed her direction and surrendered to the moment. The melody of her voice and the sight of her magnificently contoured torso arched over him completed the interchange. Felicia Moretti had invaded all of his five senses. At this moment in time, in a house at the edge of the mighty Atlantic Ocean, Walter Plews happily relinquished his free will.

Moonlight reflected off the surface of the ocean and streamed through the bedroom window. Within the dimly illuminated chamber the two lovers lay side by side, each set of eyes resting on the other. An hour earlier they had made love, passionately, tenderly and breathlessly made love. Walter reached the tip of his finger to Felicia's face and traced the outline of her profile, as if to convince himself that she was real.

"I heard a song driving home from work today that I hadn't heard in years. God, it brought back so many memories," he said, breaking an extended period of silence.

"Which song was that?"

"It's a song by a girl named Janis Ian. I think it's called *At Seventeen*."

"Is that the one about the girl who sings about never having a date because she's homely?"

"Yeah, that's it."

"Walter, that's a chick's song."

"Yeah, I know, but I had the same mindset as the girl who wrote it. The song just connected with me."

"What are some of the lyrics, I forget."

"Trust me, you don't want to hear me sing it."

"Yes I do. Come on, Walter, sing for me." He blushed and looked to the corner of the room, as if the lyrics were printed on the far wall.

"To those of us who knew the pain
Of valentines that never came,
And those whose names were never called
In choosing sides for basketball." Felicia reached across the bed and touched his face.

"A lot of people who have great lives in high school grow up to have miserable lives as adults," she said.

"Hell, in just a few months you've erased every bit of misery from my mind," he replied. His words brought a glint of sadness to her eyes. He noticed her reaction to his words but withheld comment.

Stretched out on the bed, his eyes closed and a contented smile reflecting from his face, Walter Plews was the picture of happiness. His eyelids lifted only slightly when Felicia ran her hand over his chest and down his body. Reaching his penis, she curled her fingers over and around his manhood. Her actions brought him out of his tired, contented trance and back to the here and now.

"What's all this?" he asked.

"It is time, again, to bring the dead back to life," she explained confidently.

"You've already performed miracles tonight. You have to be kidding! I'm not a twenty-year-old. I've got my weak ticker to think about."

"You'll take extra medication."

"It can't be done," he insisted. Ignited by his words, Felicia rolled from her back and mounted Walter, his massive, barrel chest sensitive to the warmth from her pubic region. Seeming to collect her thoughts, she looked up to the ceiling for a moment before returning her eyes to him.

"I want you to think back to that time you came to my apartment on Freeman Street. It was the time I hinted that I was ready to move on... the time you offered to buy me the car."

"I remember. You had that limp."

"Right, the limp. Anyway, I cut out while the tea was brewing and changed into a robe. When I rejoined you in the parlor I made a point of sitting by you on the couch. I knew what was going through your head. I made sure I knew what was going through your head. Do you care to confess what was going through your head or do I have to do that for you?" she asked. He looked up at the confident woman and shrugged.

"I kept thinking how you were naked under the robe," he muttered.

"Do you remember anything else about our time spent together that day?" A look of wariness passed over his face.

"I remember how you smelled. You gave off this magnificent, earthy, sexual smell. It did me in."

"That was the day I decided to see if I had you yet. Making someone fall in love with you is almost like taking possession of them. Sometimes you can think you have them but they wind up escaping. But, if you lay the groundwork right and you get your hooks in good and deep, there is no escape."

"And that day with me?" questioned Walter.

"My love, I knew I had you. I was inside your head, inside your crotch, and everywhere in between." He smiled up at her. "I want you to continue to think of me on that day," she instructed as she passed her fingertips over his exposed penis.

"Sometimes I feel like that poor slob in the movie *Alien,* the one who has the thing put a tentacle down his mouth and it eats its way out of his stomach. When I begin worrying that you might be pulling up stakes or that you've found some-one else, my stomach gets this horrendous knot and it's almost like that thing from *Alien* is going to eat its way out of me."

"Well, I do make a habit of putting an awful lot of me in your mouth," she jested. Moments later her expression grew serious again. She brought her face in close proximity to his while using a free hand to probe her own body. Following a thirty-second interlude of sexual tension she brought her warm, moist fingers to his mouth. A second later her fingers, moistened by her body liquids, were passing through his lips and onto his tongue. "We are one," she whispered in his ear. Felicia brought her body to an upright position and examined Walter. He was erect.

It was after three o'clock in the morning. Felicia stood at the bedroom window as a cool, autumn breeze blew the curtains around her perfect body. She was looking out to sea, the surface of the water lit up by a nearly full moon. She inhaled deeply and turned back to the bed. She was surprised to see Walter awake, his eyes riveted on her.

"What are you thinking about?" Felicia asked.

"Incredibly, I was thinking about my office window and the spider that spent this spring and summer on the other side of the glass."

26

The journey from the Sand Castle to the center of Newport, Rhode Island had passed pleasantly. With Felicia behind the wheel of his Corvette, Walter was able to stare long and ardently at the woman who, over the preceding twenty-four hours, had brought him the deepest physical and mental pleasure of his entire life. Walter's hotel was located in the heart of downtown Newport, overlooking the water and a series of commercial docks. Motoring through the city they spotted the hotel sign simultaneously and she carefully maneuvered the car through the entrance to the parking lot. It was shortly before six o'clock when the Corvette slowly rolled into a vacant parking spot at the front of the building. Felicia took a deep breath and turned off the engine.

"I have complete confidence in your ability behind the wheel of this car," acknowledged Walter before reaching over and tucking strands of her long, brown hair behind her ear. She turned to him. She could not mask a certain sadness weighing on her.

"I really didn't expect to turn this into a melodrama," she admitted, her voice exhibiting some degree of anxiety." She shook off the emerging show of emotion and quickly stepped from the car. Removing Walter's single piece of luggage, she circled the vehicle and joined him by the passenger door. He stood waiting for her, a look of adoration plastered across his face.

"It's seventy-two hours. That's all. I managed to live without you for thirty-nine years. This is only seventy-two hours," he reasoned. She dropped the suitcase to the pavement and promptly began nervously fiddling with the collar of his shirt.

"I want you to be a good boy while we're apart. Study your new software real hard. Get good and smart. You're only about a mile away from the mansions so try to find some time to visit them. Try not to miss me too much. Okay?" He brought his huge body down into a crouch and rested his head on her chest. He listened to the pounding of her heart and felt her body shudder as she held back a teary outburst.

"I can't believe you're taking this so hard. I hate to admit it but in some strange way it makes me feel good. It shows me that, incredible as it may seem, I do mean something to you," he said as he continued to rest his head on her chest.

"I've told you countless times that I love you."

"Yes, but it never ceases to amaze and puzzle me why." Felicia closed her eyes in mock anger and pushed him against the vehicle. She framed the sides of his face with her hands and pressed her lips on his, immediately pushing her tongue into his mouth. He returned her emotional gesture and the two embraced for the better part of a minute. It was she who initiated separation, reaching down and delivering him his suitcase.

"Be a good boy," she stated coyly. He shrugged, grabbed hold of his luggage and walked toward the entrance to the hotel.

A few steps before his movement would activate the automatic door, Walter stopped in his tracks and glanced back to the Corvette. Felicia Moretti was standing behind the open driver's door, her eyes locked onto him. He waved to her. She returned the gesture. Interestingly, it was executed in the same manner, the fluttering of her fingers, as she had done from behind the Cliff House on that spring afternoon when they had first gestured to one another. Walter proceeded through the automatic door and walked to the front desk. Behind the counter a dignified, middle-aged woman acknowledged through a hand movement that attention would be forthcoming shortly. He placed his suitcase down on the floor and turned back to the parking lot. Felicia Moretti and the Corvette were gone.

27

Frantically, Walter punched the numbers on the phone and waited. He sat impatiently through three rings before the sound of a familiar voice came through the line.

"Hello," answered Ronny Dingman.

"Ronny, first, I'm sorry to be calling so damn early in the morning."

"It's okay, big guy. I was up."

"I'm going to need a big favor from you," said Walter excitedly.

"Sure. Is everything okay? What do you need?"

"I need you to go up to my house and check in on Felicia. I think something's happened to her."

"Of course, first thing. You're out of state, right?" asked Ronny. "What's going on, buddy?"

"Felicia's supposed to pick me up tonight around five. I'm attending classes down here in Rhode Island. I called her last night to nail down details and I wasn't able to reach her. I called the house again this morning and there still was no answer. Jesus, Ronny, I think something bad may have happened to her. She was alone at the house," explained the harried man.

"Walter... relax. It's probably nothing. When's the last time you spoke to her?"

"I talked to her Wednesday night. As I said, we were supposed to talk last night to nail down the details of her trip down here to get me."

"I'm on it, buddy. I'll leave in ten minutes. Give me a number to reach you at and stay close to the phone," instructed Dingman.

"I keep a backup key in a fake rock by the side of the house. You can't miss it. It's on the north side of the building on the ocean end," explained Walter.

"Okay, Walter, now you relax. I'm on it. I'm sure she's fine. You're going to have a heart attack if you don't calm down."

His friend's demeanor helped Walter gain a measure of his composure. He provided Ronny Dingman with the hotel's telephone number and his extension. Lumbering downstairs to the lobby, he prepared himself a cup of complementary coffee and returned to his room. The digital clock by the bed read 7:09. Pacing the floor for the next hour and fifteen minutes, he imagined his friend opening the front door and finding Felicia lying in a pool of blood, her eyes frozen open and staring blankly into space. Walter tortured himself with image after image of a victimized Felicia Moretti, some grotesquely morbid, until the phone in the room finally rang. It was approximately eight-fifteen.

"Hello, Ronny?"

"Walter, I'm calling you from the house."

"Is Felicia all right? Is everything okay?"

"I've been all through the house. There's no sign of any foul play or anything like that. She's not here," Ronny reported.

"What about the Corvette... or her Honda?"

"There are no cars in the yard. The house is all in order. It barely looks lived in."

"What about Felicia's room? Are her clothes laid out?"

"Which one's her room?"

"Go up to the second floor and follow the hallway to the end. She has a way of leaving her stuff out on the bed," explained Walter.

"I'm on it," answered his friend. A moment later Walter picked up on the sound of footsteps leaving the downstairs and making their way to the second floor. He sat on the edge of his hotel bed waiting on his friend's return. Two minutes passed before there came the sound of the man moving through the house and returning to the phone. "Walter... nothing. There are no clothes in the room... on the bed or in the drawers. The bed's been made and every pin cushion and doily is in its place." Ronny stood in the kitchen of the Sand Castle waiting on a reply from his friend. Ten seconds passed before it came.

"I don't understand. This doesn't make sense," Walter finally replied.

"Walt, I saw there was a number of messages on your answering machine. I took the liberty to play them back, in case there was something on there from Felicia. I heard your messages from last night. In addition, there was a message from Jonathan Eddy of Maine Colonial Savings. He asked to talk to you about the withdrawal."

"The withdrawal?"

"That's what he said." Walter let out a deep breath.

"Ronny, you might get a call from me at work today. I might need a ride home from Newport. That's where I am, in Rhode Island," he explained, the energy in his voice deflated.

"Let me know, my friend. I'll be there."

"I'll reimburse you for your trouble."

"In a pig's ass you will. You'll buy me a beer at the pub... if they're still serving by the time we get back."

Ronny Dingman lifted his foot from the accelerator and allowed his pickup to coast down the main artery leading into downtown Newport. The city was draped in darkness while a light mist required the truck's wipers to slide across the windshield in ten-second intervals. Owing to his friend's precise directions, Dingman's eyes easily found the prominent sign for the hotel and he pulled the truck into the parking lot and up to the front door. Out of the shadows, Walter Plews appeared and hustled to the truck. He tossed his lone suitcase onto the floor and scrambled up onto the passenger seat.

"Do you believe it? I always wanted to see the Newport mansions and, finally, I'm here. It's a case of being in the right place at the wrong time," theorized Ronny. He stared across at Walter who sat lifelessly beside him, his eyes staring blankly through the windshield.

"She withdrew nearly every dollar from my account at Maine Colonial. I spoke with Mr. Eddy at the bank. She got into the safe deposit box, too," mumbled Walter.

"Felicia didn't show up for work Wednesday, Thursday or today," added Ronny. "You'll probably want to report the Vette stolen tonight when we get back... or tomorrow morning." Ronny glanced across at his friend again. "Wait a minute! How did she manage to do that? How could she just withdraw your money?" Embarrassed, Walter looked out the passenger window to avoid any eye contact.

"She was on the account. I put her on the account six weeks ago."

"What! Are you out of your goddamn mind?"

"I can't believe this is happening. There has to be an explanation for this. She wouldn't do this to me."

"Walter, she's done it. Trust me, she's done it. She took this time off from work to screw you over, and she's gone," argued Ronny.

"Ronny, I know Felicia could never do something like this to me. Never!"

"Earth to Walter Plews, come in. She robbed you blind and left you stranded in Rhode Island... and she apparently left in your car! What do you need... a goddamn safe to drop on your head?"

"No, Ronny, this isn't her." Dingman shook his head in exasperation and directed his eyes straight ahead to the road.

Ronny brought the pickup to a stop behind the Sand Castle and sat quietly in place, the only sounds invading the cabin of the truck being the rhythm of its engine and the cadence of crashing surf a hundred yards to the east.

"You're a damn good friend, Ronny. You do know I'd do the same for you, right?" Dingman reached over and slapped his friend on the back.

"Call me in the morning. You'll need to be getting around. It's Saturday. I'll be available. Oh, I put the key back in the fake rock. It's in its regular place." Walter snatched his suitcase and scrambled from the pickup. He stood in place as his friend threw the vehicle into reverse, changed direction, and motored down the lane, his rear lights the last thing to disappear into the ground fog. Walter turned to the house, the ponderous, empty, memory-laden nightmare of a house. There was nowhere else to go. Lethargically, he climbed the stairs and unlocked the kitchen door. He told himself she might be there, inside, sitting in the darkness. He stepped into the kitchen and listened for any evidence of Felicia. The house communicated his circumstances with brutal honesty. Walter knew he was alone, again. He was as he was the day before Felicia Moretti arrived at his door.

He trudged up the stairs to the second floor and made his way to her room. Swinging in the door, he flicked on the light. The room appeared as Ronny had said it did, spotlessly clean and tidy. All evidence of Felicia's four months of occupancy had been erased. He slid his suitcase to the wall and made his way around the room to the far window. Outside, everything was hidden in ground fog. For a moment he was reminded of the fog that enveloped the ice house on the morning he and Melinda had fled. Simultaneously, he remembered he had not eaten all day and, unbelievably, still had no appetite. His head was swimming with thoughts and memories, neither of which he wanted to entertain. He felt his head grow light and a wave of nausea was upon him. Quickly making his way from the room and down the hallway, he entered the bathroom. Leaning over the toilet, his stomach lurched unsuccessfully twice before he vomited into the porcelain bowl. He fell to his knees and cried out to God for help. He could live without the funds withdrawn from his savings account and without the Corvette. He knew he could even live without Felicia's magnificent body. However, he was not convinced he could live without her.

28

It was Sunday morning and Walter sat alone in the sunroom of the Sand Castle. Seated at the table by the window he was afforded a sweeping view of the coastline that extended south to Crescent Beach and northward to the jetty at the mouth of Wells Harbor. The elements outside were classic October, the bright sun illuminating the yellow beach and a brisk breeze from the north blowing wisps of loose sand over the surface of the coastline. Presently, the visible shoreline was peppered with a dozen or so couples, outfitted in warm clothing and walking only feet from the advancing and retreating surf. He brought a mug filled with lukewarm coffee to his lips. He stared into the distance at the sight of a lone female walking northward in the general direction of the house. Straining his eyes, his head went light, no doubt a physical reaction to a lack of sleep since the prior Wednesday. He trained his eyes on the young woman until it became quite clear that she was not Felicia. The sound of ringing from the telephone in the kitchen broke his incoherent train of thought and sent him scrambling into the next room.

"Hello," he answered anxiously.

"This is Officer Daniel Morin with the Maine State Police. I'm trying to reach Walter Plews. It's regarding his vehicle."

"This is he. I'm Walter Plews."

"Mr. Plews, I'm calling to inform you that your vehicle, a 1994 Corvette, has been towed from where it was left on Friday on request of the neighbors. You are free to come pick it up anytime after eight A.M. tomorrow morning. Overnight parking is not permitted on that roadway for any reason without specific approval. We're assuming there were mechanical difficulties with the vehicle. We have no record of the car being reported stolen."

"No, officer, there was no report filed on a stolen car. Pardon me, where are you calling from?"

"Sir, I'm calling you from Bangor. Oh, and I must advise you, there will be a fee charged when you pick up the vehicle for towing and possibly storage," added the trooper.

"So, I take it the car's in Bangor."

"No, Mr. Plews, the car was towed to the nearest garage. You can retrieve the vehicle at B&D Automotive. It's an auto repair shop in Cutler."

"Cutler! How far is that from Bangor?"

"It's a good distance away. That would be a good two hours from Bangor. It's in Washington County. I take it by your reaction that it was not you who abandoned the vehicle on Friday."

"No, it was my girlfriend. Was there anything in your report about the driver? Her name is Felicia Moretti," said Walter.

"No sir, we just have this report on the vehicle."

His conversation with Officer Morin completed, Walter rummaged through a kitchen drawer and came up with a map of Maine. Unfolding it over the surface of the sunroom table, he located Washington County and quickly pinpointed the town of Cutler. He studied the map, attempting to piece together some logical sequence of events behind the vehicle's appearance in this small, coastal town. Painfully, he began piecing together a fact pattern: Cutler was well up the coast, close to Canada and, particularly, Campobello Island. There was a very good chance that Canada was Felicia's final destination point. But why would she abandon her vehicle in a small town thirty miles from the border? She would need an accomplice and a second car to pull this off. Perhaps she did not dare to cross the border in the Corvette for fear it had been reported stolen. Then, there was the possible existence of a second person. No doubt, it was a male. Perhaps, it was a handsome, physically fit male. They would have hundreds of thousands of dollars to spend on each other. An image flashed through his mind. It was the vision of Walter's Corvette pulling to a stop beside a second car. Felicia emerges from the Corvette and greets her handsome lover with a passionate kiss while carrying a bag full of cash. Walter sprang to his feet, ripping the cloth covering and everything resting on it from the table and onto the floor.

His heart still pounding thirty minutes after his disturbing vision, Walter punched Ronny Dingman's number into the telephone and waited.

"Yellow," he answered in the tired, comical salutation.

"Ronny, they found my car. I was hoping I could impose on you, again, to give me a ride. I insist on paying you something this time."

"Dinner and a beer. Oh, and you still owe me a beer from that Newport trip."

"Dinner, any number of beers, the cost of gas back and forth and a gift to be named at a later date. How does that sound?" asked Walter.

"Where are we going?"

"Cutler, Maine."

"And where is that?"

"It's up north... a little past Machias."

"Holy shit! Why can't you do anything in Portsmouth or Sanford?"

"It's my special talent," explained Walter. His words were followed by a few seconds of uncomfortable silence before Ronny spoke.

"Any more word about the bitch with the car recovery?" Dingman's words sent a jolt of torment along the walls of Walter's stomach.

"No, there was nothing," he answered.

It was decided that the two men would get an early start on their trip to Washington County. Ronny stayed with Walter at the Sand Castle on Sunday night. By now, Walter had moved back to his apartment in the basement of the building. Ronny brought over a small, overnight bag and the two retired early. The plan called for them to be on the road by four o'clock the next morning. Their strategy was to hold off on breakfast until they reached Machias, far up the coast of Maine. Apparently buoyed by Ronny's presence in the house, Walter managed his first restful night of sleep since his return from Newport.

29

*R*onny blinked open his eyes and focused on the sight of his friend standing over the bed, a mug of steaming coffee extended in his direction.

"This is more warmth and consideration than I got my last two years with Helen," he quipped as he reached out for the warm beverage.

"That, and I'm marginally prettier," joked Walter.

"Oh, so you've seen the little witch in the morning." Plews laughed and moved toward the light illuminating the hallway.

"It's three-thirty and I've already showered. So, if my good buddy gets right out of bed and showers right away, we can be on the road by four, as scheduled," announced Walter.

"You got it, buddy. God, I love the sound of the ocean at night… very relaxing and conducive to sleep." Walter made his way back to the kitchen and filled a pair of thermos containers to the brim with coffee while his houseguest noisily prepared for their road trip to Down East Maine.

Dingman rolled his pickup slowly away from the Sand Castle while the community of Wells Beach slept. The sky was as black as pitch and the roadways deserted. The vehicle rumbled its way past the darkened houses and made its way to Mile Road. The brakes on the weathered truck groaned as it rolled to a stop. Across the street, the Beachcomber, a gift shop dating back to the early part of the century, would soon be boarded for the long winter, the last tourist having purchased the last souvenir of the 1995 season.

"You know the thing about living in a coastal, tourist community that I really love? I love the way it hibernates like a bear every year," observed Walter as he stared out the passenger window.

"Would you really want tourists crawling over us twelve months a year?" Ronny asked.

"No, I like it the way it is. The handful of people who come over the fall and winter are the best. They love it in spite of the wind and the cold and the storms. I love it when it really quiets down and you pretty much have the beach and the estuary to yourself. I had really looked forward to sharing it with Felicia." His voice tailing off on the completion of his final remark, Walter leaned back against the seat of the truck and closed his eyes.

After following the highway north beyond Portland, the pickup rejoined Route 1 at Brunswick and motored northward along the coast toward Washington County and the tiny town of Cutler. Sticking to Walter's plan, they stopped only to refuel, hit the men's room, and refill their coffee containers.

Coming out of a short nap, Walter opened his eyes and saw the truck was moving through a stretch of expansive, crimson fields. They had reached the blueberry fields of Washington County, Maine.

"How long have I been out?" Walter asked.

"Let see, you talked me out of stopping for breakfast in Ellsworth. After that, you fell asleep. That means you've been out for about an hour. Machias is only a couple of miles up the road. We're finally going to eat," groaned Ronny. Walter brushed the sleep from his eyes and glanced around at the landscape cloaked in a dark red carpet, the color taken on by the blueberry bushes two months after the harvest. The pickup followed Route 1 and crossed the town line into Machias a few minutes later. They coasted down a slope toward the center of town, passing over a dated bridge spanning a stretch of fast moving water.

"How about pizza at eight in the morning?" joked Dingman, a reference to the pizza shop thirty yards in front of them.

"Let's hold out for someplace that might actually serve eggs," came back Walter, his eyes darting from one side of the road to the other. He rolled down the passenger door window for some fresh air. His actions were rewarded with a rush of cool, autumn air and the sound of cascading water. Two hundred yards up the road they spotted a parking lot scattered with pickups and family cars.

"The Blue Bird Ranch," muttered Ronny. "Looks like it's popular with the locals. That means they've got to serve eggs. Walter, what do you say?"

"I say it's a go. The towns up here are getting farther and farther apart."

The two men entered the restaurant and quickly determined they should seat themselves. They walked toward the sound of female voices and claimed a booth by the window. Outside, less than thirty feet away, the flow of north and south traffic on Route 1 sped by. Walter and Ronny found themselves seated apart from a majority of the male customers who appeared clustered in the adjoining room along the lunch counter. They were surrounded by a half-dozen occupied tables and booths. The customers were largely comprised of working women and elderly couples. Presently, one particular waitress was holding court, her voice booming out over the low drone of the customers.

"So, Gary and I were seated next to Isaac and Vicky Beal and their little puff of a granddaughter who's taking some time off from school to find herself. Well, we haven't even gotten to our first sip of coffee when this spoiled, little Twinkie starts in on how hard it is to buy what she needs… that she has to go all the way to Ellsworth, and, even then, she may not be able to find what she needs." Over the course of her account, the waitress picked up two menus and delivered them to the table. She smiled down on the two men. She appeared to be in her early forties with perfectly groomed, brown hair and brown eyes. "Coffee, gentlemen?" The men nodded yes and she filled both cups. With that accomplished and without missing a beat, the waitress returned to her account of the evening spent at a church supper. "I looked up at Gary and I could see he was tightening up like a spring. Girls, you have to understand, this spoiled brat talked in this whiny, little voice. It was enough to make you want to wring her skinny, little neck." Walter glanced over at Ronny and smiled.

"God, you have to love the accent up here," he whispered across the table. The two men redirected their attention down to their menus.

"So, Dottie, did you wind up moving to another table or did you stick it out for the whole meal?" asked a middle-aged woman from a nearby table. Carrying her pot of coffee back in the direction of the kitchen, the waitress continued.

"I knew Gary wanted to move but we stayed put. That was when this prissy, little puff started up on how the hard water at her grandparent's house was ruining the luster in her hair. Well, that was the last straw. I looked across the table at her and informed her that some of us had real hardship growing up. I told her how some of us have had real hardship, like having to lug buckets of water up to the kitchen from the stream nearby… because there was no running water in the house! Oh, she didn't like that." The woman's account of her inter-action with this young girl brought a squeal of laughter from her listeners. The waitress concluded her anecdote with a satisfied smirk and approached Walter and Ronny.

"So, have you decided what you'll be having?" she asked of them.

"Dottie, I have a question," said Ronny. She gestured to him to continue. "If I order the ham and eggs, will I get the same size slice of ham with my eggs as everyone else here seems to have?" She looked down on him warily.

"No. I'll be putting a mark on your slips showing you're flatlanders and the cook will be sure to give you just a sliver of ham," she answered sarcastically. The two men burst out laughing and handed her their menus.

"Ham and eggs for both of us with that blueberry bread for toast," blurted out Ronny. She smiled down on the two before turning from the table.

Walter and Ronny had sat silently for a few moments before Dingman spoke.

"Walter, I hope you don't plan on taking this whole matter with Felicia lying down. Even if she's managed to wipe out your cash and take one car legally, and I'm not sure that is the case, she stole your Corvette. You have to call the cops and report this." Walter peered across the table at his friend, the same strained look fixed on his face.

"I'll wait two weeks for her to come back to her senses. Then, I promise, I'll call the police and report this."

"Two weeks! Are you kidding me? Her trail will be cold in two weeks."

"Ronny, back off. You don't know her like I know her. She won't go through with it," assured Walter. Dingman shook his head in frustration and glanced through the window at the traffic passing on Route 1.

Following five minutes of prolonged silence, Dottie returned to the table carrying the men's breakfast. She placed the identical orders down in front of them and offered to refill their cups of coffee.

"You know, Dottie, I hope you really don't believe you had it tough growing up the way you came off saying you did a few minutes ago," injected Ronny behind a serious face.

"What? Do you think it's a picnic carrying water from fifty yards to the house?"

"Hell, growing up, my family looked with envy on people like you. You see, my family wasn't rich enough to own buckets. In fact, we were jealous of the bucket people. My mom told us it wasn't Christian being jealous of them but we couldn't help it."

"Oh really. And, pray tell, what did you *bucketless* people do to fetch water?"

"Remember those free glasses you got when you bought Welch's jelly and jam?"

"Yeah, our cabinet was stacked with them." Ronny nodded his head knowingly.

"That's all we had…and it made for a lot of trips from the stream," he answered while reaching for his utensils. Dottie stood over the table for moment, no doubt searching for a pithy response.

"And all these years here I was thinking my mother had made up those stories about the pitiful people without buckets. It just goes to show, even at the ripe, old age of twenty-two you can still learn something." Her comeback brought more laughter from the men.

"You're okay, Dottie. You're okay," acknowledged Ronny while knifing through his generous cut of ham.

A few miles north of Machias the men left Route 1, joining Route 191 in East Machias and starting the final leg of their journey to Cutler, Maine. Leaving the main road through Washington County, the men encountered less traffic as they snaked their way along an extended ridge toward the small, harbor town. The air this day was crystal clear and at times the road afforded them a brilliant view of the Atlantic Ocean. Intermittently, they literally passed within a hundred yards of the sea and they observed locals harvesting clams in the tidal areas.

"Backbreaking work," muttered Walter as they motored by a half-dozen individuals bent over the packed sand below.

"It's almost hard to believe that we're in the same state," Ronny commented, a reference to the more basic lifestyle of Down East Mainers compared to their more gentrified cousins back in York County. "Whoa, what's that up ahead of us?" Dingman's question regarded a series of towers visible from a few miles in front of them.

"That must have something to do with the Naval station up here. I saw it on the map last night when I was looking over our trip."

"Man, those have to be real monsters. I mean, they have to be three or four miles away and look at the size of them," said an astonished Ronny. The pickup motored forward along the winding road. Residences were fewer and farther in-between along this stretch, the roadside dotted with a handful of small, private cemeteries.

"Is it possible Felicia came up here to hook up with some Navy guy?" asked Walter as he pondered the story behind her disappearance aloud. "Why else would she come up here to this unbelievably remote place?"

The road skirted away from the open ocean for a mile before a road sign directed them to bear left toward the town of Cutler. Ronny reduced speed and the pickup rolled another mile until they reached the crest of a hill overlooking the town.

"If Hollywood should ever want to film on location in a sleepy, New England harbor town, I think we've found it," muttered Walter while the pickup coasted into the village. "Why don't you slow up and I'll ask this lady walking her dog how to find the garage." Dingman slowed the vehicle to a stop beside the elderly woman and her cocker spaniel. Rolling the passenger window down, Walter poked his head from the truck. "Pardon me, ma'am, but could you tell us where B&D Automotive is?" The woman appeared confused for just a moment then responded.

"Oh yes, Wayne's place. You're heading in the right direction. Just follow this road out of town and drive maybe three miles. It'll be on the left side of the road. There's a sign." The words scarcely out of her mouth, the dog tugged on his leash and pulled her away from the vehicle and up the road. The men called out their thanks and they set out on the final leg of their journey north.

The woman from town's directions proved accurate and Ronny turned his truck off Route 191 and into the garage's parking lot. Walter was quick to spot his Corvette parked close by the building and away from the road. He hopped from the truck, asking his friend to hang around until he was sure his car was ready for the long trip home. Entering the garage he spotted a pair of legs and feet jutting out from beneath a jacked-up Toyota. He only had to stand by the vehicle for a few seconds before the individual working on the car rolled out from under it and peered up at him.

"Hi, my name is Walter Plews. I'm here to pick up the Corvette you towed in. Are you Wayne Dennison?" The man nodded and began brushing himself off. He was young, probably in his twenties, with a spattering of premature grayness in his hair and beard.

"You have some ID I can look at?" Walter nodded yes and produced his driver's license. "I hope you brought a set of keys." Again, Walter shook his head yes and produced his backup set.

"The state police said I'd owe you for the tow and possibly storage." Dennison smiled for the first time and waved Walter off.

"Fifty dollars for the tow. No charge for the storage," he came back. Walter opened his wallet and peeled the man off his cash. "I like cash. Cash never bounces," he added, then gestured to the far wall where a handful of personal checks were tacked in a row.

"Was there any sign of damage to the car?" Walter asked.

"None that I could see."

"Just out of curiosity, where did you tow it in from? Did it just run out of gas? If it did then I'll need a little gas, too."

"I towed it in from the bottom of Little Machias Road. I don't think the tank's empty but you'll know once you turn the key."

"And how can I find this Little Machias Road?" Dennison turned his body in the direction of town.

"Head back through Cutler and then drive another mile or so. There'll be a hairpin turn in the road. That's when you get off 191. That's Little Machias Road. There's a cemetery at the corner. You can't miss it. Your Vette was at the end of the road just before the timbers blocking it." He stuck out his hand and thanked the man a final time for minding his car.

Walter was greatly relieved when he turned the key to his ignition and the Corvette's engine came to life. Furthermore, he was amazed when the gas gauge showed nearly a full tank. He carefully made his way out of the garage parking area and made the return trip to Cutler with Ronny following closely behind. Reaching the picturesque village, he pulled the car off to the side of the road close by an impressive wooden wharf. Within seconds, Dingman's pickup had rolled up behind him and his friend was walking up to the vehicle.

"Buddy, it's running fine. I should be all set. If you want to head right back to work then feel free," exclaimed Walter. "I'm going to be heading back in a while. First, though, I'm going to go take a look at the place she abandoned the car. Just in case there's some kind of a clue about what she's up to or who she might be with." Dingman reached inside the vehicle and slapped his friend on the back.

"Remember what we talked about. Don't let her get away with this."

"I promise. I'm not going to just roll over like some kind of chimp," Walter assured his friend. "And Ronny, thank you for everything. You're a real buddy." Walter sat behind the wheel of the Corvette and watched Ronny's truck retrace its path along Route 191 before it disappeared from sight. Outside the vehicle the sound of men unloading a fishing boat wafted up from the edge of the water.

Walter pulled his car to the side of the road and to the edge of a dated cemetery and turned off the engine. His directions from Wayne Dennison had proven to be quite accurate. A glance down at his watch told him it was barely ten o'clock. The day was still young. He was having second thoughts about visiting the exact location where Felicia had abandoned the vehicle. What did he think he was going to do? Would he walk up to the doors of complete strangers and ask them about the Corvette that was left on their road? Could he stand up to an account of a man and woman coupling at the end of the road and driving off together? He seriously played with the idea of driving away before taking an extended breath and turning the key to the ignition. Slowly, he rolled the car from the shoulder of the road and moved forward. He would face his demons.

Little Machias Road was two-laned and paved. In truth, he did not know if it ran for five hundred feet or five hundred miles. His windows were down, allowing the sound of the tires rolling over pavement to dominate the cabin of the vehicle. Presently, there was no sign of life or traffic. He learned, in short order, that the sides of the roadway would be dominated by thick overgrowth. This dense vegetation was only broken on the approach to any residence. These houses, in some instances separated by three to four hundred feet, had well manicured lawns and reflected a general pride in appearance. About a half mile down the road there was a considerable disconnect in the vegetation and line of trees, affording a wonderful view over a stretch of inlet water and the imposing radio towers of the Naval station. He brought the car to a stop for over a minute and stared across at the tall pillars of steel. This place was unlike anywhere he had ever been. The bright October sunlight streamed into the car and partially blinded him. He continued down the alternately rising and falling road for a considerable distance until a particular sight grabbed hold of his imagination and demanded of him his complete attention.

Walter directed the Corvette to the very edge of the overgrowth and rolled out of the car. Seconds earlier his eyes had picked up on the dark outline of something standing within the snarl of overgrowth. What he saw were the remains of a long unoccupied house, positioned corpse-like, within the bounds of the vegetation. Completely inaccessible, it had long ago ceased to be the domicile of any human inhabitants. He left the car and walked a few feet up the road to gain the most unobstructed view of the structure. He looked on in a state of subdued awe while his mind tried to visualize a young family growing up within the walls of the deteriorating building before him. How could any of them have ever imagined the slow, tormented fate of their homestead? He turned and walked further up the road, away from his car and the small house being swallowed up in the advance of the thick brush. Thirty feet away his eyes fell upon the remains of a single car garage, it, too, having fallen prey to the ever-advancing vegetation. The structure's roof was in the process of collapsing, no doubt from under the weight of too many snowstorms over too many blustery, Maine winters. In its time it had perhaps protected a Studebaker or a DeSoto from the elements. He paused, his mind conjuring up the image of an elderly woman sitting alone in the quiet corner of a nursing home. Communicating nothing to anyone around her, but inwardly reliving her days as a young girl. She thought of a time when her mother, father, and brother, Bill, were still alive. At Christmas, they traveled to Bangor to be with aunts, uncles and cousins. Perhaps this year Daddy would finally buy her the sled she so wanted and she would test it out at the steepest point on Little Machias Road. Finally, tired of torturing himself with depressing thoughts, Walter shook the images from his head and walked back to the car. He knew he was oversensitive. It was best for him not to entertain thoughts that could undermine his spirit.

Returning to his car, he passed his eyes over the conquest of man by nature a final time and continued down the road. Ahead, there were more dated structures, particularly garages, dotting the sides of the roadway. Finally, the pavement sloped decidedly downward and the ocean came into sight. He was close to the end of Little Machias Road and, in all likelihood, the final resting place of his relationship with Felicia Moretti. Walter lifted his foot from the gas pedal and allowed the Corvette to coast the last hundred feet. Here the roadway abruptly ended with two parallel timbers laid out before him.

Walter stepped from the car and was greeted by a rush of fresh, ocean air. It was a beautiful spot, the road ending and replaced by an expanse of lawn that reached eastward a hundred yards to the edge of the sea. Between himself and the Atlantic Ocean sat a white, colonial home, no doubt a survivor from the nineteenth century given the architectural simplicity of its lines. Directly behind the rear entrance to the noble building was a curious composition, a four-posted, shingled wooden roof covering the opening to a well. Hesitating at the edge of the property, he continued to look beyond the empty house and out to sea but found his eyes returning to the stone encirclement at the cap of the well and the unusual covering above it. There was something about the simple yet unusual addition to the property that triggered a recollection from his past. Again, however, his eyes were drawn back to the ocean. The morning sun shimmered off the surface of the blue water, lending a hypnotic beauty to his surroundings. He yielded to temptation and walked to the edge of the property where he followed the line to the back of the oversized parcel of land. There, he stood on the edge of an abrupt drop down to a rocky beach. He was standing at the edge of a perfectly formed cove. Approximately a mile out to sea, there extended a line of jagged ledges. A mile beyond the ledges sat a humped-back island. After standing transfixed for no less than a full minute, Walter remembered the purpose of his visit and began the walk back to the car. He was practically abreast of the house when he spotted the tops of a number of the radio towers over the far tree line. A second later he picked up on the fluttering of something collected by the front door of the house. He glanced up the road. It appeared he was alone. Turning ninety degrees he walked in the direction of the entrance to the imposing structure. He was halfway to the door when he felt his heart begin to pound inside his chest. He was within ten feet of the entrance before he made a positive identification of what was lying by the doorway; a tightly bound quantity of yellow and white flowers. They were cosmos.

Slowly, he crouched toward the ground and lifted the blossoms from the stone surface of the step. He brought the flowers to his face and breathed in their pleasant, delicate fragrance. For a brief moment he felt close to Felicia. His next thought came in the form of a revelation. Walter walked to the nearest window and gazed through the glass. Inside was an open dining area complemented by an interior fireplace. Excitedly, he moved down the building to the next window and stared inside. There he saw the vaguely familiar layout of the living room where he and Melinda Klaus had ridden out the December ice storm in 1985.

"My God, oh, my God," he said aloud. He strained his eyes and peered through the reflected images on the surface of the glass. The couch, chairs and table are the same, he thought to himself. He fixed his attention on the hearthstone and thought back to the hours spent with Melinda in front of the open fire. Following a full two minutes of running his eyes over the interior of the living room he turned his back to the window and slumped slowly to the ground. Following ten long years of frustration, he had found the house, he thought. He stared up the road and thought how different it looked in fair weather. For a moment he wondered how they had not seen the radio towers ten years earlier. Within seconds he answered his own question. He and Melinda had arrived at night and in the midst of a driving ice storm. They had hurriedly vacated the house and region in the thickest fog he had ever witnessed in his life. Under both conditions, visibility was no more than a hundred yards. He sat quietly for the next fifteen minutes with his back against the house, the yellow and white cosmos clutched in one hand.

Walter lifted his three hundred pounds from the ground and made his way back to the front entrance. He pulled back a screen door and closely scrutinized the wooden door behind it. Primarily interested in the nine panes of glass on the top half, he leaned in and examined the bottom right pane. He saw that this window reflected light in a slightly different manner than the other eight panes. It was a replacement pane of glass. It was the final evidence he needed to assure himself that he had found the ice house.

"And what exactly do you think you're doing?" called out a woman's voice from a distance away. He whirled around to see who had called out to him. A woman walked toward him and the house with an air of authority. She was young, perhaps thirty, with black hair and glasses. There was refinement in her pretty face that seemed out of step with her mode of dress, an oversized plaid shirt tucked into a pair of faded blue jeans. "Do you always go around peeping into other people's houses?" Walter let the screen door close and took a step toward the female.

"I really wasn't up to anything. That's my car back there on the road. It was taken and left up here a couple of days ago. I just picked it up from Wayne Dennison," explained Walter. The woman looked him over for a second and softened her expression.

"We get a lot of nosy tourists down here. Most, however, don't go so far as to peek in our windows." Walter noticed that the woman did not have the regional Maine accent. "It was my mother and I who reported your car parked down here overnight."

"Well, I can't thank you enough for that. I wasn't sure how long it would be before I got it back. You saved me the cost of a rental. And, as far as looking into the house, ordinarily I would never, ever do that. Trust me. But, a long time ago, this house literally saved my life." The young woman looked up at him curiously. "My girlfriend and I got stranded down here in an ice storm. If it weren't for this house we probably would have frozen to death that night," he confessed. The woman reached over and gripped his forearm.

"Oh, my God! You aren't the one who left Rita the money and the apology note, are you?" Walter blushed and dropped his eyes to the ground.

"Guilty as charged."

"Rita tells that story to everyone. You left her quite a bit of money for that broken window."

"I left her every dollar I had on me, except for what I needed for gas to get home. I mean... her house saved our lives." A smile broke over the woman's face. "By the way, I'm Walter Plews," he said, reaching out his hand.

"Susan Robinson," she answered while completing the handshake.

Walking in the direction of the Corvette, Walter seized the opportunity to talk to the woman about the circumstances that brought him here.

"Susan, by any chance did you see anything or anyone when the car was left here?"

"You know, that was the strangest thing. Last Friday my mother and I worked outside in the yard all day. It was a perfect day for yard work and by October you don't know how many more perfect days you're going to get. At about three o'clock, I remember looking up from my weeding and spotting the Corvette at the bottom of the road. I asked mom if she'd seen it come by and she said no. It was just so strange. I mean, our house and yard is right by the road. How in God's name did we not see or hear it go by?"

"And you didn't see another car come down and pick her up?"

"Her?"

"It was my girlfriend who took the car," he explained.

"Nope, there is absolutely no way that a second car came down here that afternoon without us seeing it. No... way." she stated emphatically. He looked down thoughtfully at the woman, trying to make sense of the circumstances as explained. "What I find really puzzling is where she went after parking the car? She didn't walk up the road because mom and I would have seen her. She would have had to leave by water. Bizarre... just quite bizarre." Walter asked for and received the phone number of Rita Douglas, the owner of the house, and thanked Susan Robinson for all of her help. He had much to mull over on his long drive back to Wells Beach.

Much of Monday afternoon and evening was spent considering the revelations unearthed in Cutler, Maine that day. Walter tried in vain to reconcile the discovery of the ice house with Felicia Moretti. To his knowledge, no one, aside from himself, knew the complete story behind the actions taken by Melinda Klaus and himself on that miserable night in 1985. Had Melinda confided the details of the ice storm to anyone prior to her death? If so, how did Felicia manage to hear of it and find the house? As far as Felicia's mysterious disappearance following the abandonment of the car, Walter believed he had that figured out. He theorized Felicia was picked up by a male accomplice in the cove at the end of the road. No doubt, she and Walter's money were escorted by dingy out to his craft where their lives together commenced.

30

*W*alter lay in bed staring up at the plastered ceiling. He was not expected at work until noontime. His morning would start with a trip to the Maine Colonial Savings Bank in Kennebunk where he would survey the damage within his safe deposit box. He felt there was a good chance Felicia was not able to completely empty the large box of all of its contents. His assortment of coins would have proven quite heavy and, no doubt, would have required a strong satchel to carry off the sum total of his collection. After Maine Colonial he would visit his other two banks and determine what funds remained, if any.

Jonathan Eddy rose from behind his desk and joined Walter in the lobby of the bank. Escorting him into his office, he closed the door and returned to his desk.

"Walter, there is just under five hundred dollars left in your account. We issued Ms. Moretti a cashier's check for $92,000 on Friday morning. Legally, our hands were tied," he reported solemnly. Walter spent the next five minutes assuring the man that he knew the bank had made a prudent effort to protect him and his interests.

Descending a flight of marble steps, Walter entered the most secured area of the bank. He reached the window behind which the safe deposit department custodian sat and asked for access to box 117. The conservatively dressed woman slid him an access record form to sign. An uncomfortable twinge curled through his stomach at the sight of Felicia's name scribbled across the preceding two lines. He signed his name and was escorted to the far wall. He provided the stern woman with his individual key. After inserting his key, the cumbersome tray slid from its compartment and was handed over to him. His first reaction to the exchange was one of optimism. The metal tray was quite heavy, seeming to indicate that Felicia was unable to cart off the coinage portion of his wealth. With the tray cradled in both hands, he walked to a nearby privacy room and closed the door behind him.

Seated on a particularly uncomfortable chair Walter drew in a deep breath and lifted open the lid to the metal box. Resting on top of the contents within was a handwritten note on lined, yellow paper.

My dearest Walter,

Did you actually believe I would rob you of what was yours?
Sorry for the drama.
You know my flair for the dramatic.

Love... always,

He plucked the note from within the tray and placed it on the table. Atop the items contained within the safe deposit box was a check written on the Maine Colonial Savings Bank to Felicia Moretti for $92,000. He turned the check over and read: Pay to the order of Walter Plews. The words were followed by Felicia's signature. His eyes returned to inside the box. There were two more bank checks visible, one for $94,000 and the other $93,500. They were written on the other two local banks where Walter had savings accounts. He felt his eyes welling with tears as he pawed at the contents of the box. He came up with a roll of currency. Inside the rolled wad of one hundred dollar bills was a copy of a bill of sale. The Honda had been sold the prior Thursday for $3,300.

Walter returned to the main floor of the bank with the three cashier checks and $3,300 in hand. He deposited the $92,000 check and all of the currency into his savings account. After informing Mr. Eddy of what he found downstairs in his safe deposit box, he visited his other two banks and re-deposited the checks in each respective institution.

31

On the Saturday morning following his trip to Cutler, Walter hopped in the Corvette and sped southward on the interstate toward Portsmouth, New Hampshire. Twenty-four hours earlier he had contacted Jerry and Beth Karcher, Felicia's landlords on Freeman Street. His plans for that day already included some early Christmas shopping in the city's trendy downtown area and he seized this opportunity to meet the Karchers and perhaps gain some additional information on their enigmatic renter.

The Karchers lived in what had to be one of the city's oldest neighborhoods, the street lined with colonial after colonial homes, most shadowed under the protection of ancient oak trees. Walter ignored the brass knocker at the center of the door and announced his arrival through a series of courteous raps. He only needed to wait a few seconds before the door swung open. He was greeted by the woman of the house. Beth Karcher sported short, blonde hair that framed a youthful face. She immediately invited him in. She had what Walter thought of as an Irish smile. It was bright, sincere and probably capable of no small amount of personal charm. He was led into the kitchen where he joined the other half of the real estate partnership. Jerry Karcher sat at the kitchen table, staring down on the business section of the Portsmouth Herald. The man had sandy brown hair that, at the moment, lay tossed over his forehead. Immediately pushing the newspaper aside, Karcher reached over the table and shook Walter's hand. There was a friendly manner about him that instantly put Plews at ease.

Following an interlude of introductory chit-chat, during which he learned that the Karchers were frequent guests at the Cliff House, Walter directed the conversation toward his topic of choice; Felicia Moretti.

"I'm trying to go back and collect as much information as I can on this woman whom I am very fond of. She's been missing for about a week and I don't have a clue where to even start looking for her. I want to assure you, I'm not some predator or stalker." He reached inside his pocket and produced Felicia's note from the safe deposit box. "I thought you might have gotten some reference information from her for the apartment."

"No, I know *I* never did," answered Beth. "You have to understand Mr. Plews, she was sub-renting from Gary Tillotson. Gary paid the rent and, I'm assuming, the girl paid him for her share. As a matter of fact, I don't think I ever even met or spoke to the woman. What about you, hon?"

"No, not once. There was no reason. We got the rent on time and we got no complaints from the neighbors. There was no reason to see her," added Jerry.

"But what about when Gary left? Didn't you want to know who would be taking over the apartment?"

"Gary was in New York but the rent was paid. It was none of our business how much or how little he was there, as long as the rent was paid," Beth explained.

"So you're telling me that Gary never abandoned the apartment?"

"No, he knew and we knew he was coming back. He had a chance to make some very, very good money for three months and he jumped on it. He prepaid three months rent around Memorial Day," added Beth.

"Yeah, and rumor has it that someday I may even get to see my share of that rent money," clowned Jerry.

"Now, dearest, we've discussed this before. There are partners who handle the finances and partners who do all the work. You're the latter," recited the woman sweetly. The table shared a laugh before Walter rose to his feet.

"Is Gary back?"

"God, yes. He's been back in the apartment since September," reported Jerry.

It was mid-afternoon before Walter tossed his last shopping bag into the back of the car and followed the narrow streets of Portsmouth to Route 95. For ten minutes he played with the idea of returning to the apartment on Freeman Street and dropping in on Gary Tillotson. He was more than halfway home when he abruptly turned the Corvette onto Route 1A and motored toward the village at Short Sands and Freeman Street.

Walter pulled up along the far side of the street and stared up at Felicia Moretti's former apartment building. His mind drifted back to the night of the torrential rain when he went to her door in a state of mild inebriation and made something akin to a fool of himself. He exited the car and felt the cool October air rush at him. He knew there was a chance that Gary Tillotson would not be at home. He crossed the road and climbed the familiar stairs toward the second-story apartment. Close to the second floor he remembered his first visit to the house and the sensation that ran through his body when Felicia had unexpectedly kissed him. The recollection reminded him how much he missed her. Reaching the door, he knocked and stood patiently. Behind the glass the outline of a male materialized and approached the door. The wooden door swung in and a short, trim male of about thirty addressed him.

"Yeah," stated the man, curtly.

"Hi, my name is Walter Plews. I'm a friend of Felicia Moretti. I'm contacting as many people as I can who knew her, trying to gather any information I can to help me find her. If I'm not mistaken, you roomed with her for a couple of months."

"We shared the same roof but not much else," answered Tillotson. "Here, come in. There's too much cold air getting in." The man stepped aside and Walter entered the apartment. The furnishings brought back memories. He was led to the kitchen and offered a soda. He declined. "Felicia really kept to herself so I'm not sure I'll be able to help you much."

"Gary, if you could remember anything, like where she grew up or where she worked last?" The meticulously groomed man shook his head.

"Sorry."

"How did you meet her?" Tillotson looked across the table at his visitor, visibly recounting something from his past.

"How did I meet her? Now that was freaky, man. I met her the same way I just met you… at the front door. She saved my ass back in April." A confused expression broke out on Walter's face so Tillotson set out to clarify himself.

"Earlier this year I got myself into some trouble with gambling debts. It wasn't so much the amount of the money I owed but who I owed it to. I'd been given a twenty-four hour notice to pay up the six hundred dollars I owed… or else. They knew where I lived. We're talking about a broken arm or maybe a few missing teeth. I was absolutely broke and there were no friends left to turn to. I called my mom and asked her to wire me the money but she didn't have it. I remember she said she'd say a prayer that something would turn up. I lost it. I started cursing her, calling her a religious idiot and using foul language on her. Imagine, using foul language on your own mother! I hung up on her and was pacing around the apartment when there came a knock at the door. I almost didn't answer it. I thought maybe a goon was coming to collect early. The knocking continued and got louder until I finally had to answer the door. And there she was… Felicia. She said she had heard that I was looking to sub-rent the apartment. I think I just stared at her, not knowing what the hell to say. That's when she took six hundred and fifty dollars out of her pocket and dangled it there in front of me. How the hell she knew what half the rent was I still don't know! Needless to say, I took it. You can't make this kind of shit up." Walter shook his head in amazement.

"Wow!"

"Yeah… wow!"

"And did you apologize to your mother?"

"Oh yeah, many, many times over. She's had me on a perpetual guilt trip over that episode ever since."

32

The main entrance door to the Cliff House swung open and Walter Plews stepped out into a brisk, mid-October breeze. Lingering for a second in the doorway, he assisted two elderly women into the lobby before turning in the direction of the ocean. Reaching the backside of the building, his jacket began flapping wildly in the wind. He lifted the jacket collar to protect his ears from the blast of cold air off the Gulf of Maine and followed the path along the crest of Bald Head Cliff toward the ledge beyond the flume. He descended the steps of stratified rock and reached the circular walkway above the chasm. Hugging the rim of the back wall, he gingerly rounded the protruding face of rock and climbed down and over to the far ledge. His arrival at this familiar place was greeted with a feeling of overwhelming despondency. He eased his backside down on the flat surface of an elevated section of ledge and allowed the wind to blow over his face. The constant rush of air stirred the ocean below, furiously driving the seawater up and through the chasm thirty feet down. He wasn't meant to be here alone, he thought to himself. He would not stay long. He was expected at the pub in a few minutes and he did want to lose any time with his friends. Walter reached inside his jacket and produced three vials of prescription medicine. Standing high above the churning saltwater, he dropped each of the three plastic bottles of pills down into the agitated sea where they were rapidly swallowed up in the cold water.

The Corvette coasted into the village at Short Sands and made its customary sharp left at the Goldenrod building. Walter glanced down at his watch and realized he was on time. The setting sun illuminated the top half of the Union Bluff Hotel as he coasted into one of three empty parking spaces behind the now silent bowling alley. It was the off-season at York Beach. Columbus Day had come and gone and the magnificent rocky coast was gradually being returned to the locals.

Sticking his head through the doorway of the pub, he instinctively glanced right in the direction of the group's table of choice.

"Hey, Walter," called out Ronny, waving his friend over to their table by the window. The big man shuffled into the room and joined his two friends, applying a squeeze to Ronny's shoulder as he circled the table.

"Well, guys… and then there were three," mouthed Dingman, a reference to the relocation of Chris Jacobs since their last meeting.

"Jacobs was an egomaniac, a shameless womanizer, a know-it-all and a liberal weenie… and I'm going to really miss having him here," admitted Dave Durette in his typically gruff manner.

"Seconded," added Walter. "Why don't we toast our buddy as soon as I hail down our waitress?"

"We got Susan tonight. Look for Susan, Walt," advised Ronny.

"Oh, and what's this I hear about a certain accountant from the Cliff House recovering every cent of his money from a certain devious chambermaid?" Dave asked. Walter shook his head in the negative.

"There was nothing to recover," he answered. "It turns out she never took it in the first place."

"Walter, you're living an enchanted life. When I heard what that little witch of yours pulled while you were out of town… damn, I figured you were down and out for the count. You are one friggin' fortunate guy," exclaimed Durette. Walter nodded in agreement as his beer arrived at the table.

"Okay, it's time to toast our departed buddy," proclaimed Ronny. "To Chris Jacobs, who busted our balls in '92 after his hero, Bill Clinton, won the election. And he did bust our balls! And to Chris Jacobs, who had the balls to come and face us after his hero, Bill Clinton, through his incompetence and arrogance, gave us back both houses of congress in '94 after a forty year wait. And, sweet Jesus, we did bust his balls. To Chris," proclaimed Ronny. The three men raised and touched their glasses.

"To Chris Jacobs," said Dave, again elevating his glass. "To all his female conquests, the details of which he generously shared with his friends… and to the little broad who finally did him in. Sometimes you eat the bear… and sometimes the bear eats you." Again, the three men raised their glasses of beer and saluted their departed friend.

Following the rousing start to the evening, the conversation progressively grew more and more nostalgic and eventually tender. Ronny Dingman surprised his friends with a heartfelt story from early in his marriage to Helen. Dave and Walter sat in attentive silence as the man recounted a romantic weekend spent camping on a beach along the eastern shore of Cape Cod with the woman who was soon to become his ex-wife. It was following Dingman's warm recollections that Walter surprised even himself by sharing, for the first time, the details of his two days spent with Melinda Klaus at the ice house in Cutler. Dave Durette was last to reminisce. Not surprisingly, he shared with the men an account of a day spent in a sleeping bag on the top of a New Hampshire mountain with the girl named Janette from Berlin.

Following three beers, a satisfying meal, and insight into their friend's most fond memories, the three men sat quietly around the table.

"Gentlemen, I have an announcement," blurted out Dave Durette.

"Shoot," responded Ronny.

"I've been offered and accepted that job in New Jersey," he said soberly. Walter and Ronny looked up from their beers, surprised expressions on both faces. "Tomorrow I'll give the Chilton-Weatherly clowns my two week notice."

"Any chance of a severance package?" asked Walter. His question caused Durette to nearly cough up his beer.

"They're not even giving severances to the people they're letting go. In fact, they're even trying to chisel some of them out of their accrued vacation pay. I hardly think I'll be offered anything but the closest door."

Dave Durette's announcement threw a blanket of gravity over the last few minutes of the evening. Both Walter and Ronny threw bear hugs around their friend by the front door of the hotel as the three old friends prepared to set off in different directions.

"You have to meet with us one more time before the move," insisted Ronny as Dave walked back to his vehicle.

"Absolutely, I give you my word on it," he called back.

That October night was the last time either Ronny or Walter set eyes on their friend; David Durette was dismissed from his position at Chilton-Weatherly the following day only minutes after tendering his two-week notice. He was escorted by security to his office to pick up personal effects and ultimately to the front door. On his final pass by the acting treasurer's office he was heard to call the man a 'worthless son-of-a-bitch' in a voice loud enough to be heard two hundred feet away in the cafeteria. In the final days before his relocation to Tom's River, New Jersey and his new job, he was unable to coordinate a meeting with his friends at the Union Bluff Hotel.

33

The ocean and sky were set off in competing shades of gray as Walter looked out from the front of the house onto an unpopulated Wells Beach. Thanksgiving Day was less than a month away as was the recurring dread he had for this time of the year. In September he had cultivated a premonition of his first joyous Christmas in ten years but that was before Felicia's disappearance. The faint hope of her return he had nurtured a month earlier was gone. Reaching down to the floor, he took hold of a suitcase filled with fall and winter clothes and made his way to the stairwell and eventually to the second floor. He could no longer bear the sight of the basement walls. He needed to move closer to the rooms where Felicia had spent the better part of the summer of 1995. Her former bedroom retained the slightest residue of her scent and he was desperate to hold on to anything left behind by Felicia Moretti.

Walter rolled onto his side and opened one eye. It was a few minutes after two o'clock on a Wednesday morning and the ocean churned and rolled incessantly against the retaining wall below. His mind wandered back to the image of Felicia standing naked in front of the window. He thought back to the sight of her turning from that same window one night and staring down on him. He was listless and burdened by a strange, oppressive feeling in his head. Lifting himself up from the mattress, he stepped over to the south window and gazed downward. The lights from a nearby house bled down on the dark water outside. He closed his eyes and hoped the strange pressure inside his chest would recede back to where it came while a kaleidoscope of images rushed through his consciousness: Felicia standing on the ledge above the flume, the light from the fireplace flames reflecting off Melinda's face at the ice house, the first, yellow cosmo falling onto him at the Cliff House, the wasp snared hopelessly in the spider's web, the house swallowed in brush on Little Machias Road, his circle of friends at the Union Bluff table, the magical white house on the cove in Cutler, the trail of flowers leading up the stairs, and eventually to a reclining Felicia laid out on the hallway floor...

Ronny Dingman looked up from behind his workbench to see Pam LaBossiere approaching. She was dressed for the cold November weather, clearly on her way out of the building.

"Ronny, by any chance did you hear from Walter today? Did he have any plans today that I didn't know about?" Dingman stared blankly at the woman momentarily.

"No, not that I know of."

"I wasn't in yesterday so if something came up I wouldn't know about it. He's usually pretty good about leaving a note or something," she explained. Ronny glanced into space, recounting his work schedule that week.

"I know I saw him Tuesday. We took our afternoon break together. Yesterday I was working in the parking lot all day. I don't think we crossed paths yesterday."

"Any chance of you following up on this and making sure he's okay? It's not like him to just not come to work without anyone knowing."

"Yeah Pam, I'll try ringing him and maybe even take a drive up to Wells if I don't have any luck." The woman extended the man a grateful smile and made her way from his work area.

Ronny had called twice and been forwarded to Walter's answering machine on both occasions. Leaving work at six, he pointed the truck northward and followed the coastal route toward Wells. It was already dark, his headlights and the occasional vehicle moving in the other direction providing most all of the light along the winding stretch of road. Eventually the darkness gave way to a myriad of lights from the steady cavalcade of businesses that lined the main streets of Ogunquit. Although well lit, the sidewalks of the tourist town were void of pedestrians. It was off-season and most locals were already at home. Ronny followed Route 1 for a couple of miles before peeling off a right turn and making his way back to the coast. A mile later he was at Fisherman's Cove where a quarter-mile expanse of cement and huge, granite boulders stood between the Atlantic Ocean and a string of summer cottages sitting precariously at its doorstep. On this night the seawater was moving against and over the seawall leaving water and seaweed in the roadway. He turned the pickup onto the beleaguered coastal road and headed toward the Sand Castle.

The house rested in total darkness as his Chevy crawled up the side street toward the enormous residence. Dingman felt a wave of apprehension pass through him as he stepped from his vehicle. Walter's Corvette sat parked in the back yard. After climbing the darkened porch stairs, he found his way to the kitchen door. He pounded on the wooden, storm door and called out Walter's name for the better part of a minute before descending from the porch and searching out the key hidden on the far side of the building. Returning to the kitchen entrance, he turned the key and gained access to the house. After fumbling for a few seconds, his hand made contact with a light switch and the room was illuminated.

"Walter, are you home? It's Ronny," he called out to the silent rooms. One room at a time he made his way around the first floor of the building, flicking on lamps and overhead lights until he reached the sun room. There was no sign of his friend. The room temperature was probably less than fifty degrees. A foreboding feeling descended over him. He did not want his search to lead him to the basement apartment. Ronny re-entered the living room and took the stairs to the second floor and the ring of bedrooms above. Remembering his trip to the Sand Castle some weeks earlier, he instinctively followed the hallway to Felicia's bedroom. He pushed in the door and saw his friend seated and slumped by the far window, his body held partially upright by a bureau.

"Oh, Christ… Walter," Ronny said quietly. Dingman crossed the room and looked down on his friend. Walter Plews' eyes were closed and there was no evidence of trauma on his face. Ronny brought his hand down on the large man's shoulder.

"Buddy," he said softly while tears began to run down his cheeks.

Ronny phoned the Wells Police Department for assistance and returned to the second floor. He waited on the arrival of a patrol car with Walter, speaking to his friend until flashing blue lights lit up the window and he was needed downstairs.

34

*T*wo weeks had passed since Walter Plews was laid to rest in Massachusetts, and Ronny Dingman still had a difficult time fully accepting it. Over the last week he had reached for the phone on numerous occasions and began dialing Walter's extension number before realizing the gentle giant would not be there to take the call. Over and over he ran the circumstances of Felicia Moretti's arrival and departure through his mind. He had called both Dave and Chris and advised them of Walter's passing. However, because of their short time on the new job, neither was able to make it back to New England for the funeral. Ronny blamed Felicia for his friend's untimely death at age thirty-nine.

On a clear and quiet Tuesday in December, Dingman jumped into the cold cabin of his pickup and motored down the driveway away from the Cliff House. On an unexplainable impulse, he pointed the Chevy south at the shore road and headed for Short Sands. The roadway was dark, cold and deserted with a few wisps of snow occasionally visible in the headlights. Less than ten minutes later he saw the lights of the village through the windshield. He decided to visit the Union Bluff pub on this night for reasons beyond his own comprehension. Tapping on the brakes, he glanced to his left and eyed the sign for Freeman Street. He thought back to eight months earlier and the sudden appearance of Felicia. Walter had shared stories of visiting her apartment on Freeman Street with him. It was her presence in that apartment that had set Walter Plew's life into a downward spiral, he thought.

Ronny reached the intersection at Short Sand's village, his eyes focusing on signs for Goldenrod Kiss's and Whispering Sands Gifts as if seeing them for the first time. He turned the vehicle left and rolled slowly up the road. He remembered Walter's tendency of parking behind the bowling alley and did the same. He decided he would walk the extra hundred feet to the door of the Union Bluff on this night.

Dingman harbored a terrible melancholy as he entered the front door of the hotel and turned right into the pub. It was a quiet night with only a handful of tables occupied and two stragglers arched over the bar. He walked halfway to the bar and glanced right. The group's table of choice near the window was empty, as was every other table in that section of the establishment. Dingman paused for only a moment before shuffling to the table and taking the chair Chris Jacobs was so fond of claiming. He was partially out of sight in this darkened corner of the room but he was in no hurry to be served. If it took a waitress ten minutes to spot him, then that was all right. He glanced over his shoulder out the window. Somewhere out there Felicia Moretti was warm and comfortable, he thought. Did she even know Walter had passed? Did she care? His eyes returned to the empty chairs surrounding the table and marveled on how everything had changed so quickly. The words from a Roy Clark song came to mind:

The friends I made all seem somehow to drift away,
And only I am left on stage to end the play.

Ronny had sat quietly by the window for nearly ten minutes before the waitress appeared. It was the black-haired girl named Susan that Chris had dated briefly.

"Will you be wanting a beer while you wait and how many more can I expect?"

"Yes, to the first question, and there will be no more coming tonight." She looked up from her pad as if in disbelief.

"So, you need a table this size just to accommodate you and your inflated male ego?" she fired back.

"Nothing to do with egos. Right now you'd need a microscope to find my ego… male or otherwise."

"I know where Chris is but where are the others?"

"Dave's moved to Jersey and Walter, the big guy, he passed away a couple of weeks back." Susan's mouthed dropped, shocked by his words.

"Didn't you two guys work together at the Cliff House?" Dingman nodded yes and let out a sigh.

"Sorry about that ego crack I made. You see, right now I'm real down on men and I'm willing to take it out on anyone within snapping distance."

"Hey, women aren't exactly at the top of my hit parade at the moment either," responded Ronny. "No offense taken." The waitress stared down on him for a prolonged moment before speaking.

"Miller?" she asked with uncertainty.

"You got it."

Fifteen minutes after the arrival of his beer, Ronny was both surprised and pleased when Susan both brought his meal and slid onto the chair next to him.

"It's a slow night and you look a little lonely over here in the corner," she explained.

"Be my guest," he answered while reaching for his utensils.

"Chris told me a little about you guys when we went out. We only wound up having one date before his world caved in around him and he had to relocate to back home. I heard the story about an overweight guy with a really hot girlfriend. You're not overweight so that must have been the other guy who worked at the Cliff House… the one who died."

"Yeah, that was Walter."

"And he told me about the guy whose wife ran off with some doctor she worked for. That must be you."

"Live and in living color," attested Ronny.

"So, you're divorced?"

"Not officially until mid-January."

"I found out yesterday that my ex-husband pulled some shit on our taxes a couple of years ago and now I'm on the hook along with him for over six grand. The bastard's run off somewhere and can't be found and the IRS's coming down on me for all of it. My taxes were all withheld and paid for the year they're going after us. He was self-employed and as crooked as hell."

"Did you guys break up over money?" asked Ronny.

"No, it was over what your wife did to you except there were two women," she explained. Someone gestured to Susan from across the room and she excused herself from the table. For the first time all evening the wind blew audibly against the window. Ronny turned to the sound and remembered the incident with the girl in the bikini and the distraction she created at the table. He thought of poor Walter seated with his back to the window and fondly laughed.

Ronny's eyes followed Susan around the room for the next five minutes as she visited each of her parties of customers. She was a very pretty woman, pretty enough to catch Chris Jacob's eye. He wished he had any one of his friends at the moment to advise him on whether he should ask her out. She didn't look too, too young, perhaps in her early thirties, he thought. He felt a knot of nervous energy begin to build in his stomach. He didn't need rejection at this point in his life. Perhaps he could wait until after the divorce was finalized to come back and ask her out. He barely knew the woman, he reasoned.

Susan gestured toward Ronny about refilling his glass. He nodded in the affirmative. She returned to the table a minute later with his glass of Miller and deposited herself in the seat to his left. She glanced away from him and out at the room. He took the opportunity to look closely at her shiny, black hair and smooth, fair skin. He hated himself for not having the courage to ask her out.

"I've got a truckload of problems and decisions to sort out after work. What I usually do is walk the beach and think them through one at a time until I've made up my mind. I wouldn't mind some company. I'm off at nine-thirty," she said matter-of-factly. She turned to him, her blue eyes searching his face for a probable response.

"It's awfully cold out there tonight," Ronny answered tentatively.

"For a sissy boy it might be too cold," she snapped back.

"Then again, I am a good listener," he reasoned.

"You do know the offer's not going to be on the table all night," she warned.

"And if I got too cold, you'd find a way to warm me up?"

"Within reason," she promised. He stared at her admiringly. "Tick tock, tick tock," she cautioned.

"I'll be waiting by the door for you... or at this table." She slapped him on the knee.

"Good." Susan rose to her feet and walked in the direction of the bar. A second later she stopped in her tracks and turned back to him.

"By the way... what's your name?"

"Ronny... Ronny Dingman."

Epilogue

My last meeting with Ronny Dingman took place in late April of 2008. Explaining he needed to show me some last evidence on the matter of Felicia Moretti, he drove up to Wells and visited with me at my cottage there. Seated together at the kitchen table, he reached inside a leather carrying case and produced a sheet of paper. It was the obituary of Melinda Klaus. He gave me a few seconds to examine it. I stared down on it for two or three minutes, running the details of the account of this woman's life against the details reported to me by him a year earlier. I explained to him that this sort of validation was not necessary. The story of Walter Plews, Melinda Klaus and Felicia Moretti would be presented in the form of fiction.

Not fazed by my assurances he produced a second sheet of paper. It contained Felicia Moretti's obituary and photograph. My mouth must have dropped open as I gazed down on it. I asked him if the photograph matched the image of the girl who invaded the life of Walter Plews in the spring of 1995 and he stated in absolute terms that it did. I must have stared at her image for a full five minutes without speaking. She was as pretty as I imagined but not as ethnically Italian-looking as I had envisioned. Felicia's obituary explained how she had drowned in a swimming accident along the New Jersey shore at the age of twenty-six. Following over five minutes at the table, Ronny grew impatient with me. He rose from his chair and stood over me. He told me to study the particulars of the two documents more carefully. Another sixty seconds passed and I turned back to him in frustration. What had I not picked up on? From over my shoulder he pointed down at the dates of death on both obituaries. It was only then that I realized that Melinda Klaus and Felicia Moretti both died on August 28, 1987.

A Merry Christmas?

Thomas E. Coughlin

Susan Butler sat quietly in the passenger seat as the auto cut through the falling snow and headed eastward toward home. The once familiar sight of the Merrimack River sporadically came into view through the falling snowflakes as the roadway traced the course of the river from Route 93 to the city the mills built. She would be home soon. Home was Lowell, Massachusetts. Twelve years and a husband had passed from her life since she pulled up stakes and moved to Boston.

"You're going to have to give me some kind of directions on where to leave you off. I'm not a freakin' taxi service or mind reader," complained Doris Sullivan from behind the wheel. Until this morning Doris had been her landlady, providing Susan with a furnished, studio apartment. "What the hell am I doing driving sixty miles in a goddamn snowstorm on Christmas Eve?"

"You're driving me thirty miles, as we agreed, in exchange for a damn nice stereo system," Susan added calmly.

"Thirty miles up, thirty miles back…sixty miles," snapped back the gray-haired woman. "And for a stereo that's older than dirt." The passenger started a response but caught herself as the first syllable formed in her mouth and remained quiet. The vehicle had just passed the 'Entering Lowell' sign and she knew deliverance from Doris Sullivan would soon be upon her.

The thirty-six-year-old closed her eyes momentarily, her circumstances swirling in her head. In a matter of minutes she would be temporarily homeless. With any luck, and according to plan, the homeless period of her life would cover no more than forty-five minutes. She had hoped to arrive back to the city of her birth closer to noontime but Doris had caused delays that resulted in an expected arrival time now nearer to three-thirty. Her plan of action called upon a mid-day arrival at the office door of Attorney William Stiles. Susan counted strongly on his presence at the law office along with, at minimum, a skeleton crew of employees. She would shame him, the man she had nearly married thirteen and a half years before, into financially assisting her. And why not? Hadn't it been William, and William alone, who threw her life into the downward spiral that brought it to where it was today? Who pulls out of a marriage five weeks before the wedding, leaving the bride and her mother to deal with the questions, humiliation, and financial fallout alone?

"We can't be that far from downtown," mouthed Doris from behind the wheel. "Why can't you get out up here by the bridge? It can't be that far to the center of the city. It's not like you're lugging a suitcase or something," argued the woman.

"Fine, just drop me off up here by the bridge," relented Susan, anxious to transmit Doris into the past tense of her life.

After maneuvering herself and the sum total of her worldly possessions— a backpack crammed with miscellaneous clothing—from the vehicle, Susan leaned forward and wished Doris a safe trip back to Boston.

"God damn it, it would have to snow on the one day I don't want it to," she lamented in return, clearly unmoved by her passenger's situation or her final words of encouragement. Seconds later the sub-compact re-entered the flow of traffic, and Susan's landlady for the prior twenty-six months disappeared from her life. With that chapter in her life closed, she hoisted her bundle of clothes over her shoulder and turned toward the downtown section of the city. At present, the snow was falling gently in the form of large flakes. Following a mad dash through the busy intersection, she proceeded across an impressive configuration of steel called the Bridge Street Bridge. It was about this time, fifty feet above and halfway across the Merrimack River, that the woman underwent her first pang of discomfort from the wetness and cold penetrating her sneakers. In the distance, through the falling snow, she could make out Merrimack Street, her destination, the lighted windows of the ten-story Sun Building serving as a beacon. The afternoon, what was left of it, had grown noticeably dark. Susan trudged onward; her arms slung through the corresponding straps of the knapsack perched atop her shoulders.

It only took five minutes for the trim woman to arrive in Kearney Square, the city's epicenter. She was immediately astonished by the lack of pedestrians visible on the sidewalks. Susan waited on a change in the traffic lights and flitted to the far side of the street. She knew from perusing a Lowell telephone book kept at the Boston City Library that Bill's law office was on Merrimack Street. From her best recollection of downtown Lowell, she instinctively felt it must be located within one or two city blocks. Susan had walked less than a block when she stopped in front of a Dunkin' Donuts shop and glanced up at the office building on the far side of the street. There, a few stories up, her eyes locked onto a series of windows, each with the same designation: William G. Stiles, Attorney at Law. Susan had found her ex-fiancé's office in short order but grew dismayed at the lack of any lights visible from inside. In the next instant the traffic lights a few feet away changed, allowing pedestrians to move across the frequently busy intersection. She seized this opportunity and scurried across Merrimack Street.

With the weight from her backpack burrowing into her right shoulder, and the cold from the snow and slush penetrating her sneakers, she approached the front door of the office building and attempted to enter. Her effort proved fruitless. Evidently, public access to the building had been withdrawn for the evening. This development caused a jolt of anxiety to tear its way through her nervous system, depositing a knot in her stomach. She was pretty much without funds, friends, or any form of shelter at the moment, she reasoned to herself. Susan decided to loiter in the doorway for a short while. Perhaps someone would return to the building, someone with a key to the door. Peeking inside to the obscurely lit lobby, the woman saw an area dressed in marble. At the far end of the narrow hall were red elevator doors. No doubt, these were the doors that ushered Billy Stiles to work every day for the past five or ten years of his life.

"They locked the building at three," crowed a voice from behind her. Susan turned to confront a heavy-set woman of perhaps sixty years of age. "No one's going to be doing any business in there until after Christmas. That, you can be sure of." The woman stared intently into Susan's eyes through an imposing, unpleasant face, seeming to take a proprietary interest in the old building. Her manner caused the younger woman to become outwardly flustered. "And who was it you were expecting to see?" she asked.

"Mr. Stiles," answered Susan.

"Attorney Stiles!" shouted back the woman. "You expected to meet with Attorney Stiles, now… on Christmas Eve? See here now miss whoever-you-are, I may just be paid to clean the toilets and keep the halls tidy here but I know enough to be sure you won't be sitting with Attorney Stiles until after Christmas," proclaimed the woman with an air of authority. With that said, the middle-aged female defiantly planted her feet on the sidewalk, giving the impression she was intent on policing the foyer of the building and discouraging any and all loiterers. Susan found herself capable of holding her ground for only a few seconds before yielding her position to the unpleasant character standing before her. Seconds later, the thirty-six year old repositioned her backpack and continued up Merrimack Street.

With the large flakes of snow now clinging to her denim jacket, Susan ducked her head inside of the darkened doorway to a shop and pulled out her wallet. At her back read the sign: Re-opening 10 A.M., December 26th. A review of the contents of her wallet produced no pleasant surprises. The sum total of her cash, and therefore her life savings, was four dollars. Returning the skimpy billfold to her back pocket, she quickly decided against a trip back to Dunkin' Donuts for a hot coffee and, instead, scampered across snow covered Merrimack Street and onto Palmer Street. This short strip of roadway was laid out in cobblestone, a fact not lost on Susan upon reaching it. It was at this point in her travels, with all evidence of daylight fading away, that she was visited by both desperation and fear. Around her the air was cluttered with heavy, descending flakes of snow. Halfway across the empty roadway, her eyes fell on a shop unfamiliar to her. The Coffee Mill was a small cafe new to her. Behind the darkened windows, the stacked chairs gave witness to the early release of employees for Christmas.

Susan whirled in her tracks and stared down an adjacent, darkened alley that ran parallel to the main street. She was quick to pick up on an overhead concourse that capped the passageway, providing some measure of protection from the elements. Within seconds she was walking tentatively into the poorly lit avenue, her eyes darting from side to side in search of any potential danger. Above her head, the stone overhang was chiseled with the numbers 1874, an acknowledgement of the structure's bookmark in the city's historical past. Susan walked forward into the byway, the sides strewn with an assortment of garbage receptacles. Her feet had reached bare pavement when she stopped, hoping to allow her night vision to slowly adapt to her surroundings. This might be her best option for the evening, she thought, deliberately moving herself to a position by the near wall. Dropping her backpack to the pavement below, she eased herself to the ground and nestled against the wall of bricks that bordered the alleyway. The pavement surrounding her was cold but reasonably dry. The woman drew in a deep breath and grimly pondered her circumstances. She soberly connected the dots that were her life for the last twelve years, trying to determine how it all had led to this; homeless, crouching out-of-sight in a darkened alley on Christmas Eve. The subject of the air temperature and her overnight survival out in the elements raced through her mind. Fifty feet away on the cobbled surface of Palmer Street, the traffic flow was practically non-existent. She was assuredly alone.

The crunch of shattering glass under foot broke through the night air and delivered Susan from a unsubstantial sleep. The abruptness of her awakening sent a jolt of fear through her nervous system as her eyes opened and scanned the darkness around her.

"You can't be very comfortable lying on the ground down there," voiced a male from close proximity.

"It's fine," she responded timidly.

"Here, let me help you up," answered the voice from out of the blackness.

"No, I'm fine," fired back the woman with added assertion in her tone. With that said the man moved and took a position directly above her. Muted light from the street dimly illuminated the figure of a hulking male. He was middle aged, his features lost behind a swirl of disheveled facial hair. He bent forward with a bronchial grunt and brought a hand down on her left breast. "What do you think you're doing?" she called out with an element of alarm in her voice. An instant later the brute was kneeling atop her, his hands pawing at her body as he moved the bulk of his weight onto her delicate frame. "Please… please, someone help me!" cried out Susan while her attacker's hands ferociously probed the length of her torso.

"Keep your fuckin' mouth shut. No one's fuckin' comin' to the rescue," snarled the man, his face suddenly right against her own. His breath, weighted heavily with the odor of alcohol, invaded her senses and sent a wave of nausea through her. She struggled frantically for the next few seconds, unable to free herself from the stranger's grip. Her efforts only brought a howl of satisfaction from the brute.

"Is everything okay down there?" called out a voice from the end of the alleyway.

"Mind your own fuckin' business," snarled the monster astride the woman, his voice particularly menacing.

"For God's sake, help me," screamed Susan, her back pinned against the frigid concrete.

"A family disagreement and none of your goddamn business," hollered the attacker from his position atop his victim.

"Help me," she called out again. She felt herself go limp as the full weight of her attacker crashed down on her. Pain tore through her knee as concentrated weight drove it against the cold, frozen pavement. The voice from the roadway forty feet away went silent as the assailant pressed his mouth to hers, the stench of his breath sending a surge of revulsion through her. She pushed her face away and cried out in horror. Unexplainably, a sequence of images from her childhood sped through her mind, the faces of her parents, grandparents and pre-school playmates crowding her consciousness. Amid the chaos Susan questioned if she was dying, identifying with the reported thought processes of many faced with pending doom. At that instant she felt the weight atop her shift, then fall away, as an outburst of energy roared over her position on the ground and that of her attacker. The brunette glanced up to see a second man now reigning blows on the assailant. In the subdued light of the alleyway, Susan was able to make out the outlines of two figures. Within seconds, the scuffle was ended and her would be attacker hustled away under unsteady legs. Breathing heavily, the second male turned back to her.

"Are you all right?" he asked. "How in the world were you lured into the alley?" Susan stared up from the ground at a face largely concealed in shadows. She deliberated briefly before responding.

"I'm afraid it was he who found me here," she confessed while attempting to raise herself from the ground. Her effort only spawned a grimace as she winced from the pain shooting up from her knee. Following a moment spent in search of an object to support her weight, she made use of the rim of a garbage can and hoisted herself to her feet, avoiding the temptation to direct any of her weight onto her right leg.

"Suzy. Suzy Butler?" Susan redirected her attention back to her rescuer who stood a few steps away and in the shadow of the building. Squinting her eyes, she gazed purposefully across the alleyway and into the face of the stranger.

"Bill? Is that you, Bill?" The man moved closer and into what artificial light there was bleeding into the alley. Susan's eyes widened in recognition of the man she had loved more than a dozen years before. William Stiles slowly approached her, stopping an arm's length away. He stared intensely into her eyes, as if searching out an explanation for their unusual state of affairs. "Believe it or not, I'm here of my own accord," she explained, making no attempt to mask a hint of desperation. Her words prompted a short period of silence while the attorney pieced together the woman's words and apparent circumstances.

"Let me help you to your car," he said, his tone taking on a noble, gentrified quality.

"No, it's fine. I'll be all right. You've seen to that," she insisted.

"No, don't be foolish. Let me help you to your car."

"Please, you can run along. I'm fine."

"I insist." His affirmation caused her body to go rigid in frustration.

"There is no car!" Her voice reverberated between the nearby buildings and out onto Palmer Street. Susan turned from her former lover and hobbled toward the street.

"You're forgetting something," he added in a gentle voice and plucked her backpack from the ground. Frustrated and fuming from her oversight, she whirled and limped back in his direction. Reaching him, she snatched the pack from his hand and was about to turn away when he leaned forward and hoisted her into his arms.

"Putting any weight on that leg could be worsening your injury. Let's go back to my office and sort this whole evening out, shall we?"

Emerging from the alley, Stiles turned toward Merrimack Street and stepped cautiously over the snow-covered sidewalk toward his office building. Momentarily speechless, Susan accepted the man's gesture by looping one arm around his neck. The downtown sidewalks were practically deserted at this hour. With her face in close proximity to his, Susan took this opportunity to closely inspect the man she had nearly married a decade and a half earlier. She thought to herself that he looked slightly older than his years, his hair receding and his features perhaps the victim of stress and the pressures of his profession. Impeccably dressed, his thinning hair razor-cut and styled, William Stiles transmitted the appearance of an individual on familiar terms with financial success.

"My office is less than a block from here," acknowledged Stiles, unaware the woman had stood in the doorway of his building less than two hours earlier. For her part, Susan remained silent. She was somewhat taken aback with the unfolding of events. Finally, at the intersection of Merrimack and Central Streets, he scurried across the roadway and up to the front door to his office building.

With Susan's one hundred and thirty pounds balanced between his arms, the lawyer paused in front of the door to his building.

"Why don't you reach into my pocket and fish out my keys," he suggested before shifting her weight higher against his chest. She shot him an innocent smile and immediately took to reaching down through his outer garments and into his pants pockets. She was quick to pick up on the warmth from the man's body as her hand fumbled along the inner fabric clinging to his leg.

"My overcoat pocket," he added blandly. Susan hastily withdrew her hand.

"Well, you could have given me a little more information on the whereabouts of the keys," she said defensively. A smirk broke over the lawyer's face while his former sweetheart searched his overcoat pocket, eventually finding the ring of keys.

"It's the large, gold one," he said, indicating to her that she was expected to find the keyhole and get the door open.

Susan heard the building door slam behind them as William Stiles carried her down a marble-floored lobby toward a bright red, elevator door. The passageway was illuminated by a series of steamed glass globes that only gave off muted light. The far wall by the entrance to the elevator had only two buttons. Stiles gestured to his passenger to summon the elevator and she did.

"Now is your office down in the cellar or do I send this sucker up?"

"Go with your woman's intuition," he answered dryly. They arrived on the third floor seconds later. It was there that Susan quickly deduced that half the floor was the domain of William's law firm, his name prominently spelled out on the windows of a half-dozen doors.

"The first brown key on the ring should get us in the door in front of us," he instructed. The brunette glanced down at the ring of keys and acted as directed.

The front door to his office swung open and William immediately carried his guest through a reception area and into a large, impeccably furnished office with four windows looking out over Merrimack and Central Streets. Pausing just inside the doorway, he leaned down and flicked on the overhead, florescent lights.

"Is this your office?"

"Yes. Do you like it?"

"I'm afraid you're asking the wrong person. I'm not part of your world. I look at this and think how wonderful it must be to just come to work everyday," she confessed. He did not answer her. He glanced around the familiar office as if seeing it for the first time before carrying Susan to a leather couch extended along the far wall and cautiously laid her down. She took a deep breath then watched as he ran his hand along her denim jeans and finally over her sneakers.

"My God, you're soaking wet. You could catch pneumonia."

"I'm fine, Bill, really."

"Are there dry clothes in your backpack?"

"I assume they're still dry."

"Then why don't you change out of these wet things and into something dry while I go out to the kitchen and warm us up some tea." The tall lawyer did not wait on a reply. Within seconds he was out of the room. Soon came the sounds of opening and closing cabinets. It provided evidence of his efforts. Hurriedly, she plucked items from her backpack and gingerly peeled off her saturated jeans, socks and sneakers. Her replacement wardrobe consisted of a form-fitting pair of cut-off, denim jeans and pink, ankle socks. Her blouse and flimsy sweater had remained dry throughout the evening and warranted no change of wardrobe. Rendered self-conscious by the length of exposed skin between the top of her ankle socks and the bottom of her cut-off jeans, the shapely thirty-six-year-old curled her legs beneath her and waited on her host's return.

"Is it safe for me to come in," asked Attorney Stiles from behind one of the office's side doors.

"If you're asking if I'm suitable for mixed company, then the answer is yes. They may have to slap a PG rating on me but certainly not an R." The lawyer pushed open the door with his body, his hands carrying a tray and steaming beverages. Entering the room, his eyes were visibly drawn to his company's exposed legs folded atop his leather couch.

"I had a pair of sweat pants but they were a little damp from their time spent outside," she explained.

"No complaints from this side of the room," he answered while placing the tray down on his desk. "How do you take your tea?"

"Two sugars and a little milk," she purred, her eyes trained on him. Following no more than thirty seconds of preparation, Stiles carefully brought the two cups of tea across the room to the couch.

"Is the room warm enough?" he asked while delivering Susan her warm drink.

"Well, seeing that you asked, I wouldn't mind if you inched the temperature up just a little," she confessed. Immediately bounding to his feet, he crossed the room and fiddled with the thermostat until there came an audible click.

"You should be warm as toast in no time." He returned to the far end of the couch and balanced his cup and saucer in his lap. Susan thought she detected the faintest of smiles breaking out over her host's face as the two exchanged glances and nursed sips of tea over the rims of their cups.

Susan Butler and William Stiles sat quietly on the office couch, both staring blankly across the room, when a gust of cold, December wind blew snow against the office windows. In unison, their eyes were diverted to the far end of the room.

"It is so much better being in here than out there," she confessed wistfully.

"Which brings us back to the question of what the hell you were doing in that alleyway." Susan took a methodical drink from her cup.

"I've been living in Boston for well over ten years now. A couple of months ago I decided to move back home to Lowell. I don't have family here anymore but... you know... it's where I grew up. It's home." She glanced over to the man and seemed to catch his eyes trained on her folded legs. He recovered quickly, shifting his eyes upward to hers.

"Where or with whom were you planning to stay?"

"I didn't have a plan in place," she replied, sounding slightly embarrassed. Stiles shook his head and raised his eyes to the ceiling. "No, that's not exactly the truth. If nothing else, I should be honest with you. I had a plan...a stupid, half-baked plan. I actually came by your office earlier this evening. I was going to ask you for money." The attorney's eyes widened, puzzled by her statement.

"You were coming to me after all these years? You were coming to me for money!"

"Yes. I was going to lay this whole guilt trip on you about leaving me at the alter... and leaving me and my mother with a whole bunch of debt... not to mention the embarrassment." The woman's eyes began to tear up as she reached the end of her confession.

"So what made you change your mind?"

"Nothing made me change my mind. The truth is I wound up getting to Lowell much later than I planned and by the time I got to your building, it was locked." Susan watched his eyes drop to the floor, a thoughtful expression now etched in his features. "Of course, this was all before you came to my rescue and maybe even saved my life." William remained in a state of deep thought, his mind, it would seem, wandering back through the darkened hallways of their shared past.

"Susan, I know what I did to you was wrong," he confessed listlessly.

"Forget it, Bill. I'll be fine. For the time being, I'm out of harm's way, thanks to Attorney William Stiles," she said lightheartedly. He rose from the couch and walked across the office to the window, his back to her.

Quiet descended on the room as the two estranged lovers attempted to make sense of their current predicament. Susan stretched her body lengthwise atop the leather couch, producing an audible moan from the surface of the furniture. William turned from the window and trained his eyes on her.

"That came from the leather, not me," she hastily explained, clearly flustered. Her words brought a crackle of laughter from the man.

"I know it came from the leather. I was just afraid you were getting up to leave," he answered.

"Leave! And go where? I'm here until you toss me, Bill." He shuffled back to the couch and collapsed onto the far end. Turning his head towards her, she was able to pick up on a certain element of desperation in his stare. "Bill, what is it? Are you okay?" He broke eye contact, looking out beyond the boundaries of the room's four walls.

"A few years after you and I separated I brought home a woman my parents approved of. Brenda was everything they wanted me to hold out for. Educated at Smith, a career woman with limitless potential, Brenda Griffin brought so, so much to the table."

"A hell of a lot more than Susan Butler would have," she injected. "I never got the feeling that your folks were big fans of mine."

"They did a lot to poison me... first against marriage, then against you."

"What was she like? This Brenda Griffin, I mean."

"First and foremost, she bore a great resemblance to you... the hair, the eyes. Incredibly, my parents never picked up on it. They were totally oblivious. Anyway, for all the wrong reasons, we married. I'd like to be able to say we grew apart but I don't think we every really came together. No matter what I did, we never grew close. We were like live-in business partners. The marriage lasted less than two years. She's the one who finally took the initiative and called an end to it. I don't want anything from this pathetic excuse for a marriage except my car and my bank account. Those were her exact words." Susan extended the man a sympathetic smile.

"I didn't think anyone's marriage went up in flames quicker than mine but you have me beat. I was Mrs. Duane Gilman for a little over four years. Sometimes I couldn't figure out if I was his wife or his sparring partner. The drinking and the beatings got to be too much and I walked out while he was out on one of his benders. That was the beginning of my fall from financial grace. Now I'm here at rock bottom." She folded her legs back from their extended position along the couch, wrapping her arms around them and resting her chin on her exposed knees. The lawyer's eyes followed the maneuver with exaggerated interest.

"Bill," she exclaimed, hoping to disconnect the attorney's attention from her anatomy.

"Why don't I fetch you a blanket from the other room," he suggested, immediately jumping to his feet.

"It's still a wee bit cool in the room. I think I could make myself quite comfortable under a blanket or two."

Susan fidgeted at the end of the couch and listened as William Stiles rummaged through a closet, thirty feet away. He re-entered the room with two blankets in hand, and a blue pillow.

"Here, cover up before I make a total ass of myself," he exclaimed, tossing the blankets onto the couch in front of her. "My God, you'd think I could keep my eyes off of you for a few minutes…and on Christmas Eve, damn it." His admission brought a guarded outburst of laughter from the woman.

"Aw, I'll bet you say that to all the trollops you pick up in the alley," she wisecracked.

"You're anything but a trollop," he reassured her. The shapely brunette pulled the blankets up over her legs and torso, her eyes never leaving his. "Now, out in the kitchen there's enough food to keep you fed until I return tomorrow. There's half a gallon of milk, a dozen bottles of soda, an assortment of cans of soup and, I swear, a year's supple of Oodles of Noodles. I have to carry out the family tradition of staying the night at my parent's house on Christmas Eve. Trust me, I'd much prefer to spend the evening with you. Then, after a late breakfast on Christmas morning and the opening of a few presents, I'll come back and get you."

"I'll be perfectly fine right here in your warm, dry office, snuggled up on your couch… with all the Oodles of Noodles I can chow down in eighteen hours."

"I'd take you with me to my folk's house but I'm not sure they're up for a surprise guest."

"Particularly this surprise guest," added Susan.

"Now promise me you will be here when I get back tomorrow."

"I'll be here."

"Promise."

"I promise, I'll be here. You saw what my knee looks like! Boy, did you ever see what my injured knee looks like. That, and the other knee… and pretty much every square inch of both my legs…"

"Okay, I get it. You'll wait for me," he acknowledged, his face slightly blushed from embarrassment.

"You know, Bill, we're sort of making plans here but I don't remember any meeting of the minds relating to our situation. I mean, granted, I'm in need of your help and I appreciate all you've already done. If you had been a total stranger, I'd never have let all of this transpire. I mean, what's happening here?" He squatted down beside her at the edge of the couch.

"What I hope is happening is that we're taking full advantage of this unbelievable crossing of our paths this evening." Reaching out, Stiles clasped Susan's hand between his own.

The lawyer rose to his feet and made his way to the far side of the office where his overcoat lay strewn over a chair. Glancing down at his watch, he let out an exaggerated sigh and made haste to put on the garment.

"Bill, before you go I want to make sure you know how much I appreciate everything you've done for me tonight. In all likelihood, you saved my life back in that alley. I owe you so very much. It took a brave man to run into that dark alleyway and save a woman, a woman he thought was a complete stranger. You had no way of knowing if that low life had a gun or a knife." Halfway to the door the attorney stopped in his tracks. Glancing at his watch a second time, he turned, took hold of an upholstered chair, and dragged it across the room to within two feet of Susan. After seating himself, Stiles stared down at her for a moment before speaking.

"I'm thinking that maybe it was you who saved me tonight," he muttered in a low voice.

"Don't be crazy."

"No, hear me out. I'll share something with you that I can't believe I'm sharing with anyone. Tonight when I left the office and made my way to the parking lot, I had one thing at the forefront of my brain: how to end it all and when. I had pretty much decided to do it right after Christmas… certainly before the end of the year. I wanted to give my parents one more happy Christmas. This was not the first time I'd set my mind on just checking-out on my own terms… at a time and place acceptable to me. The first two times I had gotten cold feet but this time was going to be different."

"Billy, you can't be serious with this kind of talk," insisted Susan.

"Oh, I was dead serious. It comes from hating your life, hating your profession, and feeling so miserably alone. This had a lot to do with my willingness to walk into a dark alley when every fiber of my being told me to run and find a cop. You see Susan, I didn't much care what happened to me when I tangled with that hoodlum. I thought maybe fate was handing me an easy way out. It was only when I realized that I had inadvertently come to the rescue of Susan Butler that something resembling sanity came over me. I'm not half the hero you think I am." The confession over, the attorney's head dropped forward. Susan reached out from beneath her blankets and curled her fingers through his hair.

"And you say I saved your life?"

"The thought of returning here tomorrow afternoon and taking you back to the house is enough to lift my spirits up into the clouds."

"And there'll be no more of this crazy suicide talk, right?"

"None," he answered adamantly. She pulled his mouth to hers and kissed him for the first time in nearly fourteen years. They fell into each other's arms and remained there until Susan called a halt to the passionate embrace.

"You've got to be getting to your parent's house," she insisted. He applied a final kiss to her mouth and broke away. "The next time you see me I'll be lying here in a sea of empty, Oodles of Noodles boxes, my stomach bloated from overeating." Her words brought a spontaneous laugh from the man. Reaching the door, he turned.

"I'll be back here to pick you up tomorrow at one-thirty, two o'clock the latest. Next week, we spring you on mom and dad."

"Oh Billy, one more thing."

"What's that?"

"Merry Christmas."

If you enjoyed reading

Prey to the Butterfly

By

Thomas E. Coughlin

Look for his other works of fiction

Maggie May's Diary

Brian Kelly: Route 1

Obscene Bliss

The Odyssey of Sheba Smith

Miss O'Malley's Maine Summer

About the author

*T*homas E. Coughlin is the author of the best-selling Maggie May's Diary. He is a practicing certified public accountant and former radio announcer. He was born, raised and educated in Lowell, Massachusetts. Mr. Coughlin resides in Chester, New Hampshire.

In Memory of Rich Henderson III; who put his all into being an artist. musician. photographer. father. husband and friend; lover of laughter. life and family.

1959 - 2008